CAT OF THE CENTURY

"[Rita Mae Brown's] animals are as witty as ever."
—*Kirkus Reviews*

"There are plenty of suspects with motives in a well-constructed cozy that readers will enjoy in this one sitting read."
—The Mystery Gazette

"The mystery part of *Cat of the Century* is quite good. The clues are there but the reader is still left guessing."
—Jandy's Reading Room

SANTA CLAWED

"Fun and satisfying . . . an essential purchase for all mystery collections."
—Booklist

"[A] whodunit . . . that fans of the furry detectives and their two-legged pals will appreciate."
—Publishers Weekly

"Fearless feline and clever canine sleuths."
—*Kirkus Reviews*

"For all mystery collections and essential for series fans."
—Library Journal

"Captivating . . . will keep readers guessing whodunit to the very end. A delightful Christmas present indeed."
—*The Free Lance-Star*

"Anyone who's a sucker for talking animals or who simply enjoys fantasizing about the thoughts running through a beloved pet's brain will find heaps of guilty pleasure in Brown's latest addition to the Mrs. Murphy series."
—Rocky Mountain News

"The animals once again provide . . . the best comic moments."
—*Alfred Hitchcock's Mystery Magazine*

"[A] satisfying whodunit with a wealth of Virginia color. And, as always, the real fun comes from Tee Tucker, Mrs. Murphy and Pewter. . . . In *Santa Clawed*, they're the true Christmas angels."

—*Richmond Times-Dispatch*

THE PURRFECT MURDER

"Brown provides a perfect diversion for a cold night, complete with a cat or a dog on your lap."

—*Richmond Times-Dispatch*

"Veteran readers . . . will not be disappointed in this outing."

—*Winston-Salem Journal*

"The well-paced plot builds to an unpredictable and complex conclusion."

—*Publishers Weekly*

"The pets steal the limelight . . . [and] offer pleasure to fans of animal sleuths."

—*Kirkus Reviews*

"The plot moves easily and those non-humans who speak to each other, if not to their people, are a real pleasure and well worth one's time."

—*iloveamystery.com*

PUSS 'N CAHOOTS

"Such a delight to read."

—*Albuquerque Journal*

"The novel's tight pacing, combined with intriguing local color, make this mystery a blue-ribbon winner."

—*Publishers Weekly*

"This clever mystery strikes a comfortable balance between suspense and silliness."

—*Booklist*

CAT'S EYEWITNESS

"Thirteen is good luck for the writing team of Rita Mae Brown and her cat Sneaky Pie—and for their many fans. The Browns know how to keep a mystery series fresh and fun."

—*Winston-Salem Journal*

"This mystery, more than the others, has depth—more character development, a more intricate plot, greater exploration of the big topics. I give it nine out of ten stars."

—*Chicago Free Press*

"This book could not have arrived at a better time, the day before a snowstorm, so I had the perfect excuse to curl up by the fire and devour *Cat's Eyewitness* virtually at a sitting. . . . Entertaining, just the thing for a snowy afternoon . . . well worth reading."

—*The Roanoke Times*

"It is always a pleasure to read a book starring Harry and Mrs. Murphy but *Cat's Eyewitness* is particularly good. . . . Rita Mae Brown delights her fans with this fantastic feline mystery."

—*Midwest Book Review*

"It's terrific like all those that preceded it. . . . Brew the tea, get cozy, and enjoy. This series is altogether delightful."

—*The Kingston Observer*

"Frothy mayhem."

—*Omaha Sunday World-Herald*

"[An] irresistible mix of talking animals and a baffling murder or two . . . the animals' wry observations on human nature and beliefs amuse as ever."

—*Publishers Weekly*

"Delightful . . . Grade A."

—*Deadly Pleasures Mystery Magazine*

WHISKER OF EVIL

"A page-turner . . . A welcome sign of early spring is the latest sprightly Mrs. Murphy mystery. . . . There's plenty of fresh material to keep readers entertained. For one thing, the mystery is a real puzzler, with some subtle clues and credible false leads. . . . [They] have done it again. Give them a toast with a sprig of catnip."

—*Winston-Salem Journal*

"Rita Mae Brown and Sneaky Pie Brown fans will gladly settle in for a good long read and a well-spun yarn while Harry and her cronies get to the bottom of the mystery. . . . The series is worthy of attention."

—Wichita Falls *Times Record News*

"Another winsome tale of endearing talking animals and fallible, occasionally homicidal humans."

—*Publishers Weekly*

"The gang from Crozet, Virginia, is back in a book that really advances the lives of the characters. . . . Readers of this series will be interested in the developments, and will anxiously be awaiting the next installment, as is this reader."

—*Deadly Pleasures Mystery Magazine*

"An intriguing new adventure . . . suspenseful . . . Brown comes into her own here; never has she seemed more comfortable with her characters."

—*Booklist*

"Another fabulous tale . . . wonderful . . . The book is delightful and vastly entertaining with a tightly created mystery."

—*Old Book Barn Gazette*

"Undoubtedly one of the best books of the Mrs. Murphy series . . . a satisfying read."

—Florence *Times Daily*

The Big Cat Nap

THE 20TH ANNIVERSARY MRS. MURPHY MYSTERY

RITA MAE BROWN
& SNEAKY PIE BROWN

ILLUSTRATED BY MICHAEL GELLATLY

BANTAM BOOKS • NEW YORK

The Big Cat Nap is a work of fiction. Names, characters, places, and incidents either are the product of the author's imagination or are used fictitiously. Any resemblance to actual persons, living or dead, or locales is entirely coincidental.

2013 Bantam Books Mass Market Edition

Published in the United States by Bantam Books, an imprint of The Random House Publishing Group, a division of Random House, Inc., New York.

BANTAM and colophon are registered trademarks of Random House, Inc.

Originally published in hardcover in the United States by Bantam Books, an imprint of The Random House Publishing Group, a division of Random House, Inc., in 2012.

ISBN 978-0-345-53045-5
eBook ISBN 978-0-345-53239-8

This book contains an excerpt from *The Litter of the Law* by Rita Mae Brown. This excerpt has been set for this edition only and may not reflect the final content of the forthcoming edition.

Cover design: Beverly Leung
Cover illustrations: © Daniel Pelvin (cat), © Shutterstock/Mister-Elements (yarn)

Printed in the United States of America

www.bantambooks.com

9 8 7 6 5 4 3

Bantam mass market edition: April 2013

Dedicated to

Mrs. Harriet Phillips, Ph. D.

*A Smith graduate, a wonderful mother,
and a steadfast friend.
I don't know what I'd do without her.*

Cast of Characters

Mary Minor Haristeen—Harry, at forty, has just faced down breast cancer. She's making a go at farming; some days are easy, some days less so. She's a good-natured soul, but her flaming flaw is she's much too curious.

Pharamond Haristeen, D.V.M.—"Fair" specializes in equine reproduction. Married to his high school sweetheart, Harry, he's a powerfully built man. He reads people's emotions much better than his wife does.

Susan Tucker—She's a friend of Harry's since they were in the cradle together. Much as she loves Harry, her nosy friend can drive her right up the wall.

Miranda Hogendobber—A woman in her late sixties who worked with Harry when Harry was postmistress of Crozet, she has good sense. She's a good gardener, is very religious, and possesses a pure soprano voice.

Olivia Craycroft—"BoomBoom" has known Harry and Susan since kindergarten. She's tall, blonde, beautiful, and has blue eyes. She runs her late husband's concrete business; although we usually don't encounter her there, we do just about everywhere else.

Alicia Palmer—A gorgeous woman in her fifties, she was a major-motion-picture star in the 1970s. Like most people in the biz, she whipped through a few husbands, affairs, etc., but then wisely walked away from all of that to return to a farm in Crozet she inherited from her first lover. She's blissfully happy.

Deputy Cynthia Cooper—This lean woman lives next door to Harry, on the farm she rents. The two enjoy a strong relationship, even though Harry meddles in Cynthia's business from time to time.

Sheriff Rick Shaw—He's a decent man, wise, overburdened, and underfunded, as are most county sheriffs in America.

The Very Reverend Herbert Jones—A Vietnam veteran, he's the pastor of St. Luke's Lutheran Church, which is over two hundred years old, and a graceful, peaceful sanctuary. He is a man of deep conviction and deep feeling.

Victor Gatzembizi—Although only in his early forties, he's built ReNu, a lucrative collision-repair business, with shops in various Virginia cities. Attractive, good with people, he has the typical trophy wife but he takes good care of her, as he does his employees. He's been generous to the breast cancer fund.

Latigo Bly—Also in his early forties, he's even more successful than Victor is, as he's built a highly profitable auto-insurance business, Safe & Sound, that's currently powerful in the mid-Atlantic. Many people think he'll take the company national.

Yancy Hampton—Basically he's a greengrocer who owns and operates Fresh! Fresh! Fresh!, an upscale food emporium. He considers himself green in all things.

Marilyn Sanburne, Sr.—"Big Mim" runs Crozet. She's not much in evidence in this volume, but you can be sure she will reassert herself in the future.

Marilyn Sanburne, Jr.—"Little Mim" is often in her mother's shadow and resents it. She's vice-mayor of Crozet to her father's mayor. As they both represent different political parties, this can be interesting. She's slowed down on the politics for a bit, as she is expecting her first child.

Blair Bainbridge—Little Mim's husband is beside himself with joy at the prospect of being a father.

Aunt Tally Urquhart—She's one hundred, and Big Mim is her niece.

Inez Carpenter, D.V.M.—Aunt Tally's classmate at William Woods University, she's ninety-eight and has shepherded Fair Haristeen's career.

Mildred Haldane—Now widowed, she still runs the salvage yard she operated with her late husband. She knows more about cars than many mechanics and body-shop workers do. She is passionate about old cars.

The ReNu Mechanics

Walt Richardson, Nick Ashby, Jason Brundige, Sammy Collona, Lodi Pingrey, and Bobby Foltz.

The Really Important Characters

Mrs. Murphy—She's a tiger cat who is usually cool, calm, and collected. She loves her humans, Tucker the dog, and even Pewter, the other cat, who can be a pill.

Pewter—She's self-centered, rotund, intelligent when she wants to be. Selfish as she is, she often comes through at the last minute to help and then wants all the credit.

Tee Tucker—This corgi could take your college boards. She is devoted to Harry, Fair, and Mrs. Murphy. She is less devoted to Pewter.

Simon—He's an opossum who lives in the hayloft of the Haristeens' barn.

Matilda—She's a large blacksnake with a large sense of humor. She also lives in the hayloft.

Flatface—This great horned owl lives in the barn cupola. She irritates Pewter, but the cat realizes the bird could easily pick her up and carry her off.

The Lutheran Cats

Elocution—She's the oldest of the St. Luke's cats and cares a lot about the "Rev," as his friends sometimes call the Very Reverend Herbert Jones.

Cazenovia—This cat watches everybody and everything.

Lucy Fur—She's the youngest of the kitties. While ever playful, she obeys her elders.

The Big Cat Nap

1

A red-shouldered hawk, tiny mouse in her talons, swooped in front of the 2007 Outback rolling along the wet country road. She landed in an old cherry tree covered in pink blossoms, which fluttered to the ground from the hawk's light impact.

"Will you look at that?" Miranda Hogendobber exclaimed from behind the Outback's wheel, as she drove to the garden center over in Waynesboro.

"Raptors fascinate me, but they scare me, too," Harry Haristeen remarked. "Poor little mouse."

"There is that." Miranda slowed for a sharp curve.

Central Virginia, celebrating high spring, was also digging out from torrential rains over the weekend.

Harry, forty and fit, and Miranda, late sixties and not advertising, had worked together for years at the old Crozet post office.

When Miranda's husband, George, died, Harry, fresh from Smith College, took his position as head of the P.O., never thinking the job would last nearly two decades. Miranda, despite her loss, showed up every day to help orient the young woman whom she'd known as a baby. Harry's youth raised Miranda's spirits. In mourning, it's especially good to have a task. Over the years they became extremely close, almost a mother–daughter bond. Harry's mother had died when Harry was in her early twenties.

Noticing fields filled with the debris of the now-subsiding waters, Harry observed, "What a mess. Can't turn out stock in that. You just don't know what else is wrapped up in all those branches and twigs."

"Hey, there's a plastic chair. Might look good in your yard." Miranda smiled.

"Well," Harry drawled the word out, like the native Southerner she was.

The younger woman, generous with her time and happy to feed anyone, could be tight with the buck. Miranda couldn't resist teasing Harry about a free if ugly chair.

"This is sure better than my 1961 Falcon," the older woman said. "Initially I resisted the Outback's fancy radio. I mean, this is a used car and had the Sirius capabilities, but I didn't want to pay extra. How did I live without it?" Miranda mused, now a Subaru convert.

"Regular cars can now do more than Mercedes or even Rolls from ten years ago. That's what amazes me: the speed with which the technological developments of those high-end cars became commonplace in much-lower-priced vehicles. But I still love my old 1978 F-150 and you still drive your old Falcon. Hey, want me to wax it?"

"Would you? What a lovely offer."

"You know how crazy I get with anything with an engine in it. I'll clean the tires, refresh your dash. I'm a one-woman detailing operation."

Her eyebrows knitting together, Miranda said, "Uh-oh."

An odd pop, then a lurch, made holding the Outback on the road difficult.

"Put on your flashers and brake."

They slid toward a narrow drainage ditch, and the air bags billowed up inside as the wheel dipped in the ditch. Miranda couldn't see.

If there was enough room, narrow drainage ditches, about one to two feet deep, paralleled the country roads. Occasionally, small culverts passed the runoff under farm driveways or sharp curves, moving the water, which could rise very quickly, away from the roads.

Even without vision, Miranda was not one to panic. She braked smoothly, and the right side of the car dropped into the ditch. The car rocked a little.

Asleep on the backseat, Harry's two cats and dog rolled off.

"*Hey!*" Pewter, the rotund gray cat, howled.

The tiger cat, Mrs. Murphy, and the corgi, Tee Tucker, scrambled back up on the seat.

"*No other cars,*" the dog noted.

The tiger cat looked around. "*Right.*"

"*I was asleep.*" Pewter hauled herself up to sit next to her friends.

"*We all were,*" Mrs. Murphy drily noted.

"*Well—I was more asleep.*"

Harry, already outside, having punctured the air bag

with the penknife she always carried in her hip pocket, crouched down to look at the undercarriage. Then she walked to the right front side of the car, front end in the ditch.

"See anything?" As best she could, Miranda rolled up her air bag, which Harry had also punctured.

Harry called back, "Your right tire is cracked; the rubber's flat, too. Do you have Triple A?"

"I do." Miranda slid out as Harry helped her. "But I'm going to call Safe and Sound instead."

Safe & Sound, founded and run by Alphonse "Latigo" Bly, was headquartered in Charlottesville. Specializing in auto insurance, the company covered the mid-Atlantic and coastal South. Many business people believed Safe & Sound would go national, sooner or later.

As Miranda called, Harry opened the back door of the Outback.

"Does anyone need to go potsie?"

"Must she put it that way?" Pewter grumbled. *"And I am not about to get my paws wet."*

"We're okay." The corgi answered for the rest of the animals. Not seeing one of her best friends budge, Harry closed the door to the rear, then did her best to fold her air bag back into the dash.

Miranda was already on the phone with Safe & Sound, spilling out details, perhaps too many.

With difficulty, Harry opened the glove compartment, pulling out the manual.

Having concluded her phone conversation, Miranda informed Harry, "Someone will be here in twenty minutes. Says don't call Triple A. He takes care of this stuff all the time."

"Always best to do business with friends," Harry observed. "When you try to save money, you usually waste time or spend even more money. Safe and Sound is local."

Miranda sighed. "The older I get, the more I realize time is more precious than money."

Harry, flipping through the manual, stopped at a schematic drawing of the auto frame. "You're not old. Anyone who sings in the choir, gardens like you do, and is a member of every 'do-good' group in the state of Virginia isn't old." Changing the subject—a habit with dear friends—Harry declared, "Whatever happened, it wasn't the engine. It may be a defective wheel, but there was that odd pop sound."

"Yes. I couldn't steer after that."

"Weird." Harry glanced back at the manual. "Subaru makes great cars for the money." A fresh breeze brought the aroma of blossoms, flowers, and hay coming up, filling her nostrils.

"I'll be curious to find out what happened. How lucky we were that the car swerved to the right, not the left into oncoming traffic. Better yet, there wasn't any traffic." Miranda exhaled.

"Monday afternoon. Everyone's at work or in the fields. Herb's truck is in the shop, too, after his collision last week," Harry said, thinking of the minister at St. Luke's Lutheran Church, the Very Reverend Herbert Jones. "Things go in threes. Maybe I'm next."

"I don't know what happened, but I bet that will

cost Herb an arm and a leg. Truck's still at ReNu," Miranda said, naming the garage favored by the insurance company. "He was driving his Chevy truck. His 'big fib' truck."

They laughed, because the Chevy, used for fishing and filled with tackle, was also filled with fish stories. Oh, how Herb could wax poetic on the one that got away! He was also all too happy to show what he had actually snagged, though the cats generally proved more interested in the display than did the humans.

"If you're going to be stuck on the side of the road, best it happens on a beautiful spring day." Harry smiled. "We were lucky. Unlike Tara Meola."

Harry shuddered at the thought of the poor young woman killed last week in the hard rains when a deer smashed into her vehicle.

"True." Miranda nodded.

"You just never know," Harry sighed.

2

*A*fter a bitterly cold winter, spring had stayed cool until late April. It was now late May. Nights in the mid-forties or mid-fifties promised days in the sixties. Late-blooming dogwoods dotted the forests and manicured lawns. Over pergolas, the wisteria hung pendulous with lavender or white blossoms. The roses threatened to riot.

Harry walked through her tended acres. The farm maintained a healthy balance of crops, hay, and woodlands. Mrs. Murphy, Tucker, and Pewter followed, taking numerous side trips to investigate rabbit warrens and fox dens. The butterflies danced together, swirling, fluttering their beautiful veined wings.

Eyeing them deviously, Pewter crouched down.

"*They see you,*" Tucker said.

Ignoring the ever-practical dog, Pewter wiggled her gray butt, then leapt upward.

Without breaking rhythm, the butterflies flew away.

"*Almost had 'em.*"

"*Dream on,*" the corgi teased.

Mrs. Murphy at her heels, Harry turned. "Come on, you two."

"*She's always giving orders,*" Pewter grumbled.

"True," the handsome dog agreed. "*And she also always feeds us on time.*"

Considering this, the fat cat trotted toward Harry, who was now leaning over to inspect the tops of sunflower plants just breaking the surface.

"With a little luck, I'm going to have a good year." Harry smiled, then moved on to her quarter acre of Petit Manseng grapes.

Dr. Thomas Walker, Thomas Jefferson's guardian after Peter Jefferson died, tried to grow grapes. Jefferson did, too. The types they wished to grow didn't flourish. With the passing centuries, viniculture advanced, thanks to people on both sides of the Atlantic. The wine industry now poured millions upon millions into the area's coffers, a boon to growers and a boon to Virginia.

The horse business alone contributed $1.2 billion to the state economy. Not that any horse wishes to be compared to a grape.

Shortro, a very athletic Saddlebred, and Tomahawk, an old Thoroughbred, hung their heads over their paddock fence.

"*This will be the first year she can sell her grapes,*" Tomahawk noted. "*Remember, she had to let the first year's stay on the vine.*"

"*Even the broodmares know that.*" Shortro laughed. "*Harry's obsessed with her grapes and her sunflowers. She's just sure both will bring her money.*"

In the adjoining paddock, one of the broodmares heard Shortro's comment. "*I resent that.*"

"*Ah, Gigi*"—Shortro called the Thoroughbred by her barn name—"*I didn't mean anything by it. You girls are all wrapped up in your foals.*"

Gigi tossed her dark bay head. "*If she makes money, she overseeds the pastures in alfalfa. We all want Harry to succeed.*"

The other broodmares nodded in agreement. Their foals, the youngest only a month old, hung by their sides.

Blissfully unaware that she was the topic of conversation, Harry chatted with her house animals. "I can put up scarecrows and big plastic owls, but, you know, gang, sooner or later the birds figure that out, so I mustn't do that too soon. I'll wait until the grapes appear—tiny—on the vine, then I'll put that stuff up." She shook her head in exasperation. "Tell you what, birds and deer can wipe you out."

"*I can take care of the deer.*" Tucker puffed out her broad chest.

"*They're nothing more than big rats.*" Pewter was never one to keep her opinions to herself.

"*Oh, but they're so beautiful.*" Mrs. Murphy loved watching herds of deer, with fawns still dappled, as they crossed the pastures and meadows before melting back into the woods.

The *1812 Overture* began to play. Harry fished her cellphone out of her jeans' hip pocket.

"Yes, baby."

Her husband's deep voice answered, "Good greeting."

"What do you want?" She laughed.

"You and only you."

Pewter could hear Fair's voice, as could the other two animals, their senses much sharper than a human's.

"*So sappy.*"

"*Oh, Pewter, you're such a spoilsport.*" Tucker wagged her nonexistent tail.

"Heard anything from Miranda?" Fair asked.

"No. Latigo Bly picked us up himself. Drove her home, then me. He said not to worry. The company would take care of everything. The car was hauled to ReNu, where there's a backlog. Latigo said they've been overwhelmed with claims. There were quite a few accidents during all that rain."

"Never thought of that."

"Fair, we aren't in the insurance business." She laughed.

Fair believed that if you did business with friends, you had the advantage of speaking with someone whose native language was English. Although growing fast, Safe & Sound still seemed like a local outfit to Harry's husband. Fair got his insurance from Hanckle Citizens, as did Harry. Both their parents had used the company and been well served. "We'll hear about it tomorrow. Herb sure had a tussle when he had his little accident. He could only use ReNu, when he actually wanted to use Tom Harvey's garage. He told me Safe and Sound insisted on ReNu, since the repairs are cheaper. That was the only time I heard our Very Reverend Jones cuss a blue streak."

Harry smiled. "I'd pay to hear that."

"Called to tell you that I ran into BoomBoom"—Fair named a childhood friend of theirs—"and she told me to be sure to tell you if you intend to sell your sunflower seeds this fall, you ought to get down to the health-food store right away. Yancy Hampton is buying now."

"Yancy is what? Why on earth now? The crop's not nearly ready."

"She didn't say. Oops, call on the other line, and it looks like Big Mim. See you tonight, darlin'."

Harry hung up with the thought that he'd be late for supper, as one of Big Mim's best mares suffered from lactation problems and the foal needed that milk. If the mare couldn't produce, Fair would need to find a surrogate. Since the stud fee had been $75,000 for this particular breeding and the foal was correct, it was imperative to keep the little guy healthy as well as get Mama back right.

Harry flipped shut her cellphone. She neither liked nor disliked Yancy Hampton, but, for Harry, neutrality bordered on suspicion. Still, money was money. She'd think on it.

3

The triple-sash windows, wide open, allowed a fresh breeze to fill the comfortable room at St. Luke's Church, where the vestry-board meeting was now in progress. The administrative offices were connected to the church itself by an old stone arcade, so one could walk without getting soaked in those sudden hard Virginia rains. The St. Luke's complex was built around a lovely symmetrical inner quad, and parts of the church were some two hundred thirty years old. The entire site radiated calm and encouraged contemplation.

The early parishioners and pastor rested in a large rectangular cemetery behind the huge quad at a lower level. This lower large square was surrounded by a row of eighty red oaks, in front of which a border of climbing roses cascaded over the stone retaining wall. The current pastor's living quarters anchored the far southern side of the large outer quad. The Very Reverend Jones's fishing gear could be seen leaning against the garage. It was a hopeful sight.

Also attending the vestry-board meeting were the Lutheran cats, Elocution, Lucy Fur, and Cazenovia. As the humans—Harry being one—discussed and occasionally argued about funds or the social calendar, the feline parishioners languidly sprawled on the windowsills. Their kind were once gods in ancient Egypt, but all had the good sense to keep that to themselves. Then, too, they loved their reverend. Why upset him with a competing theological view? Humans could understand so little of cat communication. So all felines—not just Elocution, Lucy Fur, and Cazenovia—recognized that the feline–human relationship was often one-way. They pitied the two-legged creatures, but when that tin of Fancy Feast was opened, they utterly adored them.

"The riding mower needs a new air filter, and the blades must be sharpened." Susan Tucker, Harry's childhood friend, now in charge of buildings and grounds, read from her monthly report. "This isn't terribly expensive. Jimmy Carter is excellent and more than reasonable, but because of that there's a long, long wait time."

"We can't let the grass grow. It will look awful." BoomBoom Craycroft, a smashing beauty, knew people would grumble about unkempt grounds, and not just parishioners.

"Can't we borrow a mower?" Harry sensibly inquired.

Craig Newby, in his first year on the board, replied, "In theory, yes, but everyone is mowing. It's been a wet spring. Some people are mowing three times a week."

Herb's gray eyebrows shot upward. "Three times?"

"Martha Stewart, maybe," BoomBoom quipped, and all laughed.

As the problems of mowing the large expanse of church lawns and the cemetery occupied the board, Elocution looked out the window. "Brown creeper."

The creeper was a small bird, rather large chested, with a slightly curving slender bill. It worked its way up a locust tree.

"Bet we could catch it." Lucy Fur's eyes widened.

"They're pretty quick," Cazenovia remarked.

Lucy Fur murmured her agreement, then wondered, "They're so social, always hanging out with woodpeckers and chickadees. The chickadees you can sometimes distract and nail, but the woodpeckers, never. Doesn't matter what kind of woodpecker."

"I wouldn't want to eat a woodpecker," Elocution declared. "Now, a fat little mole—tasty."

As to the mowing problem, Harry agreed to haul in her zero-turn mower until the church's old John Deere was repaired. The discussion moved on to moles.

"Put poison down the holes." Craig shrugged his shoulders.

"All creatures bright and beautiful, all things great and small, the Lord God made us all." Herb folded his hands. "Did I get that right?"

"Sounds good to me." BoomBoom beamed a megawatt smile, then turned to Craig. "There's an ultrasonic deterrent. You put a small stake in their tunnel and they'll leave. Doesn't kill them." She glanced at Harry. "Not expensive."

"Yes, but do we have to buy them luggage?" Harry laughed.

Finally the meeting drew to a merciful end, after which they all stayed for coffee, tea, or a Coke. Usually these meetings started at 6:00 P.M., but it so happened that this one had been scheduled in the morning.

Miranda's odd accident was discussed, as was Herb's truck problem.

"Did I ever tell you all the story of when I had three accidents in one day?" Herb smiled.

"*Another trip down memory lane,*" Elocution, the middle kitty of the three, remarked.

"I was sixteen, had my first vehicle, an old 1939 Chevy. Ran like a top. Anyway, I pulled out of the farm, didn't get a mile down the road, and was rear-ended by old Kitchie Richards. Remember her?"

The older board members did. They also remembered that Kitchie was deep in the grape.

"Then what happened?" Craig asked, as if on cue.

"Aunt Tally drove by, turned around, drove back to Rose Hill, and called the sheriff. While I waited for the sheriff, wouldn't you know I was rear-ended again, this time by John Barrow. He just wasn't looking where he was going."

"What happened to Kitchie?" BoomBoom asked.

"Kitchie apologized as best she was able, turned around, and left. So up drives the deputy, sees that I've been hit twice. I hated to finger Kitchie, but I didn't know what to do. Anyway, it was Tom Ix, still living, who was on duty. Took down everything, including John's statement. So he told me to go on. I get in the Chevy—engine, wheels fine—and head toward Char- lottesville. Didn't get two miles down that road when I was hit again. As luck would have it, Tom passed me as I sat by the side of the road with the culprit. None of these accidents were my fault. Well, Tom looked at me and said, 'Son, you need to go home.' So I did."

They laughed, chatted, then the group dispersed. Harry, BoomBoom, and Susan remained to clean up.

"Are you taking Herb down to ReNu?" BoomBoom asked, tying up a trash bag.

"I am," Harry answered, while placing glasses in the cabinet. "Two accidents. Things go in threes."

"Harry, don't say that," superstitious BoomBoom reprimanded her.

"Well, they do."

"Maybe we'd better do like old Deputy Ix told Herb. Go home."

"Finished!" Susan called out to Herb, who'd ducked back into his office.

"All right. Any of you other girls want to ride along?"

"What? I thought I was your only girlfriend," Harry teased him.

"Yes, but what man doesn't want to be surrounded by beautiful women?" Herb's eyes lit up.

"Good answer." BoomBoom smiled at him, then kissed him on the cheek. "I need to get out to the farm. We're putting in a new well down at the main barn. The storms finally ruined the barn well. We're still cleaning up the debris."

"I got some of that, too, but I think you got more than me," Harry replied.

"Mother Nature doesn't pick favorites." Susan added

her two cents. "I'll ride along as long as you brought the station wagon, Harry. Otherwise, we can go in mine."

"I did."

Soon the three sat comfortably in Harry's Volvo station wagon, a gift from her husband. Harry—a motorhead, as was BoomBoom—marveled at how well the wagon handled, given its dimensions. If she put the seats down, she could haul a lot in the back.

They drove out Route 240, turned left on Route 250, heading into Charlottesville. After twenty minutes in medium traffic, they moved along Route 29 north and pulled in to ReNu Auto Works. Harry stepped out of the Volvo, as did BoomBoom. They'd wait to make sure. So often a vehicle was supposed to be ready, then you'd show up and it wasn't finished yet.

The front office had a counter with a young man behind it. Herb said he was there to pick up his truck.

A badge on the young man's left pocket read "Kyle." He spoke into a phone. The three friends could hear the announcement in the back to bring up the 1994 Chevy half-ton.

Nothing happened. Kyle asked for the Chevy again. No Chevy.

Slightly irritated, he looked up at Herb. "They should be back from lunch by now."

"I'll just go back and find them," Herb declared. "The keys are back there?"

"They are."

"And you're in touch with my insurance company?"

"Oh, yes. Safe and Sound is always on time paying the bills. I can go back if you'd prefer," Kyle said.

"We can't service a customer in the front office as well as you can." Herb smiled. "We'll go back—I don't mind. If there's a problem, you'll see me again."

With that, Herb headed to the garage, Harry and Susan with him.

Entering the spacious garage, they saw all the pits clean, cars raised on every lift. ReNu had two buildings set fifty yards apart, with cars parked in between. The garage sat on the left, the body shop on the right. The inner parking lot was jammed. Miranda's Outback sat on an outside row.

Not a soul was to be seen in the garage.

"Long lunch," Susan stated.

Harry noticed a tire iron sticking out from a stack of engine parts under a wall of shelves. Ever curious, she walked over.

"What the—" Blood and brains coated one end of the heavy metal iron.

Then she saw a pair of work boots peeking out from behind the cartons.

"Come here."

Due to the urgent tone of Harry's voice, Herb and Susan hurried over.

They stepped behind the cartons to view the body of a mechanic, still in his greasy uniform, his brains bashed over the floor.

There was a problem.

4

*D*eputy Cynthia Cooper stepped out of the squad car. While Albemarle County hosted a few murders a year, most of them lacked much mystery or spectacle. X shot Y or stabbed him. The victims were usually men. A woman might be killed in a domestic dispute or a female student snatched from the University of Virginia only to be found months later. Fortunately, such loathsome killings happened rarely. Years would go by before another female was murdered, but the males could be relied upon to dispatch one another with regularity.

The sheriff, Rick Shaw, with whom Coop usually rode in the squad car, happened to be in Richmond with other sheriffs for a meeting with the governor to discuss crime.

Compared to that of other states, Virginia's homicide rate was reasonable, but as far as Coop was concerned, one murder was one murder too many. Then, too, how would the state ever live down or recover from the horror in 2007 at Virginia Tech? Much as the long, lean blonde officer hoped people could settle their differences responsibly, experience had taught her otherwise.

She walked in to the garage, where the mechanics and men from the body shop were still absent. "Where is everybody?" Coop asked, hoping the forensics team would soon appear. Harry, Susan, and Herb waited for her.

Coop was Harry's neighbor, renting the old farm that had been the Reverend Jones's home place.

"Couldn't take it," Harry tersely replied. "Half of them ran outside to throw up when they finally came back from lunch. I believe they're now in the front waiting room."

"Ah." Coop strode over to inspect the body. Putting on thin rubber gloves, she knelt down to feel his flesh.

"How long do you think he's been dead?" Susan curiously inquired.

"I expect when you found him he'd just been killed," Coop said before standing up. "He's still warm, cooling a little."

"Whoever did it must have been frightfully angry," Herb said. "Such a violent act."

Coop looked at Herb with her pale eyes. "He—" She glanced down to read the name sewn onto the mechanic's uniform. "Walt faced his killer. I'm pretty sure of that based on how he's sprawled." She then walked around Walt Richardson. "Why don't you all vacate the premises before the circus arrives? I'll take your statements later. Actually, once you get home, write it all down before you forget."

They heard a siren traveling in their direction.

"Where's Rick?" Harry asked her neighbor and friend.

"Richmond. Politics." Coop sighed. "All life is politics. Someone, somewhere, will find a way to make this murder serve their political ends, just watch."

"I hate it all." Harry's voice carried an edge. "And whoever did this must have hated Walt. I mean, to crack open a skull, take off part of his face. That's hate."

"And power," Herb added. Then, gently, he began to herd the two women toward the door into the waiting room. The Volvo was parked out front.

"Don't say anything to the folks in the waiting room other than that someone will be with them shortly. Anyone know where Victor is?" Coop added as an afterthought.

Victor Gatzembizi was the owner of ReNu; besides this one in Charlottesville, there was a large shop in Richmond, one in Virginia Beach, one in Norfolk, and one in Alexandria.

"No. When we arrived, there was only the office fellow, Kyle."

"Okay. Move on out."

The deafening siren cut off, which meant one law-enforcement team had just arrived. And soon to follow would be the vans for the TV stations.

The three friends walked silently through a somber waiting room, where five mechanics sat looking glum and dazed.

Once in the car, Harry turned north to the next stoplight, then made a legal U-turn.

In the back, Susan leaned forward. "At least we know we all have strong stomachs."

"Farming will give you one." Harry reached fifty-five miles per hour and held steady.

"Mmm-hmm," Susan answered. Though not a farmer, she'd spent plenty of time way back when on Harry's farm, even when it was owned by Harry's parents.

Arms crossed over his chest, Herb's voice was deep. "It's always a shock, sad. Even when you find a dead deer. Sad."

Harry thought about this. "But no one there was crying."

"All men." Susan spoke as though this was a hard fact of behavior.

Herb unfolded his arms and reached for the door bolster. "Harry has a point. When something is that shocking, a lot of men would break down or show some emotion other than physical illness. No one would think less of them. It's not like how workers perceive a woman who cries because her feelings are hurt or she's frustrated on the job. This is different, and, Harry, you're right—no tears."

"Maybe no one liked Walt." Susan accepted Herb's analysis.

"It's for sure someone didn't." Harry knew she'd remember that split-open head for the rest of her life.

5

Slanting rays of late-afternoon sun kissed the fields as Harry walked through them.

"Like butter." She held her hand over her eyes as a shield. Today, even her summer straw cowboy hat didn't do the trick.

Mrs. Murphy, Pewter, and Tucker listened as the human they loved most rambled on.

Like most people, Harry happily babbled to her pets. She thought of them as pets. That wasn't their attitude.

Mrs. Murphy believed she had to think for both Harry and her husband. They were so slow.

Pewter considered herself a small gray divinity. She felt no call to think for the humans.

Tucker knew her job was to protect and defend, as well as to herd horses into or out of the barn. She used to herd humans, but their resistance to canine direction finally broke her of trying.

"The hay looks good," said Harry, "especially the alfalfa. I think I can cut it next week. That's a happy thought. Do you all know I made twenty thousand dollars last year selling hay? Now, I know that's a drop in the bucket compared to the big hay dealers, but really, really good for me." She beamed as the slender green blades brushed against her thigh.

"*Smells good,*" Mrs. Murphy noted.

"*Especially when it's freshly cut.*" Tucker lived by her nose.

To a lesser extent, so did Pewter. She stopped as she picked up rabbit scent, a fragile aroma. In her booming meow, she called out, "*Mother and baby bunnies passed through, um, maybe fifteen minutes ago.*"

"*You just figure that out?*" Tucker teased her.

"*I hate you, I really do.*" The gray cat sped through the hay, blew past the dog and cat, and shot in front of Harry, slightly knocking her leg in the process.

"Pewter."

"*Faster than a speeding bullet,*" Pewter chanted, having watched the *Superman* movies with Harry.

"*Fatter than a cannonball,*" Tucker called out.

That insult provoked the gray cat to stop abruptly, puff up like a broody hen with tail like a bottle brush, hop sideways, and hiss loudly. "*Death to corgis.*"

Tucker, knowing Pewter's temper, fell behind Mrs. Murphy.

"*Thanks,*" the tiger cat drily said.

"*She's not mad at you.*" Tucker's ear dropped in apology.

"Pewter, move." Harry reached the fearsome cat. "I don't want to make more paths in the hay."

Pewter peered around Harry's legs. "*Coward.*"

"*I am not a coward,*" Tucker called back. "*You're in one of your moods.*"

"Pewter." Harry looked down at the cat, still puffed up.

"All right." She smoothed her fur, then walked in front of Harry, her sashay more pronounced than usual.

Under her breath, Tucker said to Mrs. Murphy, *"She's so conceited."*

The sleek, beautiful tiger turned her head, swept her whiskers forward and back, then continued behind Harry, quite happy to walk in the clearing that the larger, two-legged animal made.

Finally, on the other side of the hay, expanses of rolling pasture unfurled. To their left flowed the strong running creek, its deep banks dividing Harry's farm from the old Jones place. Even though Cooper had been renting it, it would always be the old Jones place.

About a half mile in front of Harry was the base of the Blue Ridge Mountains, and she had a nice stand of timber, which itself was wrapped by a huge stand—more than a thousand acres—owned by Susan Tucker. This had been inherited from Susan's much-beloved uncle.

Harry briskly trotted across the pasture to the edge of the forest. She managed her own stand and Susan's, checking for signs of destructive bugs, curling leaves, or too many woodpecker holes—all signs of disease. The Tuckers were not really farmers or timber people. Ned, Susan's husband, was serving his first term as a representative in the state senate. Anyway, Harry loved doing it. Never seemed like a chore.

She sat down on a large fallen log, careful that no bees' nests lurked inside or nasty red ants crawled about. Not seeing any mounds or activity on the hickory trunk, she sat down and told her friends all that she had seen that afternoon.

"Awful," Tucker sympathized.

Harry dropped her hand on the dog's broad, glossy skull. "I ask myself, why would someone—in broad daylight, mind you—brain someone? What if one of the fellows came back from lunch early? What if Kyle had wandered back into the garage?" She paused. "Actually, Kyle doesn't seem like a young man motivated to do any more than necessary." She thought, propping her chin in the palm of her hand. "The killer must have known that."

"Mom, how come you always wind up in these messes?" Tucker cast her soft brown eyes upward.

"Bad timing. I mean, it's not like she went looking for it, which we all know she can do and has." Mrs. Murphy raised a silky eyebrow.

"Car accident with Miranda, now this." Pewter washed one paw.

"It seems to me that the killer had a narrow window of opportunity, clearly knew that, and acted. It could be I'm missing something, but that's what I deduce so far. Oh, and another thing: No one appeared too sorry over Walt's demise. I mean, when something like this happens, you generally hear the workers or friends expressing pity, sorrow, how many children he left fatherless. Stuff like that. Well, walking through the waiting room I didn't hear a peep or see one tear." She lifted her head as a large bird flew over the treetops, letting out a raucous call. "My God, that's a golden eagle. You hardly ever

see them here." Harry stood up to watch the huge bird continue on.

"*Better not come down here.*" Pewter puffed out her chest.

"*Pewts, that bird could have any one of us for lunch,*" Mrs. Murphy said, as she also watched the eagle fly away.

The gray cat didn't reply, instead focusing her attention on a little slithering lizard, which easily eluded the one exposed claw meant to impale it. Pewter retracted the claw, then returned to her toilet as though she hadn't cared one iota about the lizard.

Sitting back down, Harry said, "I'll be glad when Fair gets home. He often has good ideas. I called him after I dropped off Herb and Susan. You know, he is just the sweetest man in the world. He said he'd take the day off, get another vet to cover his calls, and come home if I was shaken up. I'm not, really. I mean, it was gross. Gross. Bits of skull and brains and not lots of blood actually." Looking intently at her three friends, she said, voice loud, "Do you know that brains are kind of blue?"

"*We know.*" The three chimed in unison.

"And another thing: Why a tire iron? Well, a gun would draw attention, but a knife would work. Then again, you have to get closer to stab someone. But Walt could have ducked. Maybe he did. Still, a tire iron. Must be a big hate."

"*She's off and running,*" Tucker noted with resignation.

"The killer had to be a man. First of all, it was so violent. You need a lot of power to bash in someone's brains. But then, well, I could do it. BoomBoom's strong enough to do it. Know what I mean? Anyway, this really troubles me."

"*We know.*" Again, the three chimed in unison.

Harry tickled Mrs. Murphy's ears as the cat sat next to her on the log. "I think I know people. Then I wonder."

"*Start with yourself,*" Pewter smarted off.

6

"*D*aylight savings time starts so early now." Harry washed snap peas in the sink, tossing them in a pot when clean.

"I like more light when I get off duty, but I don't like getting up in the dark." Cooper sliced little strips of bacon on the small butcher cutting board.

Pewter leaned on Coop's leg as the tall woman performed this task.

"You're not getting any," Tucker predicted.

"Yeah, you're just saying that to make me let my guard down. If she drops any, you'll scarf it up."

"You snooze, you lose." Tucker blinked.

Mrs. Murphy, on her side, tail slowly rising and falling, stayed out of it. Her two companions had been sniping at each other all day. It wearied her.

Harry opened the oven. "Ought to be ready when he gets home. Now that foaling season is over, we can once again have regular meals. Fair works so hard."

"Yes, he does." Coop appreciated Fair's many fine

qualities, perhaps even more than Harry did, since she didn't have to deal with any of the irritating ones.

"You're staying for dinner." Harry raised one hand. "You've had a long day, you're helping me with the snap peas, so just agree with me."

"I need to weed my garden."

"I'll help you do that tomorrow. Unlike most people, I actually like weeding the garden." Harry paused long enough to pour a little butter over the roasting chicken, then closed the oven door. "When's Rick get back?"

"He'll be back at work tomorrow. I'll be glad to see him. The crime-scene team, the photographer, they all did their usual professional job, but something about this murder doesn't sit right. Usually, when you go to a crime scene, what happened is pretty obvious."

"That's not how the TV shows present it," Harry wryly noted.

"Wouldn't be any show if they did, now, would it?" Coop finished up with the bacon, scraping it into the pot with the snap peas. "What next?"

"You can wash the lettuce. I'm making a simple salad. I've got to get my husband to eat more greens."

Pewter grimaced. *"Rabbit food."*

"Yeah, I need to do that, too," Coop said.

"So what's different about this murder?"

"Oh, like I said, if you've been in law enforcement for a while, most of the murders you see aren't premeditated. Some are, but most of them are fights that escalate, maybe domestic violence that got out of hand or the wife finally decided to fight back. It's cut-and-dried. I'll tell you what bothers me a lot about this murder. All those guys at the garage drag race. Walt, on the other hand, restored old cars. Still, they seem to have all gotten along. Setting aside Kyle, the five mechanics working that day all gave exactly the same statement."

Harry turned to look at the younger deputy. "Which is?"

Coop wiped her hands. "Hold on."

She ran out to her car, took out her reporter's notebook.

"Maybe she'll take the grease from the chicken and pour it on our crunchies." Pewter would have made a wonderful chef had she been human—a step down, in her mind.

"Good idea." Mrs. Murphy sat up.

Coop returned to the kitchen, leaving the door open. A light breeze wafted through the screened-in porch off the kitchen; all the windows were open, too.

"Okay. 'We stayed late at lunch.'" She read from her notebook.

"That's it?"

"Every single one of them said just that, followed by, 'We figured we'd stay a half hour late and make up the time later that day.'"

"Hmm."

"They also agreed that Walt left early for lunch and returned to ReNu earlier than the other workers." She looked up from her reporter's book.

"Sounds rehearsed," said Harry.

"Well, it's got me thinking. Usually in a situation like this, someone or another gets all shook up and rattles on. If there's a group, they speak over one another, contradict one another. It can get emotional."

"Well, some did go outside and throw up when they saw the gore."

"Did you see them throw up?" Coop put the notebook on the table, grabbed the head of romaine lettuce, and began washing it.

"Coop, I'm not going outside to watch people puke."

"I understand that, but I didn't see any evidence of lunch."

Harry made a face. "You looked." She stopped, hands idle for a moment. "I used to think I'd make a good detective. You're proving me wrong."

"What you are is a nosy neighbor—a good neighbor, but a nosy one who stumbles on evidence." Coop elbowed her lightly. "But you see things I don't. I have to go by the book. You can rely on inspiration."

They both laughed at that.

"*Last thing our mother needs to hear,*" Mrs. Murphy said. "*Now she'll really be nosy.*"

"*Odd that humans use that particular word when they have such terrible senses of smell,*" Tucker mused.

"I gave a call to Susan and then Herb," said Harry. "To check in. They're okay."

"When I first came to the department, the reverend was driving a big Bronco. They're so cool. The old Jeep Wagoneers are, too."

"Listen to you, and you're not even a motorhead," Harry teased her. "Speaking of motorheads, maybe you should go to the drag races. Just a thought."

Cooper smiled. "If I don't, you will."

"Ah, come on, Coop. I love cars. Why shouldn't I go?"

"Why haven't you gone before?" Cooper shrewdly asked.

"I'm so busy with the farm. Get tired at night and the weekends. Fair's home more now, but he's not much for any kind of racing."

"Odd. You think he'd like horse racing." Coop waited a moment. "When's your next checkup?"

"Next week."

"You'll be fine," Coop said encouragingly.

"I think so, but it's always in the back of my mind that the cancer may do a boomerang on me. Even when I pass the five-year mark, I expect I'll still wonder. I know, I know, they say they got it all and nothing traveled." She shrugged.

"I'd feel the same way. On the other hand, I reckon a scare like that makes you appreciate life more. You don't sweat the small stuff."

"That's a fact, but, Coop, I've been looking out this kitchen window for forty years. Mom and Dad would hold me up or carry me out to the barn when I could hardly walk. For forty years I've looked at the Blue Ridge Mountains, heard the red-shouldered hawks, seen the raccoons, the deer, the fox, the bobcats, the dogwoods, redbuds, jack-in-the-pulpits, the wild roses. I've always appreciated life. The big difference is, now I know mine can end. Oh, we all know it." She tapped her head. "But now I really know it." She tapped her heart.

"Karma." Coop wrapped the lettuce in a dish towel.

"What?"

"To know that. And for all of us to be here together. I believe it's karma."

"And what about what happened to Walt? Was that karma?" Harry wasn't looking for an argument, just curious about Coop's thoughts on the subject.

"Yes. Had no friends. Family in Iowa. That's all I've found out so far, but, yes, his death is karma."

A devilish gleam lit Mrs. Murphy's gorgeous green eyes. *"Hey, Pewts, that means the blue jay that keeps attacking you, it's your karma."*

Pewter's eyes widened, her pupils filling out, her tail lifting slightly, her whiskers a little back. *"Tapeworms are yours."*

7

A mister on a timer released tiny droplets of cool water as Harry lingered over the various types of lettuce, some varieties named with imagination, like Tidewater Romaine and Low Country Early Lettuce. Taking a step back, Harry looked down at the produce section of fancy Hampton's grocery store. Harry marveled at the freshness of it all, beholding the bounty: shiny eggplants, deep oranges, tangerines, apples in every red and green imaginable. She also marveled that these sumptuous vegetables and fruits were truly organic.

As a farmer, Harry knew how insects, blight, various fungi, too much rain or not enough, could affect a crop. Few organic goodies glowed as these beauties did. Any of them would have been at home in a still-life painting of superabundance.

Then, too, how do you define organic? Fresh. Yancy stressed the point by naming his store "Fresh! Fresh! Fresh!" The market constantly advertised the purity of its goods.

The store also heavily advertised that it bought from

local farmers. Walking its aisles, Harry conceded that buying tomatoes might be easy after all. They were the number-four crop in the state. Tobacco was third, corn second, and soybeans first.

While she'd never seen a tobacco leaf in any store, the varieties of corn and tomatoes were prominently displayed. Maybe they were trucked in.

Virginia collected $1.8 million in wine liter tax revenue, and she could only imagine the monies that the big four brought to the state. Few people realized how crucial agricultural proceeds were to the economy of any state. They were all dazzled by green industry, high technology, electronics. At least Yancy was supporting Virginia farmers.

Few people bought raw soybeans. They were hulled and roasted. Harry had no idea if Yancy's soybeans came from Virginia or not.

She didn't know why she was suspicious, but she was.

She crossed her arms over her bosom. The temperature under the morning sun had been seventy-two degrees F when she'd exited the station wagon. Just enough for the trickle of sweat to roll down her cleavage and under her breasts. A lady didn't take a handkerchief and wipe down her glories any more than did a gentleman whose nether regions were prone to sweat. Harry couldn't help but think that those very breasts, lovely as they were, might have killed her. She banished the thought, continuing to troll the fruits. The tangerines' color was so deep, it just jumped out at her.

The price, four dollars and ten cents for three, also jumped out at her.

Reminding herself that she wasn't here to buy citrus, Harry checked her watch: ten o'clock sharp. Time for her appointment with Yancy Hampton. Although Monday morning was not a time one usually associated with grocery shopping, the store was jammed with well-groomed women and the occasional man. Rolex watches captured the light; discreet good earrings or diamond studs created tiny rainbows. Perfectly pressed blouses and Bermuda shorts were worn with snappy espadrilles to complete the outfits. No one was fat.

Yancy Hampton knew his market.

Harry knocked on the natural-wood door; a thin voice called out, "Come in."

Yancy Hampton rose to greet her and shake her hand. He motioned for her to sit in an ergonomically perfect chair and then sat back down in his own version, designed to take pressure off the back.

"Harry, last time I saw you was at the Cancer Ball."

"Thank you again for your support. We raised a lot of money from the five-K race, as you know, and then with the ball we raised a quarter of a million dollars. Of course, having the work of sports celebrities and media types sure helped."

"You know that Diane Long raised that or maybe a bit more for the Boys and Girls Club? Her husband, Howie, and Terry Bradshaw were the auctioneers. We should send that woman to Washington. She'd get things done."

Harry smiled, for she'd met Mrs. Long, a great beauty, only once and was deeply impressed by the fact that she'd been a classics major. "Hampton, she's too good for Washington."

He laughed. "What can I do for you?"

"BoomBoom told me you were buying crops before harvesting. I don't want to take up a lot of your time, but I found that concept unusual and intriguing."

"And I know you're growing sunflowers and grapes. I even heard you've got a plot of ginseng down by the creek there."

Harry wasn't surprised. Everybody knew everything in the county. Then again, she thought, maybe not. There was a dead man at the ReNu shop ready to disprove that theory.

She cleared her throat, for she'd paused a bit long to answer. "I'm trying to find niche crops. I don't have the implements for my tractor to grow corn. Ethanol has sure made that an attractive proposition, but I'm old-fashioned. If I did grow corn, it wouldn't be for fuel."

Yancy leaned back, folding his hands and putting them behind his head. "Scam. That's all I'll say about that. Anyway, you know I'm dedicated to locally grown products whenever possible and to products grown as naturally as possible. You are what you eat."

Harry almost said, "And you are what you do," but she halted, instead saying, "How can you buy before harvest? Mother Nature is a temperamental partner."

"I go out, look at the crop, make a bid based on past costs per bushel or per chicken, let's say, based on the prior five years of purchase price wholesale. I also have to figure in gas costs, since everything is trucked in. That means I'm getting an average. Now, the harvest might be excellent and the prices go down a bit. Or it may be the opposite and prices rise. The market giveth and the market taketh away. But you get what I bid no matter what, so you're taking your chances, as am I."

"What if the crop is destroyed?"

He frowned a moment, as that was not a happy thought. "Obviously, the deal is void. That's in the contract."

Removing his hands from behind his head, he picked up a folder, a bright lime green, and slid it across to Harry.

She rose, picked it up, placed it in her lap as she sat down. "Beautiful folder."

He beamed. "I have a weakness for office supplies. If I hadn't become a grocer, I'd have opened an office-supply store, a high-end one." He sat up straight. "You know, there's a woman in Richmond who prints on a hand press, invitations and the like. The more our economy shifts to the big box stores, the more room there is for quality and individuality."

"Yes, I think so, too. I'll read this thoroughly."

"Well, if you decide to sign on, I'll come out three times before harvest to inspect your crops. Heard you had a banner year with the sunflowers last year."

"I sure did. And this is the first year I can harvest my grapes. It really will take another four years or so before they'll be as they should."

"You were prudent to only put in a quarter acre, if for no other reason than to see how the soil affects the taste. Every vineyard, even if only two miles apart, creates its own terroir."

"Fascinating. Thank you for the compliment, but I know I can't become a big vintner. I'm learning so much with the help of others, but I think my real drive is toward the sunflowers, the ginseng. I'm also growing asparagus, though it won't be ready until next year."

"You staggered the planting, of course." He leaned forward, brown eyes bright.

"Had to. You can only pick edible asparagus every other year. That's one of the reasons it costs more."

"I'm interested in that, Harry. I can't keep fresh asparagus on the shelves. Doesn't matter if it's the type most people know around here or the large white ones, the European varieties."

She stood up. "Thank you for seeing me."

"My pleasure."

She left, took two steps from the office as she closed the door behind her, and ran smack into Franny Howard, owner of a large tire store.

"Harry, I'm so sorry." Franny's hand flew to her lips, pink with color.

Harry laughed. "Hey, I'm just glad you weren't behind the wheel of your car."

"I do a little better there. Not so many distractions. Isn't your checkup next Wednesday?"

"Is."

"Want me to go with you?" Franny had also survived cancer, before Harry was diagnosed.

Franny had brought Harry into the cancer support group.

"Oh, thanks, Franny. I know I'm going to be fine."

"Yes, you will. Say, I read in the papers where you, Reverend Jones, and Susan found that body at ReNu Auto Works. Must have been a shock."

"Was. No suspects yet. The guy seems to have led a quiet life."

"Those are the tough ones. You peel away the layers. There's always something bubbling at the center, I swear. ReNu undercuts everyone's prices. I guess if the killer were one of their competitors, they'd have brained Vic Gatzembizi instead." She named the owner.

"Have to catch him. He's on the move between his shops. People like you and Vic have so much ambition." Harry's lips curled upward, a wry half smile.

"Thank you." Franny nodded. "Victor, you know, just in passing recommends people to me who are looking for new tires. Obviously vehicles in his shop for repair will have to use what the insurance company will pay for. But Victor is good to me, steering shall we say— non-smacked-up customers?" She lowered her voice. "Hear he's got ladies in all his shop sites. Bet his wife would kill him if she knew. On the other hand, he gives her everything. Whatever she's doing, I need to learn. Need to develop those skills."

"Honey, I think you have skill enough in that department." Harry laughed.

On the way home, with Mrs. Murphy, Pewter, and Tucker all crammed in the front seat, Harry laughed again at Franny. Thinking about cars and tires reminded her she needed to check in with Miranda and that she'd promised to wax Miranda's Falcon. Given the backlog at ReNu, Miranda would need a loaner. Safe & Sound should supply her with one, but just in case, Harry would offer her the station wagon.

Harry drove onto the bypass as she headed for Route 250 west. Taking the bypass, she'd avoid a lot of local traffic.

That plan came to a halt, literally. Flashing lights, policemen, and firemen stopped the flow of cars, trucks, delivery trucks. The line looked to be long.

"Dammit," Harry cussed, then read her gas gauge.

Half a tank. She'd be fine, even if the wait dragged on. She saw Rick Shaw and Coop up ahead, in a heated discussion with a state trooper. He had his hands on his hips, then walked to his cruiser, got in, and called.

Seeing Harry's Volvo, Coop walked down to her.

"Hey, what's going on?" asked Harry.

"Milk truck overturned."

"So."

"Federal law: The butterfat in milk is oil. We have to treat this as an environmental hazard. I've just been read the EPA guidelines. Rick and I are trying to convince Johnny Jump Up"—Coop called all state troopers this—"to allow us to create a single lane, since the spill has flowed over the far right lane and into the runoff. But, hey, milk is a danger."

"I don't believe this."

"Believe it." Coop dealt with the endless costly mandates that spewed forth from D.C. every single day.

Coop turned as Rick called for her, slapping the side of the station wagon as she did so.

"Mom is boiling hot," Mrs. Murphy warned.

The traffic, directed into a single lane, began moving. As Harry passed the overturned milk truck, Coop winked at her.

Once finally home, she hurried to her little office in the tack room and turned on her MacBook Pro computer, bought for her by her husband, as she didn't want to spend the money. He said they needed it for his work. But he really hoped she'd learn to use it. Fair carried his own high-powered laptop. He'd go through one a year, but it was invaluable for veterinary medicine.

Harry, peering into the seventeen-inch screen, called out to her friends, "The EPA, after direction by the White House, proposed in 2009 to exempt spilled milk from being treated the same as oil and fuel spills. That was years ago." She slapped the desk in frustration. She'd made up her mind to snoop at ReNu tomorrow and wanted to avoid a slowdown in case the milk had soaked into the road on the one lane. It really was absurd.

Simon, the possum, leaned over the side of the hayloft. "Is she one step ahead of a running fit?"

Tucker, upset because Harry was upset, sat looking upward, the center aisle cool underneath her butt. "She's pretty hot."

Mrs. Murphy, on a tack trunk, added, "She has her breast checkup Wednesday. She's more irritable than usual."

"Mom isn't very irritable." Tucker quickly defended Harry.

Pewter, next to Mrs. Murphy, smiled sweetly. "True, but you are."

"I am not." Tucker growled.

"The truth hurts." Pewter puffed out her chest.

Tucker, now on her hind legs, lunged after Pewter, who easily eluded the corgi.

A frightened Simon scurried to his nest filled with treasures, in the back of the hayloft.

Pewter climbed up the side of the ladder, Tucker snapping at her heels.

Harry thumped out of the office. "That's enough. Do you all hear me? Enough!" Then she turned again, glaring at Tucker. "Tucker."

Dropping her ears, Tucker plopped down but continued to bare her teeth at the gloating cat overhead.

Tired of tormenting the dog, Pewter found Simon in his den, a big hollowed-out space in a hay bale. Harry knew the location of his den and never disturbed it.

Mrs. Murphy, having heard enough of Tucker's complaint of disrespect, no matter how well founded, climbed up the ladder to join Simon and Pewter.

"Look at this." Simon, dexterous, picked up a shiny pen with metallic lime-green dots on the surface.

"Very pretty." Pewter complimented his taste.

"And how about this? It's kind of snaky." Simon held up a narrow-gauge rubber hose, which had been reinforced with fiber put into the various layers. "It wiggles."

"Smells like oil," Mrs. Murphy, nose keen, noted. "Not burning oil, gear kind of oil."

As it came off the big John Deere tractor, it indeed smelled of gear oil.

The mention of oil provoked Pewter to recount to Simon the saga of the spilled milk.

Dear little Simon believed every word of Pewter's embellished story, and Mrs. Murphy had the wisdom not to contradict her.

8

"*S*he's mental." Pewter fastidiously stepped over a grease spot that had permanently soaked into the concrete floors at ReNu.

Asking permission from no one, Harry had driven to town to examine the garage. She'd bribed her way past the front desk.

Mrs. Murphy, also avoiding the grease, replied, "*She's never going to change. We're accused of being curious, but she's worse than any cat could ever be.*"

"*Curiosity killed the cat. I hate that phrase. She's come closer to death because of it than we have. If it weren't for us, Harry would be dead.*" Pewter was most certainly right about that, too.

Over the years, Harry's desire to solve any puzzle had put her, the cats and dog, even her friends, in jeopardy. The animals, thanks to their superior senses, always knew the hammer was dropping long before their human did. Sometimes they could nudge her out of harm's way. Other times she was knocked down with a thump. She never seemed to learn. Her husband had accepted this irritating personality trait. The animals were less flexible about it, although Pewter could always be brought around with fresh tuna.

"*What nearly killed her was giving that slug at the front desk twenty dollars to let us in here at lunchtime.*" Tucker laughed. "*Twenty dollars. She's out of control.*"

"Out of control" may have been too strong a description of Harry's behavior, but at the very least she was intrusive and foolhardy.

Nose to the ground, the corgi shot straight over to where Walt's body once sprawled. "*Mmm. Old blood. Old brains. Nothing left, but the aroma is heaven.*"

The two cats, not carrion eaters, appreciated the canine stomach nonetheless. Even Pewter, now interested, passed up this opportunity to criticize the dog.

After the forensics team left, Victor Gatzembizi had called in a special crew to clean up the mess before the next day's work. The husband-and-wife duo couldn't lift the bloodstains out of the concrete, but they'd managed to clean up all the tiny bits of hair and skull. The forensics team had collected most of it, but there were always tiny fragments left or stuck under a cabinet. It's amazing what flies out of and off a body that has been dramatically violated.

Good as the cleanup job had been, those kitty noses and that corgi nose could still detect information.

"*I think his head was here.*" Tucker stood on a spot.

"*Well, something was here.*" Pewter found the place where the tire iron had been.

Harry saw where her animals were, once again reminded of how keen their senses were. "That's the place. He didn't have a chance."

She drew in a notebook. The garage, spotless as a matter of course, shone even more now after an incredible cleaning. Each of the four hydraulic lifts had a vehicle on it. Every workstation had a tall red toolbox with many pullout doors. Taped across the front drawer was the name of the mechanic. The boxes, on casters, could be moved about. Having each man responsible for his tools was another of Victor's prudent decisions. Victor bought all the tools, but every man was held accountable for his toolbox. If anyone was fired, the contents of his red toolbox were immediately inventoried. Victor knew all about the old game of someone bringing tools to work but when the employee left claiming others. This way, Victor paid for tools but he paid only once.

One large box, four feet high, had been rolled against the wall. The name "Richardson" was still on the top drawer, black Magic Marker ink on masking tape.

The walls were covered by steel industrial shelving, with ladders attached at the top so they, too, could roll. On the shelves were air filters, fan belts, items easily stored. Ford, General Motors, Chrysler, Toyota, Subaru, Nissan parts filled boxes, all numbered to indicate the model and year.

Harry knew that most jobs required a wait while the particular engine parts were shipped to the collision repair shop. No one had the space for the inventory required when repairing all makes and models. But the basic easy stuff was there: batteries, windshield wipers. No tires, however. This puzzled her.

Wrapped up in her drawings, she lost track of time. Jason Brundige, a young mechanic, walked in from lunch. His buddy Nick Ashby walked next to him. "Who are you? Weren't you the woman who found Walt?"

"I am."

The animals stared at the medium-size fellow.

"You shouldn't be here."

"Don't talk to my mother that way." Tucker curled back her upper lip.

"You're right." Feeling the hostility, Harry headed for the open bay.

As she strode past Nick Ashby, the young man smiled, happy to see a good-looking woman, whether she belonged there or not.

As Harry walked out, with Mrs. Murphy, Pewter, and Tucker at her heels, the other mechanics—Bobby Foltz, Lodi Pingrey, and Sammy Collona—returned from lunch.

Sammy knew her slightly. "Harry, I've heard of criminals returning to the scene of the crime, but not witnesses."

Chagrined at being caught, Harry said, "I . . . I couldn't stay away. I don't know why; I had to see it again."

"Once should be enough, lady," Lodi snapped.

With that, Harry climbed into the F-150, after lifting in Tucker. The cats were already inside.

As Harry cranked the motor, Nick Ashby trotted out, Jason Brundige glaring after him.

Making the time-out sign with his hands, the cute young Ashby said, "The guys aren't as bad as they sound. Everyone's upset, jumpy."

"Well, I was kind of trespassing."

"It's okay. Next time you want to come around, call me. Nick Ashby." He reached through the open truck window with his right hand to shake hers.

"Thanks, Nick. I will." Releasing his hand, she looked into his eyes. "I am sorry about what you all have been through. Something that shocking doesn't fade away quickly in one's mind."

He shrugged. "Things happen. You just gotta accept them and keep going. I learned a lot from Walt. He was hard on me, but he made me a better mechanic. I'll miss him, but I won't miss getting cussed out." He smiled.

"Guess for some people it's the stick, not the carrot, if that makes sense."

"Does. I'm really a carrot guy." He flashed a megawatt smile.

"I'll bring you some bunnies." Harry laughed as he patted the truck windowsill, bidding her goodbye.

She drove to Franny's shop. She left the vehicle's windows cracked and ran in. The ever-busy Franny, on her phone at her desk, waved in Harry.

Hanging up the phone, she said, "And?"

"You okay?"

"Of course I'm okay."

Harry briefly recounted where she'd been, the response of the returning mechanics, and then she said, "No tires. Not one. Strange."

"Not really." Franny stood up, smoothed her skirt, and sat down again. "Tires take up a lot of room. Most people don't know too much about tires, so a shop like ReNu will generally just put on what the manufacturer originally had on the vehicle, unless the customer asks for something else."

"Does Victor ever buy tires from you?"

"Rarely. He calls in orders from the various whole-salers or tire manufacturers, if possible. And as you may know, the whole piece comes: It's an entire wheel, tire already on it. In the old days, you'd pry the tire off with a tire iron. You can still change a tire if you get a flat, but for ReNu's purposes, it's easier to pop on an entire wheel. I think all this is economically generated, be-cause the customer has to buy so much more than, say, in the 1950s or 1960s. Though it's true you do get your car back faster."

"You've answered my question. You were close, so I dropped in without calling. I apologize."

"No apology needed after all we've been through. I just heard that Willa's cancer has returned."

Willa Reisman was a member of their cancer support group.

"Oh, no."

"She made it four years, but damned if a spot hasn't been found in her lung. That's the thing: Those cells can travel. She had breast cancer, as you know."

"Think they found it in time?"

"Hope so. She begins treatment next week. You know how viruses for computers are encrypted in something else, something that seems innocent?"

"Yeah."

"That's what I think cancer does. Malware. God, I hate this disease."

"I do, too." Harry sighed, then changed the subject. "Do you think Victor at ReNu is a good businessman?"

"One of the best."

"He hired a slacker for the front desk. I gained access to the garage during lunch break by slipping Kyle some money. So I'm thinking about that, you know. Victor is penny-wise and pound-foolish."

Franny played with her earring for a moment. "I guess we all are, to a degree. I know Victor very well, and he also respects mechanics. He probably doesn't think too much about the front desk."

"But you hired a good person."

"The front desk is your face to the public. It's the first employee of your company most people meet. You're damned right I have a good person, but I'm selling. Victor isn't. When the squashed car comes to him with the blown radiator or whatever, Victor already has the job. Still, you've given me something to think about."

"What?"

"How sharp you are and how you rush in where angels fear to tread. Once you're in a mess, you miss very little."

"I'm not really in a mess. I just discovered Walt's body, along with Herb and Susan."

"Harry." Franny lifted an eyebrow. "Why are you asking me all this?"

Harry shrugged. "Dunno."

Franny shrugged, too. "Whatever this was about—could have been anything, an outraged husband, a deal gone sour—I personally am not going to worry unless tire dealers go missing."

• • •

Back in the truck, the animals stayed silent until they reached the farm. Murphy and Pewter spilled out of the truck, ran around the yard and to the barn, glad to be away from all those machine odors. Pewter sashayed to the house.

Pewter sat under the enormous walnut tree next to the house. Matilda, the huge blacksnake with glittering eyes, silently crawled down the tree—bark easy for her to grip—until she reached the lowest branch, about ten feet up. Wrapping her tail around the thick branch, she swung down above the gray cat's head. While she wasn't near enough to touch, the blacksnake was close.

"*S-s-s-s.*" She flicked out her forked red tongue.

Pewter, ears so good, looked up. She let out a scream, ran through the screened-in porch door, which had an animal door in it, and then through to the kitchen itself.

"*Ha.*" Matilda was full of herself.

Mrs. Murphy, sitting in the center aisle, saw Pewter run, then saw the source of the dash.

"*Hey, Tucker. Come here.*"

The dog joined her feline friend, who gave her the story. They watched the large snake swing back up onto the big branch.

"*She has an evil sense of humor.*" Mrs. Murphy laughed.

"*Should we go into the kitchen? Pewter will be very upset.*" Tucker did love the gray butterball.

"*We'll need smelling salts.*"

The two laughed uproariously.

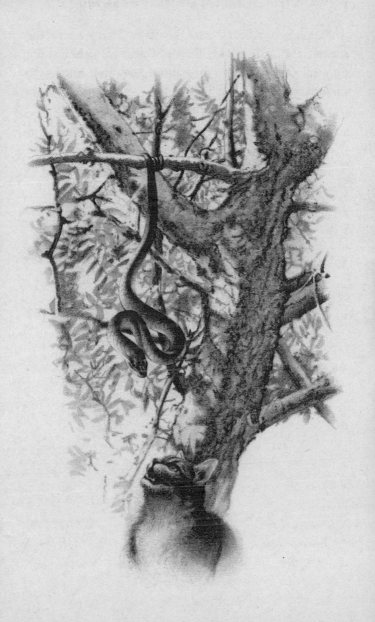

Flipping hay flakes into the stalls, Harry heard the meows and little barks, then saw her animals leaning on each other and thought about how love knows no boundaries.

For that matter, neither does hate.

9

The next day, Franny Howard, almost always the first person at work, unlocked the door to the showroom. The immaculate garage behind the showroom had three large drive-in bays where tires could be put onto vehicles. Franny ran a tight ship.

Fresh morning coolness brushed her too-rouged cheeks. No sooner did she hear the click, click of the large lock than she sensed something wrong. Opening the door, she looked at the long countertop, the desks behind that, and her own office behind that. Everything looked to be in order. She checked the counter, the shelves underneath. Nothing amiss. She turned on each of the three computers, punched up information she considered sensitive. Nothing had been stolen that she could discern.

Then she unlocked the door to her office. Again, everything was as she'd left it last night before meeting friends for an intimate dinner at Keswick Sports Club.

Hands on hips, she breathed in. Why did she feel such unease? Turning on her mid-height heel, Franny walked out from her office to the front of the long polished counter, then opened the door into the garage just as Mackie Rogan hit the button to roll up one of the doors to a big bay. He turned to face the inside of the service area at the same time as Franny stepped into it.

Both of their mouths fell open.

"What the hell?" Mackie finally gasped.

Franny hurried over to the area where the various brands of tires were kept, each clearly marked. "Goddammit! Goddammit to hell!" she cursed, a rarity.

Mackie, now next to her, intoned as though reciting a litany, "Goodyear Eagle F1 GS-D3, empty. Continental ContiSportContact 2, empty. Yokohama ADVAN Neova AD07, empty. Michelin Pilot Sport PS2, empty. All of them."

Arms across her chest, trying to assess the damage, Franny nodded. "Whoever cleaned us out knew tires and was a high-performance freak. A real high-performance freak."

"Boss, this is terrible." Mackie cast his eyes over their remaining inventory. "They left the Hankook Ventus, the Toyo Proxes, the Pirelli PZeroes, the Dunlops SPs. Damned good tires."

Swiftly calculating, Franny shook her head. "Mackie, I tote up about twenty-five thousand dollars."

He put his big hand on her thin shoulder. "Yep. They'll be on the black market by tonight."

Not one to fade during a crisis, Franny patted his hand. "I'm glad you were the first one in the service area. You can keep your wits about you. Check the security system. I'll call the sheriff. And, Mackie, let's see who notices when they arrive for work."

Mackie's dark eyes widened. "You don't think one of the boys did it, do you?"

"No. We have a good team. But what I'm curious about is how long it takes our guys to notice and what happens when they do. It teaches you about people."

Mackie nodded, as always impressed by Franny's shrewdness. He briskly walked to the metal door that enclosed the expensive security system.

Franny hurried back into the office to call the sheriff on a landline. Put it on a computer, call from your cellphone, and it was out in the world, never to be recalled. One could never control the new technology, despite loud government and corporate protests to the contrary. All this whirled through her mind as she dialed.

No sooner had she spoken to the sheriff's department than Mackie opened the door into the front area. He was a large man, and she recognized his heavy tread. Emerging from her office, she smiled at him. She trusted Mackie; they'd worked together since she founded the business in the mid-eighties, a time when it was not terribly easy for a divorced woman to get a business loan.

"Our security system was disabled. Whoever did this knew about more than tires," Mackie told Franny.

"How'd they get the door open?"

"I think with a tiny welding flame. Just sliced clean through the lock. I checked the regular door into the service area. M.O."

"Mackie, can I get you a drink?"

He smiled. "No. Tell you what, it was a shock."

"Yes." She looked at him imploringly for a moment. "Why do people steal? It takes so much knowledge, so much hard work. Wouldn't it be easier to be upright?"

He shrugged. "Greater profit, no taxes, I guess. And if this is a large operation . . . well," he fumbled, "there must be some sort of protection if the thief is caught."

"Yes, yes. You always see things I don't." She flattered him, but it was the truth. "Stupid criminals act on impulse. Intelligent ones plan and protect one another."

"I'm sorry."

"I am, too." She smiled at him, remembering how young he was when she hired him, her first hire. "But we'll get through it. We always do."

"We will," he said with conviction.

With Rick at the wheel on their way up Route 29, Cooper took the dispatcher's call. The sheriff decided they could go to ReNu after this. He wanted to question the mechanics at ReNu himself, and Coop wanted to walk through the garage to see if she or anyone else had missed anything. Given the variables at a crime scene, especially murder, things could go overlooked. But Franny's call required immediate attention.

Once there, both sheriff and deputy reached the same conclusion that Mackie had: This was the work of professionals.

Rick took notes while interviewing the other employees of the tire company as they arrived. Cooper listened intently. She was an excellent listener.

Rick respected Franny and spoke plainly to her. "This

is going on all over America. One of the biggest tire heists was a few months ago in Reno."

"Why there?" Franny motioned for the front-office girl to simply sit down when she walked into the scene. Isabelle, a bit frightened, did just that.

Coop looked over at Isabelle and said, "No one was hurt. We just need to ask you and everyone a few questions."

"Yes, ma'am," the diminutive young woman replied.

Rick leaned toward Franny. "These operations have big warehouses. Huge business. Cheap storage, dry conditions. They set up near a good airport so things can be easily shipped all over. It's easier for some companies to use those huge storage units for inventory than to take up space at the factory or, worse, build."

After Rick and Coop left, Franny sat down to write a preliminary summary of her investigation so far. Never hurt to put it on paper. Making lists, checking inventory—tasks that often bored others—helped her think. As she pulled up her inventory on the computer, she reviewed how many computer systems she'd gone through since starting up. Then she recalled a squib she'd read in The Kiplinger Letter, saying that the number of small businesses started by women was growing 50 percent faster than the number of businesses started up by men. She was especially pleased that one of the fields booming with female ownership was construction.

Franny felt no particular competitiveness against men, but she rejoiced when women succeeded in male-dominated fields. One thing life had taught Franny was that most reasonably intelligent men knew where their economic self-interest lay and put their energies into those businesses that would turn a profit.

In a tiny way, she felt that young women wanting to steer their own ships was her little victory, too. Now, if she could just encourage women to take more risks, for Franny well knew that greater risks meant greater profits.

Then she came back to the present. Seemed she had run risk enough in her youth. The funny thing was Franny, like most people, thought life would get easier as she got older. It didn't. She just got better at handling the crises.

10

"*H*e was a brilliant mechanic. Not that the other guys are bad, but they plug in the cars to the computers. They're very dependent on technology. Walt was, too, but he had a feel. Computers don't."

"How long had you known him?" Cooper asked.

As she conducted the questioning, Rick sat in the squad car using his computer to get statistics on the splatter pattern of dashed brains. Information like that could be helpful in determining just where the assailant stood.

Victor Gatzembizi leaned back in his comfortable office chair. "A long time, actually. He worked for a big Chrysler–Dodge–Jeep dealership in Richmond. When disaster struck Chrysler, he figured sooner or later he'd be fired, the dealership would close, or both. I hired him. Hadn't opened the shop here yet, but I wasn't going to let anyone that good go. As it was, I had this place opened three months after I hired him."

"No troubles?" Cooper also leaned back, then sat upright. She was tired and needed to stay sharp.

"No."

"It would appear he wasn't popular with the other men."

Victor's dark eyebrows rose. "No one complained to me."

"Would it have done any good?"

This caught the handsome forty-one-year-old man off guard, so he paused. "If the complaints piled up, had some commonality, I would have listened. Officer, you've probably not run a business."

"No." She didn't take offense.

He smiled. "You get some people who like to work, take pride in their work. You get slackers and those you need to fire right off. But most men fall into the middle; they might like what they do well enough, but it's all about that paycheck. They live for the weekends. Walt loved cars, loved engines, loved working on them. If anyone spoke badly of him to you, I'd be willing to bet there was a tinge of jealousy, resentment there—maybe because I favored him, made him the floor boss."

Cooper silently noted that none of the mechanics had mentioned this. "I see. I'm hoping you can help me, and these questions might seem tangential, but emotional relationships nine times out of ten can point us in the right direction to solving a crime. This one was brutal. A great deal of emotion may have been involved."

Victor grimaced. "I can't imagine anyone out back"— he motioned with his head toward the rear of the building, as they sat in his well-appointed office—"hated him that much. And, I repeat, I heard nothing. You'd think I would have heard some grumbling. Kyle's quick to pick up crap like that. If anything, he revels in it."

"Troublemaker?"

Victor shook his head and laughed slightly. "No. Kyle's young, and he's one of those people who pounces on the negative."

Victor was right about that, Cooper thought to herself, but mostly what Kyle had pounced on was Victor himself. The young man, without launching a frontal attack, snidely characterized his boss to Cooper during questioning as a pompous rich ass fond of flashy cars, jewelry, and (he hinted) women, despite Victor's marriage.

"Have you ever suffered any kind of robbery here?" Coop asked.

"You'd know."

"Not if it was only a slight imbalance in the till, not enough to call in our department. A muffler missing here and there. That kind of thing."

"No, I have honest people here. Although I do know that toilet paper and paper towels occasionally have gone missing, as well as far too many ReNu tablets and pens." He shrugged. "That's any business. Employees think they're entitled to those items, especially since we do give out pens and tablets to customers. But it can add up quicker than they imagine. One year I had a stationery bill of three thousand some dollars. I let everyone know I was pissed."

"Would scare me," she teased him.

Coop, good at questioning, read people fast and accurately. Some needed to feel safe, others needed to be knocked down a peg, some feared that revealing information would cost them their jobs—and, depending on the information, it just might. Others feared physical reprisals, especially with certain types of murder, and Walt's carried a hint of that. Anyone who would bash out someone's brains with a tire iron either possessed a hair-trigger temper or didn't much mind hurting someone. That could include anyone who got in the way while they covered up the first murder. Victor liked congeniality. Cooper provided that, and her good looks certainly assisted the process.

He smiled at her mock fright. "Oh, you've dealt with a lot worse than myself, Deputy."

Her turn to laugh. "Mr. Gatzembizi—"

"Call me Victor."

"Victor." She waited a moment. "Have you received threats concerning your business?"

"No." A cautious note crept into his voice. "But ReNu is a relatively new firm, founded here in 2007, as you know. I also have shops in Richmond, Virginia Beach, Alexandria, and Norfolk." He brightened. "Norfolk—all those sailors. The young ones get loaded on the weekends and it's one fender bender after another. Perfect for me." He grinned broadly.

"No threats at all?"

"You mean from a disgruntled customer or from another business? No. Well, this sounds like so much hype, but I don't have disgruntled customers. I fix their cars. If there remains a problem, I do any further work gratis so they don't have to keep dealing with their insurance companies. That's where the real problems are. By the time the client gets to me, he or she has been exhausted by all the people they've had to talk to—the claims adjuster, et cetera. It's a bit better if they deal locally. Tell you what, Officer, don't get in an accident."

"I know that. You get a lot of business."

"There are a lot of accidents in Charlottesville. As you know, hey, anywhere there's a college, there are plenty of accidents."

She flipped through her notebook. "The various insurance companies cite you as providing reasonable rates for repairs."

"Yes, I have a good relationship with all of them. And I can usually undercut other shops. I'm more efficient. It's not rocket science."

"I see. You don't think one of those other shops—let me put it this way, someone would try to harm your business?"

"The way to harm my business would be to offer quality work cheaper than I do. It would be pretty stupid to kill my best mechanic. Better to steal him away, pay him more."

"Yes, it would." She again agreed with him.

"Officer, I'm a successful businessman in a difficult time. Really. Every time I turn around it's a new law, a new ruling, a new tax. I hire good people, which is half of success. I'm always looking for better ways to provide service, and that isn't always easy, especially given the materials cars are made out of now. Entire bumpers fall off. In the old days those bumpers were made of steel. Used to be pretty simple to repair carburetors. Fuel injection is a wonderful thing, but it's more expensive

when something goes wrong. If I undercut my competitors, it's their own fault. But, still, to kill one of my
people—I can't believe it."

Coop had let him ramble a bit. Often people revealed
far more than they intended to if you let them go on. It
wasn't necessarily facts but a sense of the situation and a
strong sense of who that speaker was.

Victor Gatzembizi was intelligent and slick. She understood his self-interest—not necessarily a bad thing.
She sensed he was a ruthless competitor, although the
form that took appeared to be honest. He cared about
his appearance. He really had built a successful business.
Her own work on this told her that. Big shops across
the state, forty-six employees, a few part-time. That was
a pretty lean number, so he saved money there. By all
accounts he paid very well, rewarding good work. His
employee turnover stayed low.

Coop returned to her squad car, where Rick bent over
his laptop. He'd walked through the repair shop and the
body shop. He had wanted to see those splatter patterns on the computer and he had a special meeting that
night with the county commissioners, not public. Not
only would this murder come up, so would the budget.
He wanted to be prepared, and if he sat in headquarters it would be one interruption after another. As for
all sheriffs or police chiefs, battles over funding were a
major obstacle—a bleeding ulcer, really—yet everyone
expected law-enforcement services.

He shut off the computer. "Well?"

"Rick, everyone's been helpful. Victor Gatzembizi
freely answered any questions. He said Walt was his best

mechanic. Still, neither Victor nor anyone else seems remotely distressed over Walt's murder. Oh, they're all horrified at the way it happened. No one says they wished him dead, but no one wishes him back, either."

"Strange."

"I'll say." She cut on the motor and drove off the ReNu lot.

11

"Gotcha!" Miranda tossed a weed over her shoulder into the half-full wheelbarrow. "Death to weeds."

The Very Reverend Jones sneaked up on her as he trod softly on her beautiful herringbone brick walkway. He clucked. "Miranda, plants are living. God made all living things."

She stood up with some help from Herb. "You've come to test me, I see."

His deep voice, always soothing, replied, "I came to see one of my favorite people. And, as always, your garden puts others to shame."

She shook her index finger at him. "Now you're testing me for the sin of pride?"

"Well, it's true. Your garden dazzles and, of course, Big Mim tries hard to cover her envy about your emerald thumbs."

They both laughed, for the Queen of Crozet, Big Mim Sanburne, lavished huge sums of money on her gardens, tended by three gardeners, and while beautiful, those gardens couldn't hold a candle to the small but exquisite gardens of Miranda.

"How about some iced tea? I need a break. Un-tea, as I recall."

"I'd love some." He patted his stomach. "I do miss sweetened tea, but I am trying to cut back on the sugar."

"You've lost weight."

"Thank you." He smiled. "Thirty more pounds. Tell you what, Miranda, the pounds just creep up. Too much sitting." He smiled again. "You slimmed down."

They walked to her back porch, screened in as most back porches were in this part of the world.

"Did. Tending to Didee put me off food." She poured tea from a cooler she kept on the table when she worked outside. "Herb, it's easy to have faith when everything's going your way. Watching my sister die, well, I asked painful questions and I have no answers."

"None of us do. You were wonderful to your sister and she was grateful. You have a deep capacity for love and hard work, Miranda. You endured George's passing with similar fortitude." Herb mentioned her late husband.

"That was so long ago," she said almost wistfully. "And mercifully quick."

"I pray for a heart attack." He held up his hand. "It's up to the Good Lord, but why linger?" He paused. "Is there anything I can do, sweetie?"

"Your friendship is healing. You, Harry, Susan, and the girls." She referred to BoomBoom and Alicia as the girls. "I have such wonderful friends."

"Because you're a wonderful friend."

They drank their tea, both in rocking chairs, pushing away.

"Recovered?" she asked him.

"From what?"

"Finding that body at ReNu."

"Poor fellow didn't have a chance. It was gruesome. But somehow I can't stop thinking"—he shifted his weight—"that if only I had walked in a few minutes earlier, I might have been able to stop it. Rush forward, yell, anything. Know what I mean?"

She nodded her agreement. "I understand."

They rocked some more. A soft breeze lifted the wisteria climbing over the back porch and onto the roof, yet another chore Miranda would attend to in time: taming her wisteria.

"Herb, to change the subject. You picked up your truck from ReNu."

"Finally, yes. The sheriff's department wanted to examine every vehicle on the lot."

"Are you satisfied with the work?"

He put his glass down. "Sure, but I just got the truck back. Hopefully I won't have further problems."

"Safe and Sound gave me a list of acceptable repair garages. ReNu is the only one in our area. Now, that doesn't seem right. I'm not paying to have my Outback towed to Richmond. But Latigo Bly says ReNu does good work at good prices."

"Any idea how long it will take for your car to be repaired?" Herb asked.

"Once I get on the schedule, it should take a day. Of course, they cover themselves by making me sign a paper saying if more damage is discovered they will not perform the work until Safe and Sound agrees to it. Herb, this goes on and on."

"Well, it does. I went through the same thing. Everybody is covering their butt."

She changed the subject. "I bought a Dell. Lots of good stuff for a good price. Well, there's another company. You try getting something fixed or help from a so-called geek at Dell. What a nightmare. I'm learning about more than computers!"

"I've heard Dell's support is dreadful." He fished the mint out of his tea to chew. "Comes down to service. As long as everything works, you're fine. Those great online deals make you feel like you're smart. I'd rather pay more for a product and know the people that sold it to me will stand behind it." He smiled at her sideways. "You know I stand by my product."

She laughed. "You stinker. Did you come over here to try to get me to leave the Church of the Holy Light? I know you think I'm a Holy Roller."

"Did I ever say that, Miranda? Even once?"

"You didn't have to. You high-church people can be such snobs. You aren't, though."

"Well, now, I am a Lutheran pastor and I will always be a Lutheran pastor, but I believe we can all work together. I guess where I have trouble is reaching out to the fanatics, at least those whom I consider fanatics. The folks who preach about a God of vengeance."

"Yes." She sighed. "Sometimes Reverend Paisley gets carried away with the fire and brimstone." She brightened. "Other than that, I do love my church. I feel I have a direct relationship to God, and I don't feel that in what I think of as the high churches."

He considered this. "Yes. I know what you mean, Miranda. I really do, but I believe in the liturgy, as well. You know how I feel and I know how you feel. We both do the best we can with what we have."

"Some days are better than others. Some days I'm bitter about how my sister suffered."

He nodded. "But she's gone home."

"She has. I like to think that Mama and Daddy, and Yippy, her little Pomeranian, were there to welcome her. Well, here I am getting misty."

"Miranda, one of the reasons I cherish you is that you're not afraid to show your feelings. And while we're on the subject of feeling, you know Harry has her checkup this afternoon."

"Yes." Miranda pushed off harder with her left foot. "She'll be fine. After this checkup, she doesn't need to go back for a year."

"Our girl has trouble with feelings. Tries to cut them off." Herb got up and poured himself another glass of tea. Normally this would be rude, but they'd known each other for more than forty years.

"Now, I could have done that. I'm being a poor hostess."

He sat back down. "I dropped by unexpectedly. I'm lucky to be received." He winked at her. "Plus, you're really rocking there, girl. I wouldn't want you to have an accident."

They both laughed. She slowed down her rocking-chair rhythm.

"One accident was enough, and that happened so fast."

"Always does. Hey, you heard about Franny?"

"I'm afraid so. It's been one thing after another around here. I do have some good news, however."

"I'm ready."

"Little Mim is going to have a baby."

He clapped his hands. "You don't say."

"Big Mim called me today. She and Jim are over the moon. Aunt Tally is already taking charge—God help Little Mim when her great-aunt gets into it—and I heard that Blair bought every cigar at the shop in Barracks Road as well as the one up by Giant."

"Those are expensive cigars."

"Wonder if he'll give me one?" Miranda put her finger to her lips.

"Ask him."

"I think we should all descend upon them—calling, of course—bring little gifts, and then smoke a cigar. Well, I can't smoke one, but I can suck in a celebratory puff. I'll ask for a cheap cigar. No point in wasting one."

"When a man is about to become a father, the cost of cigars are part of the thrill." Herb clapped again. "What good news. 'Course, he'll have to buy more once the baby arrives."

"He did jump the gun, didn't he? Still, it's good news."

12

"*A*re you in there?" Susan stood outside the clinic's narrow changing booth, its brightly colored cotton curtains shutting off the occupant from the other women at the mammogram center.

"What are you doing here?" A note of surprise crept into Harry's voice.

"I longed to see you in hospital chic."

"Susan, I told you I could do this myself. It's just a checkup."

"You told me, but that doesn't mean I listened. Now, are you going to invite me in or not?"

Harry pulled open the curtain. "All right."

Susan stopped, looked her best friend up and down, head to toe. "Oh, honey, brown paisley becomes you."

"Shut up." Harry laughed as she plopped down on the bench, Susan dropping beside her.

"At least your boob's not hanging out."

"Did that." Harry glanced down at the top of her breasts, visible in the thin shift. "Ever consider what a royal pain these things are?"

"July. That's the worst. For me, anyway. You can't stop sweating. You can lift up your blouse to wipe yourself dry. You go into air-conditioning and the wet feels cold. Walk outside into the furnace again and more sweat. Ugh. Even now, May, I'm starting to sweat a little." Susan paused. "How long ago was your mammogram taken?"

"Fifteen, twenty minutes. I really don't like them."

"It's the squish that gets you. You can't move. Still, it's a wonderful tool. When I look back on some of our parents' friends who died of breast cancer, I wonder if they'd have been saved if only they'd had mammograms. The technology we have today," Susan mused out loud.

"Bet a lot would. And a hundred years from now, even these methods will look primitive." Harry crossed one leg over the other. "Much as we dislike the boob squisher, it beats a prostate exam."

They laughed.

"Been back to ReNu?" Susan asked, a slight accusatory note in her voice.

"Why would you ask that?" Harry asked, suspicious of her longtime friend.

"Because I've known you all your life. Spill it, sister."

"You're just fishing. You don't know anything."

"I ran into Nick Ashby at Fresh! He mentioned that he'd seen you. He has a good memory, because he remembered my face from that awful day."

A slight pause followed Susan's revelation. "I take it Nick flashed his big smile for you," Harry said.

"Did."

"Sometimes I hate this town. People talk too much," Harry grumbled.

"They talk too much in Istanbul, in Paris, France—and even up the road in Paris, Virginia, too. Human nature."

"Yeah, yeah." Harry leaned back against the wall.

"I'm waiting."

"Me, too. I hope my X rays don't need a second reading."

"This place is packed today. Aren't you glad Ruth let me back here to find you?"

Ruth was the head nurse, who had gone to high school with them.

"I have to think about that."

Susan punched her in the arm. "Why did you go back to ReNu? Harry, you are out of your mind. How do you know the killer doesn't work there?"

"I don't, but I keep seeing that body sprawled out, faceup. Bothers me. We must have missed something. The sheriff must have missed something."

"It's not your job to find Walt's killer."

"I know, but . . ." Her voice trailed off.

"Just think about it, Harry. That man didn't stand a chance. Maybe he stole some money, slept with another mechanic's wife—who knows? Nosing around there is not too bright."

"Motive always explains, defines a crime."

"That's exactly what I'm talking about." Susan's voice was firm. "You don't know the motive, but if it involves one of his co-workers, that guy has just seen your face again. Sometimes I swear you have no brains."

Hearing steps approaching, Harry did not reply.

Ruth called, "Harry."

Harry rose, pulled aside the curtain to face the nurse. "How'd I do?"

"Clean as a whistle. I'll see you in six months. You, too, Susan. I checked your records and you, BoomBoom, and Alicia—along with Harry, who had her mammogram when you all did last winter—you will all be due then. I'm keeping tabs."

"I'm grateful. It's a lucky thing we did come for that mammogram. Caught Harry's suspicious spot early."

Susan couldn't bring herself to say "cancer."

After Ruth returned to the front desk, relief flooded Harry's face. "I wasn't worried."

"Liar."

"Well, just a tad," Harry confessed.

"Come on, girl. Put your bra and your shirt back on. Let's blow this joint. I'll wait outside."

"Where are we going?"

"Starbucks. I'm buying you a giant Frappuccino, double chocolate, to celebrate."

From Central Virginia Medical Center to the Starbucks in Waynesboro off Route 340 took all of fifteen minutes.

Never one to fret over calories, Harry ate the mound of whipped cream before sipping through the straw.

"At least the woman behind the counter didn't call me 'Sir,'" Harry mentioned.

Susan laughed. "People don't pay attention if you come in wearing overalls with mud on them, a baseball cap, no earrings, and a bandanna around your neck. They can't imagine a woman farming, I guess."

"Remind me to wear my tiara next time I drive the tractor." Harry took a long pull on the straw.

"Great idea. You could make the cover of *The Progressive Farmer*." Susan named a farm periodical they both read.

"Better wear my evening gown, too." Harry smiled, then leaned toward her friend. "It would be easy to ship drugs in the boxes of auto parts, the hoses, headlights. Easy."

"What?"

"Drugs and porn are the two richest industries in the world. Betcha."

"I wouldn't know." Susan considered that information. "But I know you need to kill this obsession right now."

"Umm . . ."

"Just forget it, Harry."

"Okay. Should we talk about boobs some more?"

Susan put down her large cup and laughed until the tears filled her eyes. "Drugs and boobs. Has a ring to it? What's in your Frappuccino?"

Harry laughed, too. "Well, you don't want to talk about the murder, so boobs. Okay, Susan, what do you think when you see a woman with a great set?"

"Nothing. Why?"

"Me, neither. So please explain to me why, if a woman is well built and reasonably attractive, men have to be put on a respirator."

"Does Fair?" Susan asked.

"He forgets to breathe."

They got sillier and sillier.

Finally able to control her giggling, Susan replied, "I

don't know about this boob stuff, but it never hurt us. Our parts are useful."

"I will never, ever figure out why men lose their reason over cleavage, but I will figure out the murder. It might take me a long time, but I can't walk away from it."

"Girl, if you don't walk away from it, you'll wind up running away from it. Mark my words."

13

Mrs. Murphy, Pewter, and Tucker sprawled under the shade of the walnut tree in the backyard of the old white clapboard farmhouse. The front entrance, simple and gracious, was rarely used. Just about everyone came to the back door, including the dogs of friends.

Asleep in the hayloft, Simon snored. Flatface, the great horned owl, also slept, in the cupola with vents. Matilda's nest was in the hayloft, but she was anything but asleep. She was in the walnut tree and didn't miss her loftmates for a minute.

Like all animals, she kept a hunting radius and defended it. Any other blacksnake found herself at the end of a hiss and big fangs. Matilda did allow a male to visit during mating season, but her interest in the opposite sex faded rapidly soon after. Some years she laid eggs, others she did not. As for most females of any species, motherhood could pluck one's last nerve. Then again, you had to love those little things as they wriggled around.

Hanging from a branch in the walnut, Matilda focused intently on Pewter, who had been insulting her for years. All the large snake had to do was wait. Scaring the cat the other day made her very happy. Not that she'd bite Pewter. The fat gray cannonball deserved a big fright, not a fearsome bite.

Matilda's glittering eyes missed nothing, and her sense of smell was far better than humans could imagine. As for flicking her forked tongue, she gathered information that way, but, again, humans didn't get that, nor did Pewter, who complained that Matilda lacked respect because she'd stick out her tongue. Matilda could gauge temperature and the oncoming weather, and her taste buds worked just fine, too.

She arced up halfway as Harry, who'd been on her eighty-horsepower John Deere, walked back to the barn. The attractive human wasn't happy. Matilda observed it in her demeanor, but she could smell the frustration, too. Humans stank. Their unmistakable scent could be mollified by cleanliness and even perfume, which Matilda didn't like much. But when a human was angry, frightened, or getting peevish, they stank. The funny thing was, they couldn't smell it.

Matilda watched as Harry, hands in pockets, stomped into the barn. The human had come home from her checkup in such a good mood. Obviously, it had evaporated. Then the snake, muscles so powerful, formed a big "U," wrapped her upper body around the branch, dropped her tail, and climbed up on the branch. She now lay flat out, quite an impressive sight.

Pewter, dead to the world, heard nothing. Tucker also was out cold. They'd chased birds, butterflies, and even a big groundhog, until they'd worn themselves out. Mrs. Murphy, who'd been prowling the barn, was less tired and awoke when she heard her human's footsteps. She roused herself, stretched, trotted to the barn, and ducked into the tack room as she heard Harry on the phone.

"Yeah, I know." Harry sat down in the director's chair. "Just sprayed oil all over the place. It's hydraulic fluid." A long pause followed. "Yes, you did tell me the whole gearbox and hoses needed a complete overhaul. You also told me it would cost ten thousand dollars." Another long pause followed. "Let me talk to my husband. I'll get back to you by tomorrow."

"Mom, don't fret. Take a deep breath." The tiger cat rubbed against Harry's leg; the hay dust covering the thin old denim now dotted the cat's coat, as well.

Harry reached down to rub Mrs. Murphy's head. "I knew this would happen sooner or later, but I thought I could get the first cutting done. The hay is perfect, just perfect. Dammit. Dammit to hell." She dialed Fair's cell number. "Honey."

"Hey, beautiful. What's wrong?" He recognized the distress in his wife's voice. "I thought this was a great day."

"Well, it was. But the gearbox is shot in the John Deere. The dealer told me it would take ten thousand dollars to replace it, plus I have to replace all the hoses. Dammit, Fair. They did say, however, they could pick up the tractor Friday, May twenty-fifth. That's a miracle."

"Yeah."

Friday was day after tomorrow.

"We can't afford ten thousand dollars."

A deep sigh, then Fair said, "Let me go to the bank."

"Honey, they aren't making loans. If they do, it's big ones. It's just as much work to make a small one as a big one. We're screwed."

"Who told you about the loans?"

"Big Mim, at Little Mim's baby shower last night. We had a little bit of time together."

"If anyone would know, she would. God knows, the woman owns enough bank stock. Look, don't get het up." He used the old Virginia term for "hot." "Give me a little time to think."

She calmed down. "I don't know why I let stuff like this get to me. This really has been a day of good news."

"Oh, babydoll, some days are just like that: a roller coaster."

She smiled. "You're right. Okay, honey, I'll wait until you get home." She hung up the phone, looked down at her friend. "I don't know why he puts up with me."

"Because you put up with him." The cat laughed. *"And he loves you. We all love you."*

With that, the cat leapt onto Harry's lap.

Harry picked up the phone, dialing Franny Howard. "Hey, I know you're at work. I won't keep you."

"Business is good right now. I'm happy, except for the theft, of course. Victor Gatzembizi came by to tell me he'd be on the lookout if any expensive tires showed up in his shops. Given what he's going through, that was nice."

"Any leads?"

"No, but Coop said it would take a while. She had to check on other thefts to see what merchandise was taken and if the M.O. was similar. She said there's just a huge black market."

"Who would have thought about a black market for expensive tires?" Harry changed the subject. "Well, I called to tell you I sailed through my checkup. Thank you for keeping after me about my mammograms at our support group. I really am grateful."

"Oh, Harry, we girls have to stick together on this one. I've passed my five-year mark, but I take nothing for granted. You look wonderful."

"Thanks. Need anything? My asparagus is up. Lettuce, too. All the early plantings."

"I'll take whatever you've got." Franny's voice was warm. "You know I have totally, totally changed my eating habits, and I think that's one of the reasons I'm alive. I am convinced, absolutely convinced, that sugar feeds cancer cells."

"You may be right. I've cut way back on the sugar. Missed it for the first month and now I don't. I mean, I'll still drink a cold Co-Cola, but no cookies, sweets, all that stuff."

"You stick to it, girl."

"Franny, I'll drop off the greens tomorrow."

Just as Harry hung up the phone, Tucker barked a warning. She hurried out of the tack room, Mrs. Murphy following her.

Tucker stopped, because the intruder was Cooper in the squad car. Tucker adored Coop.

"Hey." Harry walked out, determined not to bitch and moan about the John Deere. It was more than thirty years old, so how much could she complain?

"I want to show you something." Cooper pulled out her laptop and headed toward the screened-in porch.

Within minutes, she and Harry sat at the kitchen table, cold drinks in hand, as Cooper brought up pictures on the screen. Harry had told her about her clean mammogram, which made Cooper happy for her friend.

"Look at these. You're a motorhead."

Startled, Harry demurred, "Yeah, but not like that."

"Bear with me." Cooper scrolled up photo after photo of naked women in old cars.

The women, quite lovely, might wear a tool belt or have a wrench in their hands. A few bent over engines, their bottoms exposed.

One photo showed a truly beautiful woman leaning over the opened hood, her breasts falling just over an impressive twelve-cylinder engine, which had been chromed.

"Sure hope the engine's not hot," Harry quipped. "Why are you showing me naked women?"

"Okay. This was on Walt's home computer. No hardcore porn or anything like that. A lot of mechanical information showed up—no surprise there; he kept up with his profession. But then we found these pictures. Can you tell me anything about them? Here, I'll go through them again. Forget the women. Look at the machines."

Harry, hands folded, tried to block out the naked beauties. Fortunately, easier for her than for a man.

A mint-colored DeSoto, resplendent with white leather interior, passed, then a restored 1939 Buick.

Image after image of beautiful women and beautiful cars filled the screen.

"Hmm." Harry unfolded her hands. "Go back one." She pointed to a golden Studebaker Avanti, a design way ahead of its time. "Most of these cars are orphan cars."

"What's that mean?"

"No longer in production. The companies are dead. Packards. Nashes. Franklins. Well, now Pontiacs and Oldsmobiles, but most of these pictures are of old grand cars. You know, like Packard. The other thing is, all the cars are roadworthy. Also, no trucks, no sports cars, and what I've seen runs from after World War One up to the mid-fifties. There was one more-recent car, again good design, and not an orphan car: the Buick Riviera from the early 1960s. But this is quite a collection of marvelous restorations and some awfully good bosoms and bottoms." She laughed.

"A car is out of production. What happens?"

Harry, picking up on Cooper's intensity, responded, "At first, nothing. People run them until they become outdated. We're primed to buy new things in America. So they sell the cars, which often wind up in the hands of kids, who can only afford an aging Hudson as their first car. Then they get wrecked or are sold for scrap, and a lucky few wind up sitting in garages. There are beautiful cars left to rust. Cars that had marvelous engines for the times. Or design, like the Auburn."

"If you find one, how do you fix it?"

"Oh, gee." Harry flopped back in the kitchen chair. "Well, you can't get parts. Although large companies are supposed to always keep in stock the parts for anything they have manufactured, they don't. A carmaker that no longer exists means spare parts that no longer exist. Think what it takes to bring back a 1959 Edsel Corsair."

"Wasn't that a bad car?"

"Not really. The Corsair was a pretty good design, but Ford misread the market. So it only lasted about three years before it tanked." She leaned forward again. "Murphy, don't."

The cat was patting the screen.

"She's okay." Cooper petted the cat.

"There are special companies that deal in parts for orphaned cars. There are others that specialize in one brand only—say, Chevy, which of course isn't orphaned, but just try to get a steering wheel for a 1957 Bel Air."

"I see. Can these parts be built?"

"Someone would really have to be good. You can build engines, carburetors, the heavy-duty stuff, but one would need access to a . . . I don't know, small foundry, plus you'd have to have the specs—another problem."

"But with computers, surely that has to be easier. I mean, to create images and blueprints." Cooper could use a computer with the best of them.

"Yeah, but you'd still need the engineering knowledge. You can't be off more than one one-thousandth of an inch. As for interiors, easier, but it's all hideously expensive."

"So if someone like Walt were involved in this, profits could be made?"

"Oh, sure. He'd be moonlighting, but, Coop, it's a big jump from naked women to a side business restoring old engines. Then again, if you throw in the naked women, big profits." Harry laughed.

"I can't imagine making love to anyone wearing a tool belt." Cooper laughed loudly.

"People have their ways. As long as they don't hurt anyone."

"I knew you'd see things I didn't. Could be the guy was just turned on by the, uh, mechanics. We're hitting a wall in this investigation. I'm trying to think of all kinds of things. Like I told Rick, I have yet to question anyone who mourns him. Walt was a loner. Not that that's a bad thing, but clearly he wasn't a person with highly developed social skills. Everyone says he was a crack mechanic, and Victor Gatzembizi swore he was incredible."

"Victor's a drag-racing nut. That can be as expensive as restoration. A top fuel dragster can cost about two hundred thousand dollars. Has to do the quarter mile in 4.9 seconds. Close to two hundred miles per hour."

"What do you think of Victor?"

Harry shrugged. "I don't know. Another rich guy with the trophy wife, big cars, big ego. He's very generous to charities. Gave thirty thousand dollars for our five-K run to raise money for breast-cancer research. He's always been nice to me, probably because I love cars."

Cooper turned off her computer. "My job is to not jump to conclusions. To keep an open mind and maybe, just maybe, to always remain a little suspicious."

"And?"

"My instincts tell me Walt threatened somebody. Yes, the crime was especially violent, so a degree of passion may have been involved, but this guy set off a trip wire."

$$\boxed{14}$$

The odor of soil reached Harry as she walked down the alleyway behind Fresh! Fresh! Fresh! Ahead of her, three trucks unloaded produce. Vegetables were carefully arranged in sturdy wooden boxes covered by thin balsam tops with air slats —the source of the dirt smell.

Box after box of unshelled peas, early kale, and lettuce that had survived the hard rains was placed on a conveyor belt taking the food straight into the back of the food market.

One backed-up truck carried oranges, their startling color leaping out from the boxes' slats. Harry couldn't believe that was the natural color. The distinctive aroma of oranges reached her—not as strong as orange blossoms in the grove, but there was still a hint of that delightful citrus odor.

No way were oranges ready to be plucked from the trees at this time of the year. Watching the boxes roll down the conveyor belt made Harry wonder where Yancy Hampton procured fresh oranges in May. She admitted to herself that just because they were out of season in the United States didn't mean they weren't organically grown in South America or wherever they might have been harvested.

Still …

She watched Evan Gruber, a distant acquaintance, back a new refrigerated truck to the second large open door.

Evan waved as he caught sight of her. She waved back, then turned, retracing her steps down the alleyway. Everything she saw pointed to clean produce carefully handled. As to exactly the source of Yancy's purchases, she had no idea, but watching his operation gave her a sense of how her own sunflower seeds and ginseng might be treated. Of course, she'd be the one unloading her produce. Why waste money having a middleman deliver it when she could do it herself? Now that she no longer ran the post office, Harry had the time.

She missed that regular paycheck. As to the benefits of being a federal employee, she doubted she'd ever see them. Harry believed there was no money in the till. Her generation would be the one to truly find out that sorry fact. Anyway, once upon a time she had known just about everything going on in Crozet.

On the bright side, now she could farm full time, her true love. And there were no bosses or rules or regulations to tell her and her animals how to get their work done.

What troubled Harry now was that she received countless mailings from the Department of Agriculture, all with long forms to fill out. The State of Virginia also sent their share of paperwork. Her attitude was, she could either spend her time filling out forms or farming, and she'd rather farm.

Watching the food being handled, she wondered what hoops Yancy had to jump through to keep his store running. While for the most part Harry trusted people, for some reason she couldn't put her finger on, she didn't trust Yancy. Maybe it was because he presented himself as so squeaky-clean.

As she reached her old truck in the parking lot, she realized she didn't want to live without trusting others, even in the face of murder. She should be alert, pay attention to character, but she didn't want to become a cynic, even as she knew she was living in cynical times.

To perk herself up, she drove down to Keller & George, the elegant jewelry store that had been in Charlottesville since 1875.

She pushed open the glass door. Gayle Lowe looked up, as did Bill Liebenrood.

"Hey, I came to visit my pearls," Harry greeted them.

Bill smiled. "I bought my granddaughter her first pearls before she was one week old. You need to catch up, girl."

Gayle walked behind the lit case wherein resided the 9mm double strand of pearls that Harry had been coveting for more than two decades. Each time the pearls would be sold, Bill would call to relay the sad news. Then in about six weeks another double strand of beauties would arrive.

"Your pearls came in today. They're awesome," Gayle would tease her with a phone call.

Elbows on the case, Harry lovingly stared down at her

self-adornment dream. Gorgeous, quiet, those pearls reminded her of her mother's dictum: "Wear the best that you can afford and don't draw attention to yourself. Flash is always new money."

Fat chance Harry would ever be new money or old money, but her mother's urging to not show off had stuck.

Before Bill could come over to tell Harry she should just try on the pearls, the door opened.

"Harry," Victor Gatzembizi greeted her, smiling. "I'm giving way to temptation."

"Oh," came her weak reply.

Bill momentarily disappeared into his small office, returning with a package. He opened a green Keller & George box, removed a necklace that could blind one, and placed it on an unfolded black velvet cloth.

Victor beamed. "Harry, come here and be my model."

Harry walked over, looked down at the pear-shaped diamond on the platinum chain, and gasped. "Oh, my God. I've never seen a diamond so big."

Bill came around from behind the counter, artfully putting the necklace on Harry. "Divine."

Victor, hand on chin, murmured, "Even with your T-shirt, Harry, a diamond becomes you. I can't wait to give it to my wife and see it just above her cleavage."

Gayle, Harry, and Bill smiled without a word. Of course the diamond would be spectacular, and of course that's where a woman would wish it to fall, but best to keep that to yourself.

Victor wasn't worrying about such niceties. He was so thrilled with the diamond that he became ever more expansive. "I told myself that when she reached her fortieth birthday, I would make it the best birthday of her life. 'You're beautiful,' I tell her. 'Forty is nothing.'" He looked again at the necklace, nodded, and Bill removed it from Harry, whose hand flew to her neck.

"For two minutes, I was a diva!" she enthused.

Bill put the diamond back in the green box. "Would you like this wrapped?"

"No. I'm going to surprise her by placing it around her neck as she puts on her makeup to go out to dinner tonight. You didn't fail me. The diamond is a perfect pear."

As Victor left the store with his gift, Gayle called out, "Warn her that if she wears that in the daytime she'll cause car wrecks."

He stopped at the door. "Gayle, she'll stop traffic no matter what."

As the door shut, Harry opined, "Love."

"And money." Bill winked. "Then again, this could be to make up for past sins."

"Oh, Bill." Gayle rolled her eyes in mock disgust.

"Do you all really think forty is that big a deal? I didn't." Bill folded his hands, resting them on the counter.

"How do you know I'm forty?" Gayle lifted a shoulder.

"Had your firstborn at five, did you?" He needled her.

Howard Hyde, the miracle jewelry repairman, pushed open the door from his workshop, heard and saw his two co-workers, smiled at Harry, and disappeared back into his workroom.

"Bill, I know you too well." Gayle nodded toward Harry.

"Don't let me stop you. I'm ready to hear all your sins and forgive you." Harry loved it when her friends carried on.

Blair Bainbridge walked through the store's front door. "Harry, is that you?" he asked.

Harry threw up her hands. "Why is everyone surprised to find me at Keller and George?"

"Uh . . ." Blair fumbled.

Gayle came to the rescue. "She's out of context."

"Right." Blair reached in his pocket and pulled out expensive cigars. "Howard!" he called.

Howard loved a good cigar.

"He's back there." Gayle pointed to the door.

Before Blair walked behind the counter to open the workshop door, he handed Bill a cigar. Then he held one up for Gayle.

The blonde smiled. "No, thanks."

Harry called to him. "Miranda wants one, according to Herb."

"Will do." Blair disappeared into the workroom.

"I think I'd better go before someone else comes in and is surprised to find me."

"Your pearls will be waiting for you," Gayle said.

Harry looked from Gayle to Bill. "How many carats is that pear diamond?"

"Eight," Bill swiftly replied.

"At about twenty-two thousand a carat," said Gayle. "The price of diamonds just went up." She thought the pear-shaped diamond utter perfection.

"Oh, my God," Harry whispered.

"And the chain was platinum." Bill smiled. "Just about two hundred thousand, all told."

"I feel faint. I had a two-hundred-thousand-dollar necklace on." Harry blanched.

Bill, ever gallant, replied, "You did it justice."

"That you did," Gayle agreed.

"Shall we assume there are a lot of car repairs in Charlottesville?" Harry laughed as she left the store, her right hand still touching her neck.

15

Sitting in the modest living room, Herb bowed his head in prayer. Sitting tightly together on the sofa, Sharon and Artie Meola did likewise. The husband and wife held hands.

"Heavenly Father, grant to these thy servants the warmth of thy love. Help them through this sorrowful trial. Let them know their daughter now resides with you, secure in the bosom of heaven. In time they will be reunited with Tara in great rejoicing.

"Grant them knowledge of her spirit united with your Son. Give them peace and show all of us the way to help Sharon and Artie transform their sorrows into deeper love.

"In the name of the Father, the Son, and the Holy Ghost." Tears spilled down his red cheeks.

Sharon sobbed. Artie put his arm around his wife of thirty-two years. He cried, as well.

Finally, Artie rasped, "Reverend, I don't know if I will ever understand. Friends told me at the funeral, this is

God's will. How can it be God's will to take our girl in such a horrible way?"

Tara, driving her old but sturdy Ford Explorer, was killed in a freak accident on the two-lane highway from Crozet to Whitehall. The old road contained numerous blind curves. Years ago, paving it was seen as a great victory by the state representative and by many residents. Others thought differently. Too much speed on a dirt road meant you'd skid out, your hind end would crunch sideways. You might go off the road. Or you might dampen your speed. Rarely were there deaths, although there were sure enough cars that crashed through wooden fences and wound up in the pastures. The paved road encouraged development, which in turn encouraged more traffic at faster speeds.

According to the team investigating the fatal crash, Tara was going the speed limit. She was on her way home to Crozet, heading south from Whitehall. As she approached a curve just beyond Chuck Pinnell's leather business—formerly a large apple shed—a deer leapt out, crashing through the driver's side windshield. Tara swerved her Explorer into oncoming traffic—which happened to be a mighty Range Rover, flying along at ten miles over the speed limit.

By the time the rescue squad was on the scene, Tara had bled to death. The driver of the Range Rover would never be the same. His only fault was speeding, but no one could foresee such an event.

Tara, just twenty-five, brimming with promise and so very pretty, had been the Meolas' only child.

After a half hour of talking, praying, drawing closer

together, Sharon asked Herb to please have a bit of lunch with them.

Some people would have refused this, fearing to put the distraught mother to more trouble, but Herb, wise in the ways of people and especially wise in the ways of Virginia ladies, readily agreed. Preparing the meal would give Sharon something to do, something at which she excelled.

She and Artie talked the whole way through a light delicious lunch about Tara's dreams, her dating, and what a good volleyball player she was in high school and college. It was a way to keep her with them. In time, the stories of their daughter would subside, as would the grief. The questions over God's plan, however, would never subside.

Herb, unlike many priests, ministers, and pastors, didn't have a ready bag of pat answers. He couldn't understand why snatching a lovely, good girl entering the prime of her life could serve any earthly purpose.

He had seen Tara grow up. He'd taught her catechism for two years, for which Tara evidenced little enthusiasm. She used to make him laugh and remember that when he was her age, he lacked enthusiasm for catechism, as well. When she took her first communion after the simple confirmation ceremony, she looked up at him in his vestments and he had to fight the urge to wink at her.

As Herb drove back to St. Luke's—his Chevy running like a top after being fixed—he, too, asked God unsettling questions. The answers he received were the ones he always received: Faith. Trust. Love. He first heard that

call as a young soldier in Vietnam. Back stateside, filled
with dreadful memories of the horrors of combat, he
entered seminary. Decades later: faith, trust, and love.
Like most of us in this life, he had no assurance that his
efforts truly helped anyone, but he nevertheless tried.
He prayed for Tara and her parents and would continue
to pray for them often.

With a heavy heart, he walked into the beautiful
stone administrative building on the St. Luke's quad.
He passed his secretary, Lenore Siebert, who was about
the same age as Tara. She opened her mouth, but before
anything came out, Big Mim walked out of the living
room, which was really a meeting room. Three cats and
Miranda followed behind her.

Big Mim took his hand while Miranda took the other
one. They walked him into the room, its windows wide
open, and sat him down.

Big Mim took charge, as always. "Nothing can make
this better, but we have something that might let the
Meolas know how deeply we all care."

Miranda handed Herb an envelope. "This is a start.
Big Mim called everyone in the parish, and the two of
us made the rounds."

Big Mim smiled. "Open it."

Inside the envelope was a check for five thousand
dollars, made out to the Tara Meola Scholarship Fund.

"Girls." Herb's eyes filled up again.

"Each year we will raise this amount or maybe more.
We will ask Sharon and Artie to select a young person
entering college who they think reflects some of their

daughter's wonderful qualities." Big Mim, not always the most sensitive of people, smiled.

"Girls," Herb repeated himself.

He was as moved by Big Mim's compassion as the check. The old girl was changing.

Elocution, knowing her human was overcome, jumped on the back of the sofa and put a paw on his shoulder to give him a kiss with her rough tongue. *"It's all right, Poppy."*

"Miranda was with me every step of the way, even if she isn't a Lutheran." Big Mim reached for Miranda's hand. "And so was Victor Gatzembizi. Catholic, you know. So many people pitched in."

Herb held the check, studied it, glanced at the two old friends. "'God moves in a mysterious way. His wonders to perform.'"

16

Standing in the equipment shed where the big tractor sat, as well as the smaller, thirty-horsepower unit, Harry took off her ball cap, throwing it on the crusher run. "I am bullshit mad."

Fair burst out laughing. He couldn't help it.

"Oh, boy, she'll really get hot now." Tucker stepped farther away from the humans.

Mrs. Murphy and Pewter, perched on the high tractor seat of the eighty-horsepower John Deere, watched, big-eyed.

"What's funny? What's so damned funny?" Not a woman given to profanity, Harry was losing her composure.

"Baby, you're acting just like your father." Fair put his hands in his pockets.

A long pause followed, then Harry laughed. "Daddy did have a habit of throwing his cap down, didn't he?"

"Hey, when his Orioles cap hit the dirt, you knew to clear out." Fair laughed. "The apple doesn't fall far from the tree."

Her voice lightened. "Well, I am mad. I shouldn't swear about it, but, Fair, if you could have heard that twit. Sanctimonious twit."

"He's not my favorite, but I only see Yancy Hampton in passing."

"Fair, he gave me a decent price for the sunflowers per hundredweight. But I just don't know if I can do business with him. I really don't."

"Why don't you wait a few days before making that decision? An early purchase is a hedge against a drop in prices. Then again, it's a loss if prices rise—but you know that as well as I do, honey. Mother Nature can and does throw plenty of curveballs. Plus, Hampton's money might help pay the tractor repair bill."

"I know." She leaned against the big tractor, unaware that the two cats looked down at her from the seat. "I canceled the tractor pickup. Too much money. I'll try to get Dabney Farnese to fix it. It will take longer, but he's reasonable."

Fair picked up her faded, worn red ball cap, handing it to her. She clapped it back on her head. "I shouldn't let it get to me. Guess I'm tired and maybe still upset over finding that body. Tara Meola's funeral service got to me, too."

"All of us. You never know."

"No, you don't." She looked up at him, wondering what would happen if he died first.

For all their former troubles, Harry couldn't imagine life without Fair. For one thing, he was much more attuned to emotions than she was. She blocked emotion, even while being aware that sooner or later those stashed-away pains and troubles would inevitably leak out.

"Sounds like he was impressed by your sunflowers and the ginseng."

"It's still early in the season, but so far so good, and I have laid them all out properly."

"You're good at what you do, honey."

She smiled at him, loving the praise. "Here comes the good part. Hampton asked me about when and how I fertilize. I said I use turkey or chicken poop and I put it down usually in the fall. I always read *The Farmer's Almanac*, though, and if they predict a drought for the fall, I wait until spring."

"And?"

"You would have thought I said the earth was flat. *The Farmer's Almanac*. He cited all the studies I should read, all the computer-generated statistics, and then— oh, this is what really fried my two remaining brain cells—he excoriated me for using chicken and turkey poop, because who knew what parasites might be thriving in the poop? I just about lost it."

Fair breathed a mock sigh of relief. "But you didn't, so he has his front teeth, thank goodness. You have a mean right cross, sugar."

"I counted to ten. A few times. I replied that my father used natural fertilizer and it has always served us well. Actually, when I was little, Papaw used to get muck from the Chesapeake as well as crushed seashells. Can't do that anymore, but each year Papaw and Dad would vary which field received what. Well, he didn't want to hear any of that. He lectured me on the proper nitrogen, phosphorus, selenium, you name it, balance in soil, depending on crops, and why commercial fertilizers are better. Yes, and right now they are three hundred dollars per ton more than last year, too. So I just said I would continue to use natural fertilizer, which reduces my reliance on foreign oil."

Fair clapped his thighs with his hands and laughed. "Good one."

"Hey, it's the truth. All that stuff has a lot of gunk in it, for lack of a better word. Given that Yancy is the type that uses curly lightbulbs and feels superior to the rest of us, he had to shut up. Ass."

Fair laughed again, moved over to the tractor, and gave his wife a big hug and a kiss. "Have I told you today that I love you? I never quite know what you're going to do and say, but I'm never bored."

She kissed him back.

As this heated up, Mrs. Murphy leaned way over to try to snatch Harry's ball cap off her head.

Pewter, whose bulk was an impediment, coached, "A little to the left. You got it."

Mrs. Murphy hooked the cap, tossing it on the crusher run.

Harry didn't notice.

The three friends observed the two oblivious humans.

"Aren't they odd creatures?" Tucker commented.

"One minute she's ready to kill Yancy Hampton, and the next she's wildly in love with her husband. One extreme to the other."

17

*N*ick Ashby lavished attention on his 2009 Subaru Impreza WRX STI. He figured for one-third the price, he got 70 percent of a Porsche's performance. Since he was six feet two, the pocket rocket forced him to bend over just to get in. Fortunately, he carried no fat, or the steering wheel might have bisected his belly.

The amazing acceleration and fine suspension made up for a somewhat hard ride. Okay with Nick. He didn't want a luxo-barge. His black coupe sped through the night, twisting up Route 22 near Cismont Manor. After work, he'd search out the best roads to push the car and himself, back roads like the old Route 635 in Nelson County or the old roads in Albemarle to Greenfield. He'd put the windows down just to listen to the engine, out of which he'd wrung more horsepower, thanks to his mechanical skills. The 305 horsepower off the lot had been bumped up another twenty horsepower and married to the six-speed manual transmission. Nick would wind that sucker up or down.

He needed all his skills at 9:30 P.M. on Wednesday,

May 30. Behind him roared the new yellow Chevy Camaro with its big V8, sold at 426 horsepower, tweaked to 444. Nick knew the car and its driver well. Sweat rolled down his face. He could feel the heat of his body as he tried to tear away from the larger car. His one hope was that the STI proved more maneuverable; plus, the Camaro suffered from dreadful sight lines. He could hope the big car would spin off the road, but so far it had not. Chevy hit a home run with the Camaro if one loved muscle cars. Except for the sight lines, the damned thing was about perfect.

Muscle cars had made a spectacular comeback with the Dodge Charger, the ever-cool Ford Mustang, and the Camaro. Those Americans who loved cars loved powerful, quick cars, and no amount of gas prices could quite kill that love.

The STI hung a curve—no slide, no nasty feedback from the steering. Nick heard the Camaro break slightly, then the roar of the engine as the driver made up for the slight slowdown. That man, too, knew the capabilities of the STI. Much as the pursuer scoffed at anything manufactured by the Japanese, he appreciated what the machine could do.

Nick knew this part of the county well. There was a dirt road a quarter mile up ahead, just after a sharp right curve off a bit of a rise in the road. It was well hidden. If he could get on that, he could cut his lights and keep moving, as he had long ago disabled the computer chip that kept lights on at night whether you wanted them on or not. As the pursuing Camaro rode up the rise, its lights might just miss him. Nick floored it, flew over the rise—wheels off the ground—and came down with a thud, despite the good suspension. Cutting his lights, he turned a hard right. He peered into the darkness, slowed, then stopped to listen. He heard the huge engine in the Camaro whine by.

Putting his head on his sweat-soaked hands, he slumped back on the seat. He laughed a short dry laugh. If nothing else, that son of a bitch in the Camaro had learned Nick Ashby could drive with the best of them. Creep never would give him credit at the drag strip, either. He waited until he could no longer hear the rumble of the Camaro, cut on his motor, cut on the lights, and drove at forty miles an hour down the dirt road. It would get him out to Black Cat Road, where his new girlfriend, Hilary Larson, lived.

He crept out onto the tarmac of Black Cat Road, drove two miles, then turned left onto her dirt driveway. He'd been planning to stop by earlier, so once he hid his car behind her house, he explained that he'd run into some trouble. He didn't tell her what trouble. And he apologized for tardiness, for parking behind the house.

A fright, a sporting event, anything that ramps up the adrenaline, also ramps up the sex drive. She forgave him, didn't seem all that put out, and Nick had a great night. He'd worry about tomorrow tomorrow. He thought he'd be safe at work. Granted, Walt Richardson hadn't been safe at work, but Nick figured Walt had just taken too big a bite out of the pie.

The next morning, Hilary made a quick breakfast, then left for work before Nick. She needed to get to the west side of Charlottesville.

Fortified, he walked out, hopped in his great little car, and headed down the winding drive. His exit was blocked by the Camaro. He saw the familiar face behind the wheel.

He popped it in reverse, but too late. A bullet crashed through the windshield, hitting him in the chest. The pain slowed him enough so the Camaro came up close and the driver finished the job with a second shot, through the heart.

18

The ambulance took away Nick's body as Cooper, Rick, and the crime-scene team carefully combed over Hilary's place.

"Smart." Rick stared down at the stone-covered drive next to the STI.

"Smart and the second murder in two weeks of men who worked at ReNu." Cooper knelt down. "The killer took his time."

"Yep." Rick moved a short distance away from the STI. "We're dealing with someone who can think ahead, is cool, and can act quickly if need be. So much easier to catch a murderer who kills in a fit of rage."

"Sure is." Cooper lightly ran her hands over the stones. "Whoever shot Ashby actually raked this, and raked it deep down, including all the way out to Black Cat Road. Not a chance we'll get a tire imprint." She stood up. "And the rake in Hilary's little garden shed was washed off. No fingerprints."

Rick smiled ruefully. "Hey, maybe the guy's a professional gardener and carries his tools."

"Right." Coop smiled back at him, then her smile faded. "Where to first? Hilary Larson or Nick's mom?"

"I'll send Jarrod over to Mrs. Ashby. He's good in a situation like this. You and I will find out where Miss Larson works and get ourselves over there." He sighed. "You know, I've had to inform people for decades that someone they love has been killed on the road or died in a brawl. It never gets any easier."

"Yeah. It's their shock, that split second of disbelief, that always gets me. This was so cold, so calculated." She shook her head.

Rick walked over to the squad car, called in to see if anyone there could find where Hilary Larson worked. "Come on."

Coop hopped into the car with him. "Let's try the neighbors, okay?"

He turned out of the driveway. They slowly drove down Black Cat Road. They stopped at three places, all off the main drag, for it was a fairly well-traveled road. No one was home; everyone was at work.

They then turned down Mechunk Road. Although this road was more miles from Hilary's place, someone might know her. Same story, though.

"Remember when this was Route One?" Rick slowed as he reached the end of the road.

"Then the post office changed everything to names. I still remember it by the route numbers and the box numbers. I guess a name is progress."

"Depends on the name." Rick smiled.

The dispatcher reached them. "Old Navy. Hilary Larson works at Old Navy in the Barracks Road Shopping Center."

Rick asked, "How'd you track her down?"

"Well, I couldn't find anything in the computer other than her address and license-plate number, so I asked around and Sherry, at the front desk, actually knows her. Small world."

"That's the truth. Thanks, Marcie," Rick told the dispatcher as he headed out to Route 64, but he didn't hit the siren. No need.

The two drove west in companionable silence.

Coop finally broke it. "ReNu is turning into a dangerous place to work."

"It could be that Walt and Nick were tied in to something outside the business. These days, you never know. Just because people pass blood tests—which Victor informed me the business does randomly—doesn't mean they aren't selling drugs."

"True. Doesn't feel like that, though, does it?"

"No."

"Then there's those racy pictures on Walt's computer. Could be some kind of sex ring. Remember years ago when I first came on the force, young girls were being recruited from the private school as well as the university?"

"Mmm-hmm. We'll never completely stop that, you know. Unless someone comes forward, that's one of the easiest and most lucrative businesses to run. All you need is a telephone and a reliable stable. And it's true we're about due for one of those scandals."

"This isn't it. Neither of these victims was the type

who could organize and operate a high-class call-girl ring. Boy, this is a town that eats up stuff like that." Coop grimaced.

"They all do. But when you consider the type of high-powered men coming in and out of Charlottes-ville . . ." He shrugged. "Easy pickings."

"I've never understood why high-powered women don't feel entitled to the same benefits." Coop looked out at the already-rich foliage.

"Do you?"

"God, no. I'd die before I'd pay for sex."

"Therein lies the difference. In sex, a woman is the center of attention, always and ever. The man has to find her, woo her, court her with goods, or, in the case of the high-class call girls, shell out the bucks. All you ladies have to do is breathe."

"Guess so, but it's so . . . I don't know. Neither one of us is a prude. We both know how the world works, but to pay for a woman, even a discreet one who comes from an equally discreet service, there's something deeply creepy about that. To me, anyway."

"As a man, I can understand it, but I think it's a little creepy myself." He pulled in to the parking lot in front of Old Navy. As they walked in to the fairly large store, customers noticed.

Coop motioned for a salesperson to come over. "Could we see the manager, please?"

"Sure." The young woman led them to a middle-aged woman moving a rack of clothes with another worker.

As quietly as Rick could, he explained they needed to see Hilary Larson in a private space. Always sensitive,

Rick asked if there was a good friend or if the manager herself would take Hilary home and someone else would drive her car. He emphasized that the young woman would be hearing some very upsetting news.

The manager, Crystal Hines, nodded and had the good sense not to ask questions. She took them to her small but comfortable office.

"I'll bring Hilary to you. Can I get you anything? A Coke, some coffee?"

"No, no, thank you." Rick sat in one chair.

Coop stood, as there were only two chairs in front of the desk.

Mrs. Hines brought the young, attractive woman to her office. She said to Coop, "Sit at my desk. It's messy. You can't make it any worse."

As Mrs. Hines left them all, Coop did just that, taking out her notebook.

Rick's voice was calm. "Miss Larson, I'm Sheriff Shaw, and this is Deputy Cooper. Please sit down. We have some sad news."

The pretty redhead was wide-eyed and fearful. She sat across from Rick. "It's not Daddy, is it? He hasn't been in an accident?"

"No. It's Nick Ashby. He was found dead in his car in your driveway."

She sat upright. "Nicky? What's happened?"

"He was shot. He's gone, Miss Larson. I'm sorry."

"Shot? Why?" Tears came into her eyes; her hands shook.

"Deputy Cooper and I were hoping you might provide some insight."

She put her head in her hands and shook it.

Coop got up, stood beside the young woman, and put her hand on her shoulder. "If it's too much, we'll come back. Someone will drive you home."

Looking up at the tall woman through tearful blue eyes, Hilary cried out, "I'll do anything to help. Anything."

Coop glanced back at the desk, saw a box of tissues, grabbed a few, and handed them to Hilary. She then returned to the desk, picked up her pen.

Rick softly asked, "Did Mr. Ashby ever mention being afraid?"

"No."

"What about his activities? Anything illegal? Drugs, prescription or illegal?"

"He wasn't into that. He could drink a little on the weekends, but he wasn't much for drugs."

"How long have you been dating him?"

"Um, two months. He was a good guy."

"Did you meet his friends?"

"Well, they were all guys who raced cars on the weekends. Those guys—Nick included—put every penny they had into their cars. That was one of the reasons Nick didn't take drugs. And when he drank it was only on a weekend when he wasn't racing."

"Drag racing?"

"Right."

"Ever sit in the car with him?"

This brought a smile. "I did. Loved it."

"The other men. Ever feel any of them had it in for Nick?"

She thought about this. "No, but no one likes being beaten, and Nick's STI beat out every car in its class. He just toasted a Mitsubishi Evo. That guy wasn't happy, but most guys know you win and you lose. They'll just haul their cars back into their garage to start working on them again."

"I see." Rick then asked, "Did you ever meet his mother?"

"I did. His father's passed."

"You got along with her?"

"Well, I don't know her very well, but she seemed to like me. She laughed that if I was going to be seeing her son, I'd better get used to him spending money on his car and not me. That was about it."

"Did he spend last night with you?"

"Yes."

"How did he seem?"

"He was late. Said he got tied up, but he seemed elated, kind of, maybe a little preoccupied. But then he settled down. He'd get that way when he raced."

"I see." Rick leaned toward Hilary. "If you think of anything, no matter how seemingly small, call me, text me. Or Deputy Cooper."

He gave her his card. Cooper rose, did likewise, and then left the room.

She returned with Crystal Hines. Upon seeing her boss, Hilary began crying again. Mrs. Hines hurried over to put her arm around the young woman.

Rick said, "Miss Larson, Mrs. Hines will help you go home." He then turned to the manager. "Thank you for your help."

• • •

Back in the squad car, the two pulled onto Route 29.

"ReNu?" Coop asked.

"Yep. What'd you think?"

"That she really doesn't know anything."

"Me, too. Well, let's hope somebody at ReNu has a thought. They've lost two employees. You'd think that would jar something or someone loose."

It didn't.

19

Long shadows lapped the lush grass of Farmington Country Club. Created in 1927 by a Scotsman named Findlay, the course boasted long fairways and beautiful approaches to small, fast greens, which tested a golfer. In the old days, land was not as expensive as it is now, so the course designer had a large canvas to paint.

What golfer could ever tire of coming up behind the club itself, originally designed by Thomas Jefferson as a working plantation, for which he was paid an architect's commission? The player faced the feminine roll of the Blue Ridge Mountains, while behind him or her stood one of America's loveliest colonial structures, red brick washed in the patina of time.

This late afternoon, the glut of players having tapered off, Dr. Nelson Yarbrough, Latigo Bly, and Susan Tucker had each smacked the tar out of the ball from the tees at Number 14. A mockingbird eagerly watched from a huge pin oak, first cocking his head one way, then another. Some birds waited for the rolling ball to disturb bugs. The mockingbird in this case took a dislike

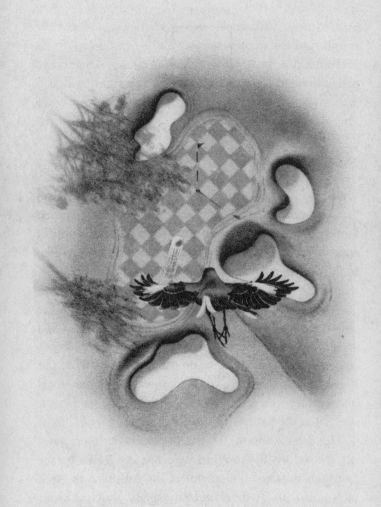

to the ball, opening its wings, lifting off the branch, and soaring overhead to monitor the ball's progress. The bird witnessed countless balls on the fairway and in the rough, and for whatever reason he felt compelled to fly over each one, be it white, yellow, or orange. The orange balls offended him the most, and, upon sighting one, a big raven call would emanate from his graceful body. The bird could duplicate any sound he heard. Raven calls, harsh, often disturbed other birds and people, too. As to just why these golf balls provoked such a response, well, you never knew about mockingbirds.

"Look at that silly bird." Latigo Bly pointed his driver in the bird's direction.

Dr. Yarbrough smiled. A former quarterback on the UVA football team, he was strong and highly intelligent. "Maybe he knows something we don't."

"Like a snake in the grass," the tall, thin Latigo thought out loud.

"Nah, it's bird Zumba dancing. He chased each one of our balls. Think of the exercise." Susan, like Harry, adored watching animals.

While men and women did play golf together, the typical group consisted of same-gender friends. Various explanations for this seemed to be accepted by both men and women—the men, of course, feeling superior, since they hit off the men's tees.

Susan Tucker had won the club championship three times. She'd won the Virginia State Women's Championship once, seven years back. She nearly always placed in the top ten in any tournament.

In high demand with the men—who silently watched

her, always hoping to figure out how such a feminine woman could send the ball soaring down the fairway— Susan kept her thoughts to herself. She knew she would never match the record of the late Mary Patton Janssen, probably the best amateur golfer FCC had produced in the twentieth century and just possibly the best amateur golfer ever in the state of Virginia. She won state six years, from 1957 to 1962, a feat never matched. She played in the British Women's Amateur in 1956 in the first all-American finals. Those were a handful of her many accomplishments, which also included riding horses over stout fences and showing dogs.

The key to Susan's game was her short game. Well, isn't it always? When she was young, she'd tag along with Mary Pat, studying every little move the attractive, dynamic lady made. When this keg of dynamite died on May 20, 2011, Susan, like every golfer who had ever seen Mary Pat play, knew an era had ended. When Mary Pat learned the game, one walked the course and often carried one's own bags or just played with six or seven clubs. When possible, a caddy would be hired, always useful. Susan, being a kid, never could hire one, so Mary Pat graciously paid for Susan's caddy, telling her to listen to her caddy, who had walked the course more times than any golfer including Mary Pat, ever could.

With the great lady's death, Susan became determined to sharpen her game and make an effort to teach youngsters. Susan couldn't have cared less if they were boys or girls, rich or poor. Of course, at FCC, those youngsters came from privileged backgrounds, although not all of them lived in happy homes. Susan also would go to the city golf course once a week in the good weather to work with young people who didn't have two nickels to rub together.

This concern for others drew Susan and Dr. Yarbrough together. Each had achieved athletic fame in their own sports, which gave them respect from the young and allowed them to reach some kids that others thought unreachable. The interesting thing about both the powerfully built dentist and the gracefully built housewife was they didn't talk about what they did, even to each other. They just did it.

Latigo Bly stood in sharp contrast to this. Given his wealth, he supported the Cancer Society, the Multiple Sclerosis Foundation, and the Salvation Army. His name and often his photo were prominently displayed. Nor was he loath to call attention to his acts of charity.

All three of these golfers lived the good life in their way, but Latigo certainly lived more of it: fast cars, faster women, disgruntled ex-wives. His garage was filled with a Porsche 911, a Camaro, a Mustang convertible, even a Lamborghini. His bed had been filled with female counterparts easy on the eyes, hard on the wallet. His wife, Vivien, instrumental in his success, looked the other way. He loved her, but he used her. Some might define him as narcissistic, others as a man driven to win, to profit.

Halfway down this snaking fairway, using an eight iron, Dr. Yarbrough ripped a tremendous shot. It arced up like an artillery shell, coming almost straight down next to the pin. A big smile crossed his rugged features.

"Show-off," Susan teased, calling from across the fairway.

She pulled out her seven iron, hit the ball with backspin. It landed on the green, fifteen feet from the pin, but then began to roll backward, stopping a beautiful four feet away. If there was one thing Susan could do, it was read greens.

Latigo was not as powerful a driver as either Dr. Yarbrough or Susan. He hit the ball, which was about twenty-five yards behind their fairway shots. It was a good, clean shot, landing just in that first halo of taller grass surrounding the green, taller by maybe a quarter of an inch. That quarter of an inch was enough to make the man stare hard at his ball and then hard at the distant pin.

Golf didn't take bravery like, say, foxhunting, but it sure could break your heart.

The remaining four holes played fast. The three, enjoying one another's company and the lovely light breeze, wrapped up on the eighteenth hole.

Susan shot a 72. Dr. Yarbrough came in at 75, and Latigo scored a very respectable 82. The three cleaned up, walked up the outside stairway to the nineteenth hole, and sat down for a refreshing drink.

"That mockingbird put the mojo on my ball."

"Latigo, if we were in Florida, you'd say it was an alligator." Susan gratefully sipped her sweetened iced tea.

"Well," the tall fellow drawled, "there are a lot of alligators on the greens down there."

"You know, they can run faster than we do," Dr. Yarbrough noted. "You wouldn't think it to look at them."

"Speaking of alligators . . ." Latigo looked intently down at his drink while a former affairette swished by, gave him a hard look, sniffed, then continued.

"Latigo, the lipstick and fingernail polish alone should have put you off." Susan winked at him.

"I beg pardon?" Latigo's eyes opened wide.

"Black fingernail polish and dark-purple lipstick. What were you thinking?"

"He wasn't." Dr. Yarbrough laughed, and his two companions laughed with him.

"Purple." Susan just shook her head. "I will never understand men."

Latigo touched her hand with his forefinger. "I think you understand us well enough."

"Sometimes I think I do, until my wonderful husband, love him to death, goes into a hardware store. Oh, my God! Hundreds of dollars later, he totters out under the weight of wrenches and screwdrivers."

Dr. Yarbrough plucked a menu off the table. "Anyone hungry? On me."

Both Susan and Latigo expressed thanks, ordering light salads.

Harry must have rubbed off on Susan, because she asked Latigo, "You send clients to ReNu. What do you think is going on over there?"

"I don't know. Victor doesn't know. It's deeply upsetting."

"Why do you refer clients to ReNu?" Susan pressed.

"Good work for good prices. Collision-repair shops indemnify their work."

"That means you're not responsible?" Susan blurted out.

"It means if they perform shoddy work, I can go after them. Even the best shops can have a lemon day, for lack of a better phrase. Insurance is more complex than you might think. The Code of Hammurabi mentions an insurance practice in 1750 B.C."

Susan, sensing he was about to warm up to his pet subject, insurance history, diverted him. "Did you ever consider that love is a fire for which there is no insurance? Even if you crash and burn."

Dr. Yarbrough laughed, both because of the sentiment and because Susan had cut off the potential lecture of boring information.

20

On Friday, June 1, the cool morning air refreshed Harry as she cut the endless lawn at St. Luke's. At ten, the turquoise blue skies were dotted with cream cumulus clouds hovering over the emerald grasses. Once Harry adjusted to the zero-turn mower—her old belly-mount conventional mower had finally died after twenty-five years of cutting grass—she wondered how she'd ever lived without the new manner of mower. Instead of a steering wheel, the driver grasped two long handles, which could move forward and back. She could cut corners so much closer than with a conventional mower. Still she'd have to use an edger along the pathways and the special gardens lining those pathways, but the zero-turn saved so much time.

Peonies, in full bloom this late in the season, crowded the long, brick-laid pathways. The gardening club of the church—now full of men as well as women, since gardening had become just about as competitive as grilling with some of them—created masses of white, pink, and magenta with the peonies. Harry marveled at how beautiful the grounds looked, regardless of season. Even in winter, the hollies shone with red berries, and pyracanthas grew up the side of Herb's garage, providing a long-distance blast of orange, often against snow. While she liked gardening, she lacked the time to devote herself to it. Her focus was her crops, the foals, and working the horses. Wistfully, she looked down at the cemetery on the lower level, old cream-colored climbing roses spilling over the stone walls. If only she had more time.

The scent of fresh-cut grass filled her, lifted her up. Something about fresh-cut hay and grass made Harry glad to be alive.

Every now and then, Herb would look up from his desk to see one of his favorite parishioners out there mowing away.

Chuckling to Elocution on his lap, he said, "See the pattern? She cuts in one direction, then comes back on the other. Takes longer, but Harry wants there to be a pleasing pattern. Her mother was like that. Well, she inherited her mother's sense of beauty and her father's practicality. Not a bad combination."

A thunk caused Harry to cut the motor.

Once on her hands and knees, Harry saw that a hidden rock, part of it above ground but covered by the grass, had sheared off one of the bolts holding the belly mount. If she continued mowing, she'd scrape the earth and the cut would be uneven. Couldn't have that.

"Drat," she muttered under her breath, then said aloud, "Well, I can fix it."

As she walked toward the administrative buildings on the quad, Herb leaned out the window.

"What now?"

"Sheared a pin. You wouldn't happen to have spare parts?"

"Don't. We don't have a zero-turn."

"Right. Well, I'll head to the dealer."

"Go to Waynesboro. Better price."

"That's the truth. Buy something in Charlottesville, add ten percent to the price. Herb, I'll need to drive over there and fetch a pin. I promise I'll get this all ready before Sunday. Actually, I think I can finish it today."

"I'll drive you over there. It's such a beautiful day. I'm getting antsy in the office," Herb volunteered.

"Okay," Harry walked inside the administrative buildings from the back door, washed grease off her hands, then met Herb out front, for he'd already pulled his truck around.

"Come on, girl. Time for an adventure, especially after your clean mammogram." The older man grinned.

"Word gets out." Harry smiled back at him.

"Your friends are very, very happy."

Handsome, overweight, the Very Reverend Jones was a barrel-chested man, not tall but impressively built. All through his high school and college years, the football coaches wanted him to play on the line. He preferred baseball instead, playing catcher, where his wonderful memory served pitchers well. His knees held up better than if he'd been on the football line, but they creaked.

He sometimes wondered how many times he crouched, rose, crouched again.

Within twenty-five minutes, Herb pulled in to the dealer's. Light traffic helped, but it was actually faster, although a longer distance, to shop in Waynesboro rather than inching up Route 29.

Harry picked up some extra parts just in case. She reached into her jeans' back pocket to pull out her wallet.

Herb grabbed her wrist. "Church purchase."

"I don't mind. It's my mower and my little offering."

"Your work is the offering." He pulled out a silver credit card and handed it to the fellow behind the counter.

"I love doing it."

"Looks good. My office affords me such a wonderful view, regardless of weather or season. I get most of my best sermon ideas just staring out the window."

After Herb paid, they hopped back into the truck.

"Ready for our next vestry meeting?" Harry asked.

"We have a good board. Makes it easier. As you know, just maintaining the physical structures takes so much money and effort. Still, I wouldn't want to be in modern buildings for all the tea in China."

"Do they grow tea in China?"

"I don't know, but they sure drink it." Herb gave her a devilish grin. "We aren't all that far from Wayne's Cycle Shop."

"Yesss?" She lifted an eyebrow.

"Think what St. Luke's could save on gas if I rode a motorcycle?"

Harry laughed, a light happy sound. "And half the board would have a fit and fall in it."

Now they both laughed at the old Southern expression.

"Ever own a bike?" he asked.

"No. I'd love to. I mean, I'd just lose my mind, go everywhere. 'Course, the real decision would be whether to buy a dirt bike or a road one. Love the sound of the big ones."

"Me, too. Like the old V8s from the fifties and sixties. That rumble."

"If Fair and I weren't facing a big bill for the hydraulic system on the old John Deere, I'd think about it. You really can save money on gas. Our gas bills have doubled, and, boy, that cuts into the budget. The estimate from the John Deere dealer—back to the tractor—is ten thousand dollars for a new hydraulic system, all new hoses, the works. We're gonna get the work done outside the dealer, I think. It will take longer. Still cost, though."

Herb whistled. "That calls for serious prayer and maybe a winning lottery ticket."

The two people who loved each other drove back to St. Luke's, chattering away.

As Herb pulled in to the driveway of the garage, the truck backfired, shuddered, and stopped dead.

Harry jumped out after Herb popped the hood. "Cut on the motor."

He did. Nothing.

As this was a truck that still had an oil dipstick, Harry took it out, put the clean end to her ear. "Okay, try again."

A click sounded, another. Click. Click. Click. But no ignition.

"I just picked this damned truck up, as you know."

"I think it's your alternator. But it could be more than that. Better call ReNu. They'll need to tow you."

He got out of the truck, slamming the door. "I do need a new truck. Or that motorcycle. But you know there's no way the church can afford new wheels. Given the hauling and odds and ends we need, half the parish uses the church truck. It has to be a truck."

"Yes, it does." She crossed her arms over her chest. "I'll call ReNu. Got the number?"

Herb easily recalled the telephone number, as he'd called it so many times.

By the time Harry had the new pin on the belly mount—an easy job once she found a block of wood to steady the mount and once she was able to dislodge the sheared pin—the tow truck from ReNu had turned onto the driveway. To her surprise, Victor Gatzembizi emerged from the passenger side; Terry Schreiber, the driver, was about as greasy as she was.

Wiping her hands on her jeans, Harry strolled down to them as Herb came out of his office.

Victor looked up. "Reverend Jones, let's hope this is a hangover from your former problem."

"Why?"

"Well, otherwise you and the insurance company are throwing good money after bad."

Herb explained what happened, then Harry piped up, "I think it's the alternator."

Victor listened. Terry, who didn't know Harry, discounted what the attractive woman said.

"If Harry didn't farm, she'd be working for you, Victor." Herb smiled.

"Given what's happened to us, I could use a good mechanic." Victor shook his head.

"It has to be a shock and a strain for you, Victor. I'm sorry."

"Thanks, Reverend. The best thing I know to do is to keep working. And I go to each of my shops at least once a week. It helps to get away. Terry here can't. I think it's harder for the boys."

"I want to know what the sheriff is doing," Terry grumbled.

"The best he can." Harry quickly defended Rick and, by extension, Cooper.

"You're right, Harry," Victor agreed. "It takes time, and even if they know who did it or have a good idea, they still have to gather enough evidence to run them in."

Harry looked at Terry, who had a smear of grease on his forehead. "I guess you guys are all pretty close."

"We have a few beers. Race our cars." Terry shrugged.

An idea occurred to Harry. Like most of her ideas involving curiosity about others, it would come to a bad end.

That evening she called Cooper, told her about Herb's truck, and asked her if she could run over the VIN number.

"I can, but that's not going to tell you anything," Cooper said.

"Why not?"

"It will tell me and CarMax, for instance, if the car has been in a wreck. Won't tell me anything about the repairs, which is what you're after since his truck was just repaired. Right?"

"Right. But surely there are repair records."

"Only insurance companies can access those." Cooper paused a minute. "From a law-enforcement perspective, we don't care about repairs. We want to know if the title, the registration, the license, is current, expired, et cetera, and we'd like an accident record."

"But what if the accident is caused by a fault in the vehicle?"

"That's not my job."

"Hmm."

"Harry." Cooper's voice rose. "I don't know where you're heading with this. I'm kind of afraid to find out."

21

"*E*ver want to do this?" Harry sat in the empty bleachers with BoomBoom, her childhood friend, competitor, sometimes enemy, and friend again. They were alone at the Central Virginia Hot Rod Track over in Augusta County, next to Albemarle County.

"I'd love it. Alicia, on the other hand, would be apoplectic if I started drag racing."

Alicia Palmer, a former movie star, was BoomBoom's partner in life—a big surprise to both of them, but it was working out just fine.

"You could use her Mustang."

"Harry, she'd kill me." BoomBoom laughed. "That's her baby. Funny, she has the money to buy any car in the world, including those gorgeous Bentleys, but she wanted that metallic candy-apple-red Mustang."

"It is pretty cool. Soup that baby up and I bet you'd win some of these races. Top fuel dragsters spend over two hundred grand on those things. 'Course, you wouldn't need to spend that much at this level. Could just fire up what I call a door slammer."

BoomBoom wondered how the dragsters managed, given the expense of low-level racing. "Even if it's a door slammer, every penny goes into their rod. The ReNu guys weren't rich."

"That's what Cooper said about Nick Ashby. All his money got poured into his STI. Raced it as a sports compact. After the police picked over and through his car, they gave it to his mother. What a little gem that car is. Tons of power, plus it starts in all weather, goes through snow, and, being a Subaru, lasts forever."

"Maybe Nick's mother will sell it to you."

A light shone in Harry's eyes. "Oh, God, to cruise around in a torpedo with four wheels. Ever wonder how you and I wound up being gearheads?"

BoomBoom shrugged. "Actually, no. Remember in our junior year when the boys took over that straight stretch from the old Del Monte plant to the train depot? Two in the morning and all of us stood guard to watch out for the cops."

"Fab." Harry grinned.

"What was really fab was, after they all ran their heats, I took out the old Trans Am and just smoked them. Ha." She slapped her thigh.

"Gallop down Memory Lane." Pewter, on the bleachers with Mrs. Murphy and Tucker, sniffed.

"Makes them happy." Tucker lay down, head on paws.

"I suppose, but the dumb stuff they talk about: drag racing, who got their ears pierced—"

"In ancient Egypt, cats had pierced ears and wore gold earrings," Mrs. Murphy interrupted.

"You're making that up," Pewter replied. "Although we were gods—then again, we still are."

"I'm not making it up. Mom has pictures in one of her history books of a cat statue with earrings." Mrs. Murphy looked out over the quarter-mile track.

"I wouldn't want to be a god," the corgi wisely stated. "You'd never be real, never truly one of the pack. I want to belong to my pack, which"—a long sigh followed this—"I guess is Harry, Fair, and"—another long pause—"you two."

Mrs. Murphy kissed the dog, licking her nose.

"Cats don't belong in packs." Pewter thrust out her chest.

"Well, you can stay by yourself, then," the tiger quickly said, as she bounded down the bleachers to follow the two women who'd started walking the track.

"Did you know this place was this well organized?" Harry asked the beautiful BoomBoom.

"No. I figured it was just a quarter-mile asphalt strip. Obviously the owners sank some bucks into this."

Both women observed the Christmas-tree lights for each driver's lane. The top two were small amber lights; below these in a straight line were three large amber lights, then a green, and last a red light. It really was a mess of lights. A high control tower on the side afforded a clear view of everything. It resembled a small control tower at an airport, except it was built of wood.

"Let's go peek inside the tower." Harry ran to the stairs, taking them two at a time. Putting her hands around the edges of her eyes, she peered through the window in the door. The tower top was all windows, 360 degrees.

BoomBoom bounded up behind her. "It's a panel like

a big computer keyboard, kinda—headphones with a little speaker on one side, lots of switches. Two seats, so two people work this. The track lights have to be automatic, so they must set them off from up here."

"Good P.A. system. And those huge clusters of night lights like at baseball games have to cost a fortune!" Harry exclaimed. "Anything electrical, computer-driven, isn't cheap."

"How about the salaries? I expect there are people groundside who are connected to the tower. There's so much potential for danger—I mean, one blown tire as you're hauling down that track. Can you imagine the cost of the insurance policy?" BoomBoom shook her head.

"When we were in grade school, before all this technology, wasn't there a death here?"

"Wasn't at this track but at the old dead-end road near what's now the Augusta County offices. The car blew up; they couldn't get the driver out." BoomBoom grimaced. "Those days it was just guys getting together and racing. The sheriff's men left them alone, because they weren't creating traffic problems and the road was abandoned." She thought a moment. "'Course, that eventually caused problems. As the road deteriorated, cracks and potholes appeared. I think that's why the racers finally left. I don't know who built this track. Must be successful, though— still here."

"Coop's investigating the track, because Nick raced here. So do some other mechanics at ReNu. She's not much of a gearhead, so she asks me questions. You know what was weird? The first guy who was killed, Walt, had photos of orphan cars with hoods that stretched into next week. Well, draped over engines, hoods, the trunk, or lolling inside those great leather interiors—tops down, of course—were women, uh, tops down."

Peals of laughter rolled out of BoomBoom. "You're kidding. Car porn?"

"Well, it wasn't exactly porn. Think of it more as a deep appreciation of metallic and feminine curves."

They came back down, the wooden steps reverberating with their footfalls. Mrs. Murphy and Tucker awaited them.

"Would a calendar of naked men and great old cars turn you on?" BoomBoom punched her old buddy on the arm.

"I don't know. Depends on the man. Depends on the car. Some hunk splayed over the hood of a 1961 Corvette would catch my eye."

"Fifty-seven Thunderbird," BoomBoom fired back.

"Pervert."

"Look who's talking." BoomBoom laughed, then became more serious. "Harry, curiosity killed the cat." The blonde looked down at the tiger. "Sorry, Murphy. Harry, I know you found Walt's body, and this other guy worked with him." Harry nodded as BoomBoom continued, "I wonder if drag racing isn't connected to Nick's death. Don't know about Walt—you said he didn't race. But seems to me all of the mechanics at ReNu knew about racing. This drag track is a small local one but look how much money went into it," BoomBoom concluded.

"What do you mean?" Harry asked.

"People look for patterns, connections. The first

connection is, both men worked at ReNu, both good mechanics. The second is this place. And if they find bountiful women pimped on cars on Nick's computer, well, that will be the third, but it doesn't necessarily follow that those ties are crucial. They may be, they may not, but what I'm trying to tell you is, be careful. Two men are dead. Let's not add one woman."

"I'll protect her," Tucker barked.

Pewter remained on the bleachers. She enjoyed looking down at them.

"Yeah." Harry paused a long time. "I did nearly get you killed once years ago. I'll behave."

The two women had apprehended a killer inside a building. Although the murderer had a gun and had fired at will, both women had remained in command of themselves.

"I hope so. Now, the next question is, when do you want to watch the drag races? I know you're going to do it, and I'd better come with you."

"Friday."

22

*L*ooking up at Dr. Nelson Yarbrough's incredible silver hair, Harry, mouth wide open, gave thanks that the former UVA quarterback chose dentistry as his profession. He was so careful as he leaned over her. She'd chipped a tooth trying to dismantle the hydraulic pump on her 2750 John Deere.

As the good dentist patiently worked, he asked in his rumbly voice, "I've seen a lot of teeth, Harry, and yours are good ones, but I've never known anyone to chip a tooth on a tractor."

Once his hands were out of her mouth, she replied, "John Deere. Good steel."

"Mmm-hmm." He smiled, getting back to work as Beverly, his assistant, handed him the bonding agent.

Nelson and his wife, Sandra, also a dentist, had in their youth been one of Albemarle County's more glamorous couples. The years had not leeched away their good looks; however, now the kindness shone through. The pair, along with able assistance from Alice Hill and JoAnne Burkholder—a former county commissioner for Greene County—kept patients happy. Amy Doss and Holly Cox kept their teeth clean. One could tell a great deal about a business by the attitude of the people who worked there. This was the only dental office Harry had ever walked in to where the first thing one heard was raucous laughter.

She did recall being in Larry Hund's office and witnessing a pretty teenager being dumbfounded when confronted by the dentist's movie-star looks. Charlottesville seemed to specialize in interesting dentists.

Once out of the office, her tooth looking good as new, Harry trotted up the outside wooden stairs to Blue Ridge Embroidery. Evan Gruber was coming down.

"Morning, Evan. Good to see you again."

"Harry, what brings you here?"

"Picking up some T-shirts for St. Luke's. Flag Day party. It's a big annual do. The kids love it; I do, too."

Evan rubbed his chin, covered with a fashionable two-day stubble. Fashionable though it might be, it certainly gave his girlfriend brush burn.

"Isn't that the day you put flags in the cemetery?"

Harry nodded. "Everyone does. All over America."

His question answered, Evan pointed with pride. "I got a new truck."

Harry turned around to look. A quilted stainless-steel refrigerated truck sparkled in the sunshine.

"Wow."

"Ford truck; the bodywork was done down in Richmond. I mean, that sucker can frost you." He beamed. "Full of dressed free-range chickens. Need to deliver them to Fresh!"

"I saw you unloading a few days ago. I don't recall you being in the poultry business."

"Not me. I just pick up the orders. I give anything extra, left over, to the Salvation Army."

"Good for you."

"Mostly drunks. Still." He shrugged.

Harry didn't know if those who used the venerable organization's services were drunks or not. She did know that about fifty-four million Americans went hungry each day. The figure so overwhelmed her that she always hoped it wasn't true but feared it was.

"Haven't been down there in years."

"I go every day. Sometimes I use my old pickup to haul furniture to them, too."

"That's good of you, Evan." She hesitated a moment. "How long have you delivered to Fresh?"

"Two years, give or take. I go over to the valley; still some poultry farms there. Stick to birds. Beef, lamb, pork, won't do it. It's not that it smells bad right away, but the odor lingers. Whatever you put in the freezer unit after that soaks up the odor."

"Never thought of that." And indeed Harry had not. She continued, "How do you define a free-range chicken?"

"I don't. I just pick up chickens when the poultry farm calls. They all look the same to me." He then quizzed her. "You found Walt Richardson. He used to work on my trucks." Evan, not one to miss the opportunity to express his many opinions, held forth on the murders of the two mechanics at ReNu. "I'll bet you it was drugs. When a man kills a woman, it can be lots of things, but men killing men: drugs."

"You've got a point there."

Leaning down toward her, he half-whispered, "They're all in on it. I tell you, Harry, this crap goes all the way to the White House. Insider trading, stock-market manipulation, Ponzi schemes, and drugs. You don't think half of Congress isn't bought with drug money?"

"I never thought about it."

"You should. As long as drugs are illegal, no taxes. Pure profit. Everyone on the take has a big—I mean big—reason to keep the stuff illegal."

"Yes, I can see that." Harry really wanted to get going and pick up those T-shirts.

"Tell you something else. This is a rich town. It's full of good weed, good coke, and all those pills the doctors write prescriptions for. I mean, there are all kinds of druggies, right?"

"Guess so."

"Meth. Out in the county. Lots of meth. It's not a city drug. If those two dead men had bad teeth, meth. Otherwise, weed or blow. You just wait and see." With a self-satisfied grin, he tipped his baseball cap and descended to his silver truck.

Harry sighed, pushed open the door to Blue Ridge Embroidery.

The proprietor, Greg, his ginger hair catching the light, looked up. "Heard the whole thing. Thought maybe I'd save you, but Evan was on a roll, wasn't he?"

"Isn't he always, but, hey, Greg, at least he didn't lecture me on how we're descended from aliens."

"Maybe he is." Greg laughed as he unfolded one of the T's for Harry to inspect.

"Perfect. Just perfect."

"Red T's, white, blue. The flag looks good on everyone."

"Herb's idea to use a small Old Glory over the heart turned out perfect. St. Luke's was founded before the Revolution."

"Beautiful, beautiful church. Let me help you carry these down the stairs."

Harry paid him with a St. Luke's check and they toted the boxes to the bottom. "Where's the Mrs.?" she asked.

"In the embroidery room."

"Business good?"

Greg smiled a slow smile. "Coming back. We had two and a half bad years."

"We all did. You didn't go under. Neither did we. You'd be surprised at how many people don't call the vet when times are tough. Fair will work with them, spread the payments out, but they figure the horse will just cure himself."

"Kinda cruel."

"Is," Harry flatly stated. "Sometimes I think I don't understand people at all."

"I know what you mean," the nice-looking man agreed. "Hearing Evan's analysis of the ReNu murders brought that to mind. You think you know someone, a neighbor, an acquaintance. Then you find out he's beating his wife or, in a situation like this, he's killed those two men. It's almost always a man."

"You know, Greg, I think you're right, though I'm willing to bet more women kill than we know. They're just smarter about it."

He laughed. "Hey, I knew that when I got married. Not that she's a killer," he hastened to add. "But my wife sees so much that I don't. I'm focused on the job."

"Greg, you underrate yourself." Harry thought him a good businessman. "But I do know what you mean about being fooled by people. 'Course, you can be fooled in good ways."

"Right. Let's concentrate on that."

23

The thick odor of high-test gasoline, rich exhaust, and burning rubber assailed Harry's nostrils. The screaming of the engines, on the other hand, thrilled her, just as Beethoven thrilled a music lover.

Waves of heat wiggled up on the tarmac from the exhaust pipes. Friday night, 7:00 P.M., the sun was still about two hours from setting at this exact spot in Waynesboro. The temperature was still in the high seventies, the day's warmth hanging on.

Racing continued throughout the weekend, but Friday nights drew the fellows fresh from work, eager to roll and without big-enough wallets to compete with the Saturday men. The semipros used Central Virginia Hot Rod Track on Saturdays and Sundays. Those big dogs knew how to use the bleach box— also called a burnout pit—to heat their tires before reaching the staging area. Warm tires held the track better. But even the fellows with lighter wallets knew how to get their front tires just right. The staging lights were lit, next the big ambers, then green, and vroom. Sometimes a driver would miscue and the front end of his car would stand up: sure way to lose a race. The top fuel dragsters could do a quarter mile in 4.9 seconds at close to 200 mph. But even at the lower level, the driver's body was subjected to close to 4.9 g-force pressure. It was a wild high.

True to her word, BoomBoom accompanied Harry. Alicia was in Richmond for a fund-raiser for the Virginia Historical Society and was only too happy to miss the noise and smell. Fair accompanied Alicia, as he, too, adored history and would read anything about Virginia history. So it worked out perfectly for both couples, each member having an escort, each member doing what he or she truly wanted to do.

The two women perched high on the bleachers.

Conventionally gorgeous, BoomBoom drew many an appreciative stare. But the men then looked at Harry, a far more natural-looking woman. Two good-looking women new to the viewing stands lifted spirits. The two high school classmates wore short-sleeved thin blouses, Bermuda shorts with espadrilles. BoomBoom fanned herself with an old-fashioned palm-frond fan, the kind that used to be given out in church during the summers.

"What do you think a paint job like that costs?" Harry indicated a flaming orange—a kind of burnt orange—on a Camaro with the black numeral 15 on each side.

"Metallic painting costs more, and that's an unusual color." BoomBoom squinted. "I guess five thousand for starters. I mean, to get that depth of color would take countless applications, and the paint would need to be really thin."

"Bet you're right. God, when you think of the money spent on these cars, it's pretty overwhelming."

"Yes, it is, but the people I worry about are the ones who don't have a passion. The ones who always worry about the money and how everything has to make sense."

"Are you criticizing me?"

"No. You worry about money too much, but you don't lack passion. You love your horses, the farm. I'd have to say you even love your crepe myrtles." Boom-Boom laughed.

Before Harry could reply, the air shattered as a lower-level drag racer thundered down the strip. Bounding up the bleachers came a perspiring Victor Gatzembizi with Latigo Bly.

"Harry, my model. This little track has never seen such pulchritude." Victor threw out his arms, then told BoomBoom and Latigo about Harry modeling his wife's fortieth-birthday present.

Latigo, less effusive, simply asked after Victor's tale of the fabulous necklace, "What brings you ladies over the mountain?"

"We live so close, we finally decided to see the action." Harry smiled as Victor plopped down next to her, Latigo next to BoomBoom.

"Some good mechanics here. More importantly, some good drivers." Victor swatted at a mosquito. "My whole crew is down there, and they're good drivers, if I do say so myself."

Latigo nodded. "Some of his boys might have made a

career in racing, but it's so tough. A person has to have the personality for it; it's not just skill."

"What do you mean exactly?" Harry's curiosity, never far from the surface, was piqued.

Latigo, who had indulged in a bit of discreet plastic surgery, crossed his arms over his pecs. "A man—well, a woman, too—has to really want to win. But more than that, they must hate to lose. In 1966, Shirley Shahan was the first woman to win a national title, and she wanted to win every bit as much as the guys."

"Really?" BoomBoom turned to fully face him. The effect was immediate: He straightened up and smiled broadly.

Victor chimed in. "He's right. Those pros, traveling from race to race, would rather win than eat. There's a high with it. Has to be. I don't have it. Raced some, truly enjoyed it, but I didn't care if I was the center of attention."

"Performer personality," Latigo said with conviction. "Now, there are a few drivers on the NASCAR circuit who are introverted, but most are hams. Love the cameras, love the interviews. Same with the dragsters."

"What about the women?" Harry shrewdly observed. "Groupies."

"The groupies are there, not quite to the level of rock stars. The funny thing is, a fair number of the big guys come from backgrounds where women are placed on a pedestal. They might go to bed with groupies, but sooner or later they want a real partner. The secret always is to look at a man's mother."

"Isn't that the truth?" BoomBoom thought of her late

husband, who, she felt, probably suffered whippings from his mama into his early forties. Kelly Craycroft, some years older than BoomBoom, never had quite enough backbone for her. After his death, a string of paramours filled her life. She finally woke up realizing that all that activity kept her from facing his death and her own inner pitfalls, as well.

Harry, on the other hand, observed closely but rarely had a clue as to the emotional underpinnings of human behavior.

"Speaking of rock stars, where's your entourage?" Victor teased Harry.

"Home. The fumes and noise would upset them. It's even pretty overwhelming for us."

Latigo, in a pleasant manner, said, "Bobby Foltz, Victor."

"Ah." Victor shifted his attention to the track, where Bobby drove up to the starting line. "One of my boys, Bobby Foltz."

Both Harry and BoomBoom kept quiet as they watched Bobby's four-year-old Dodge Charger line up next to a really souped-up new Charger. They could see the helmets on the drivers, which obscured their features.

The green light flashed; the speed of the acceleration was stunning.

"Oh, my God," Harry blurted out. "They need parachutes to stop."

Bobby won the heat.

"Parachutes are used for cars exceeding a hundred

fifty miles per hour. This class is close but no cigar." Beaming, Victor stood up. "Excuse me, ladies."

Latigo remained behind. "Vic gives his men full support. He's a wise boss. Then again, he loves drag racing."

"Was Nick Ashby any good?"

Latigo replied, a bit sadly, "Yes, and he was a good kid, too. This has hit Vic very hard. Hit all of them hard. They all race and work together. A close-knit group."

"Even Walt Richardson?"

Latigo half-laughed. "Harry, you're impossible."

She sheepishly grinned. "I can't help myself. I get to wondering, you know."

"I could put some masking tape over her mouth." BoomBoom pretended to look in her Pierre Deux cloth bag for tape.

Latigo enjoyed BoomBoom's teasing. "Harry, Walt marched to a different drum. Now and then he'd come out to the track. He worked on the other guys' cars, but he didn't race. Actually, Walt was more interested in classic cars."

Harry wanted to say, "I know." Wisely, she kept her mouth shut.

"They haven't made any progress yet, I don't think— on the murders, I mean," BoomBoom said.

"I thought it would hurt Vic's business, but it hasn't. Of course, his shop is the one we always recommend to our clients who've had accidents. No one does such good work so reasonably."

"ReNu does seem to do the work for less." Boom-Boom just made conversation as she focused on the next race. She was really getting into this.

Harry was, too, but Harry could get sidetracked. "So the murders didn't hurt Victor's business?"

"No. Vic encouraged the fellows to keep racing in Nick's memory. He made a contribution to the Classic Car Club of Virginia in Walt's name. He's keeping up morale."

Fanning faster as a result of both the heat and the fumes, BoomBoom asked, "Latigo, why didn't you found a life-insurance company? Why auto?"

Flattered to be questioned about his life choices, Latigo replied in his light but pleasing voice, "Death, really. When I started Safe and Sound, the company was painfully small—myself and three others, one of whom was my first wife. I didn't want to call on people when someone passed away, and neither did Nola." He named his first wife, who left the marriage far richer than she entered it.

Latigo always gave Nola credit for helping build the business, and he didn't shy away from the fact that he indulged in one affair too many. Nola had wearied of it, wisely refraining from retaliatory affairs of her own. She waited until after the divorce. Nola was nobody's fool.

Harry piped up. "Don't you have to call on people if the car was turned into an accordion and the driver squashed to death, too?"

"We do, but usually it's after the worst is over. By that I mean the life-insurance company has paid a call, started the paperwork, the funeral is over. Then we go. I can't take the anguish. Now that the company's big, I don't need to make those calls. Sometimes I think it would be better if we'd vaporize and vanish. Less pain and drama."

BoomBoom, having lost her husband years ago, steadily replied, "Latigo, just because you don't see the body doesn't mean you don't feel the pain. It's like getting hit in the gut with a medicine ball, but the pain doesn't go away. Not for years, really."

Realizing he'd forgotten about Kelly, Latigo apologized. "You're right. I forget that you lost your husband."

"I wasn't offended." She smiled at him. "Simply making a point. If I'm truthful, I think we would have eventually divorced. He was so driven by the business, morning, noon, and night. There wasn't time for me, and I guess I'm selfish. I want to be first."

"Oh, BoomBoom, you're always first." Harry shrugged. "But it's almost always about sex."

Latigo's eyes bugged out. He couldn't believe Harry said that. Sure, the women had known each other for most of their lives, but still.

BoomBoom laughed—such a clear, lovely laugh. "Leave it to you to tell the truth."

Sheepishly, Harry said, "Boom, something happens to men when they look at you. Their brains go right out the window."

Latigo smiled. "She's right, BoomBoom."

"All I ever wanted to be was loved for myself. That's not as easy as it sounds."

Latigo nodded. "Maybe not for anybody."

The two women had lost count of his ex-wives. He hadn't, since he had to pay alimony and child support.

"Let's not talk about me." BoomBoom stared down at the track. "I see tires smoking. Isn't that dangerous?"

"Not really. What's dangerous is not changing the tires when they need it. These specialized tires can run up to five hundred dollars apiece, and you go through them fast."

"What about those expensive tires that Franny Howard sells? The Pirelli PZerocs and stuff like that?" Harry inquired.

"How do you know about PZeroes?"

"Motorhead." BoomBoom pointed to Harry.

"Motorhead." Harry pointed back at BoomBoom.

"Ah. Victor did tell me you two were car nuts. Not too many women are. Rare."

"Well, those girls are missing a lot," Harry said forcefully, since she had long ago tired of being the odd girl out among the talon-fingernailed girl set. "But I'm friends with Franny. She was so glad the next shipment of Yokohamas came in after the theft. But why not those big-name tires?"

"In drag racing, you need highly specialized tires. Simply put, you need a lot of rubber on the road. You need grip, but not the kind of tread you'd need in mud, snow, hard rain. It's a whole different ball game. Also, these cars usually weigh less than true road vehicles. Weight is saved whenever it can be. For instance, some body repairs might be made with plastic. Not smart, but sure helps the weight problem. So, again, a driver needs a different kind of tire. People usually don't think about vehicle weight when they buy a tire." He waved his hand. "I've seen just about every kind of collision aftermath that you can imagine. Fortunately, most of them are easily repaired—well, maybe not easily, but they can be repaired. Others are scrap metal, and that's why you need really good people in the field. But I can tell you—and this is just a rough guess, no industry statistics—that I think about twenty-five percent of accidents could have been avoided if the vehicle's owner had checked the treads and replaced those tires. Everyone wants to get that extra thousand out of the rubber. It's really stupid."

"Money," BoomBoom simply stated.

"Everything seems to come down to that, but, hey, seems to me that one's life and the lives of your family are worth the price of four new tires."

"You should work for Franny." Harry liked Franny so much.

"Smart lady. Could she sell racing performance tires? I mean real racing performance tires, not just a great set of tires on a Ferrari to be driven for show. She could, but the market is so small. That woman, all by herself, has built a great business."

"Well, you have, too," Harry complimented him.

"The insurance industry has changed so much. It's a lot harder now—regulations, being demonized by the media." He shrugged. "Well, we aren't the only business unfairly singled out for censure." He laughed. "Could be a bank."

Victor, perspiring, rejoined them.

"How's Bobby?" Latigo reached into the small backpack cooler and handed Victor a much-needed beer.

He offered drinks to the ladies, who passed.

"Pumped up."

"Good heat," Latigo commented.

"He's improving. My only worry about Bobby is he wants to tear the engine apart and bore out the cylinder a tiny bit more. He's going to wind up with cylinders thin as paper."

"He'll get a bigger blast," Harry laconically said.

Victor, who knew by reputation of Harry's fascination with vehicles, thought a moment, then encouraged her. "I expect Nick's WRX STI at his mother's isn't a welcome sight. I'm pretty sure she doesn't want it. If you like, since I'm in constant contact with her, I can gently suggest she might want to sell it. She's probably already thought of it."

"Really?" Harry felt her heart beat a tiny bit faster. "I'm sure it's too expensive."

BoomBoom giggled. "Harry thinks a loaf of bread is too expensive."

"Hateful." Harry closed her eyes for a moment, but she was smiling.

"The book value for that year and model"—Latigo knew so many of these figures by heart— "is about $30,500."

"More, buddy. Nick put so much into that car." Victor looked at his friend.

"He did, but his mother will get that back only if another racer buys it, and the group that races here just doesn't have that kind of money to go buy another car or a second car. They've got all the car they can handle. If Mrs. Ashby needs the money or just wants to not look at it—too vivid a reminder—she'll go with regular retail."

"The loan should be about in the $24,500 figure."
Latigo folded his arms across his chest.

Harry's face fell. "We've got a 2750 John Deere to repair."

"Don't give up just yet." BoomBoom touched Harry's hand. "Put it in your back pocket, unless," she turned to Victor, "you think the car will sell quickly."

"No. Mrs. Ashby's dealing with so much right now. The poor woman is grief-stricken. Leave it to me. Okay?"

"Now, Victor, I'm not making a commitment." Harry felt a tug of panic.

"I know."

24

Cooper envied so many things about Miranda: her garden, her green thumb, her gift with color. On Saturday, June 9, the Blue Ridge Mountains were so clear that Coop felt she could see every leaf on every tree. The fine weather lifted her spirits, which surely needed lifting. So far the investigation into the deaths of the two ReNu employees had yielded nothing.

On her hands and knees pulling out burdock root—a miserable job, since the root surely went all the way to China—Coop reviewed the case.

Over and over again she returned to the identical statements of the mechanics: Bobby Foltz; Lawrence Pingrey, called Lodi; Jason Brundige; and Sammy Collona. You'd think the shock of seeing their co-worker with his brains bashed out would provoke an emotional torrent, if not of loss then of fear. Not so.

After Nick was found shot, Cooper had returned to ReNu. The mechanics' statements were again, while not identical, disquietingly neutral—somber, yes, but still neutral. Nick was liked. While perceived as Walt's protégé because of his talent, he still got along great with the other guys. They all raced and, besides, Nick had an infectious charm.

The four remaining mechanics knew a bit about one another's personal lives, but their real connection was cars. They all mentioned what a looker Hilary Larson was as well as the highly appealing fact that she liked cars. None of them knew Nick was making payments on an engagement ring. Given the short duration of their relationship, Nick was impulsive—not always a bad thing when it comes to romantic love.

The mechanics at the garage knew Nick's mother, whom they liked. Victor and all the body-shop men had called upon her, and they all attended Nick's funeral.

Coop had also questioned the body-shop men. The mechanics and the body-shop fellows worked in different buildings. Each group kept to their own peers. As the work was constant, sometimes pressured, this made sense. The body-shop guys liked Nick. He was easygoing. Seemed everyone liked the fellow.

In exasperation, Coop got up, bent over, and grabbed the burdock in both hands, after having loosened the soil. She pulled with all her might. The tall, strong officer sweated, cursed, wiggled the stubborn plant, and cursed some more—louder, too. Finally the root gave way, emerging from the ground like a dirty giant worm. She tumbled backward.

Coop had to laugh. There she was, flat on her back, just as Harry came down the driveway. Rolling over and getting up, she held up her hands in surrender as Harry and Susan disembarked from Susan's lime green

Wrangler, her fun second vehicle. The two cats, Tucker, and Owen—Susan's corgi and Tucker's brother—disembarked, too.

"*Are you okay?*" Tucker, a sweet animal, licked Coop's hand.

Cooper leaned over, patted the glossy head, then picked up the long, giant root, holding it aloft. "Killed in the line of duty."

Harry took the root from Coop's hand. "What a monster."

Susan's eyes gazed west at the huge timber tract abutting the back of the old Jones place before returning to the vanquished invasive root. "You should save that for Miranda. Maybe the two of you could bronze it for posterity."

"Dropped by to give you something." Harry returned to the wagon, brought out a Mason jar filled with clear liquid. "Good for what ails you."

"Illegal, no doubt." Coop smiled, taking the moonshine, called "country waters" in these parts.

"Perhaps there are too many restrictions on enjoyment and profit," Susan added.

"Tell that to your husband," Harry jabbed.

"Ned has never introduced any bills against any activities bringing income into our county," Susan countered.

"Honey, Ned hasn't introduced many bills yet." Harry's eyebrows shot up.

"Who cares?" said Susan. "Come on. Let's have a sip under the hickory."

The humans walked to the Adirondack chairs under

the two-hundred-year-old hickory. Coop ran into her kitchen, came back with a pitcher of lemonade and a box of shortbread cookies.

"I could eat a cookie." Pewter noticed the box.

"We're obligate carnivores," Mrs. Murphy noted.

"Doesn't mean I can't eat a cookie."

Murphy and Tucker ignored Pewter, taking up key positions by the chairs just in case a human wished to throw a cookie to them.

"Lemonade for a long drink. Ladies, I'm about out of food and I can't face the supermarket, so we'll make do with cookies."

"Hey, sounds good."

The three sat, passing around the Mason jar and taking tiny sips. They knew better than to take a swig.

"Smooth." Cooper closed her eyes in appreciation.

Harry nodded. "Those old boys know what they're doing."

"Where'd you get this?" Cooper asked.

"I'm not telling."

"All right." The blonde shrugged.

"I won't tell, either, except to say the waters were all clear mountain runoff," Susan added. "That's the thing about Virginia country waters—they really are country waters. Of course, some people throw in peaches, others plums, cherries, kind of like a signature, I suppose. But if I'm going to take a sip, I like it clear, clear, clear, just like the runoff from the Blue Ridge."

"Susan, I didn't know you were such a fan." Cooper used the lemonade as a chaser, quite refreshing.

"I'm full of surprises, although not as many as I'd like."

"Guess that could apply to us all. I turn on the TV and see the misdeeds of politicians, TV stars, movie stars, and realize I'm plain old white bread." Harry laughed at herself.

"You know, those people can't be happy. To act out like that, to sleep with battalions of men or women, to send photos of your genitals—I can't believe anyone who acts that way is truly happy," Susan mused.

"I'll never know." Cooper grinned.

"Hey, girls, there's still time," Harry said cheerfully.

They laughed, gossiped, talked about what was left to be done for the Flag Day celebration at St. Luke's, which would be held next Saturday, June 16, starting early, at ten, in case the heat came up. Harry told them the T-shirts looked great.

"Coop, you need a hobby other than pulling out burdock root. I'd be happy to take you out on the driving range at the club," Susan offered. "Golf can take you away from the world."

"That's what you say. Wasn't there a book written about golf entitled *A Good Walk Spoiled*?" Harry took her last little sip from the Mason jar.

"Susan, thank you," said Coop in her dark soprano. "I don't see how I would ever get the time. As it is, we're working overtime because we can't hire any new recruits. The only way the sheriff's department can hire is if someone retires. I'm not faulting the county. The financial crisis has impacted law enforcement and fire departments all over. I was lucky to get today off, but

I've worked two weeks straight. And Rick is working too hard, way too hard. I'm worried about him. The constant prodding from the media about the two murders isn't helping. My boss is a good sheriff and a good man. He wants to find the perp, as do we all, but this is quite an odd case. Like most cases, sooner or later it will crack."

"I hope so," Susan forthrightly said. "But Ned declares murder is the easiest crime to commit if you plan carefully."

"Yes and no." The deputy stretched out her long legs. "Nine times out of ten the perp is right in front of you. Most murders aren't premeditated. Sloppy jobs. Well, maybe I shouldn't say that, but there are professionals, like in every other human activity. Those people really know how to take someone out. People with big egos can plan a murder, but if they aren't professionals, they'll likely slip up."

"Think the ReNu murders bear that stamp?" Harry asked. "Professional?"

"No. No." Cooper sat up straight. "But they were committed by someone intelligent."

"So you believe the two deaths are connected?" Susan ate a cookie, crumbs falling on her thin summer camp shirt.

"I find it unlikely that two mechanics from the same company were killed without a connection."

"BoomBoom and I went to the drag races last night. I mean, I've always wanted to see them, but I was also kind of curious," Harry confessed.

"Kind of?" Susan's perfectly plucked eyebrows arched upward.

"We are gearheads." Harry's lower lip protruded slightly. "Have you been over to see them?" Harry turned her attention to Coop.

"Rick and I drove over, talked to the owner, walked the track the day after Nick was killed. We haven't found a link there, either."

"Well, why would any murders be linked to drag racing?" Susan wondered.

"Endorsements. Someone wants Castrol oil and someone is their competitor?" Harry threw that out.

"Harry, not at this level of racing. Granted, there can always be some sort of personal hatred, and I remind you that Walt didn't even actually race. The one thought that's crossed my mind and Rick's is the possibility of a gambling ring."

"Among the racers?" Susan found this pretty interesting.

"Perhaps. Or the ring could be tied to larger drag races or NASCAR. Gambling makes millions, just not for the gamblers."

"Even at the level of Central Virginia Hot Rod Track?" Susan furrowed her brow.

"Depends on how wide the clientele. Yes, even in Waynesboro, a gambling ring could be netting six or seven figures. Once you pay your workers and the setup costs, illegal activity is one hundred percent pure profit." Coop held up the Mason jar.

"So it is." Harry sat silently for a long time.

25

*R*osebushes, pink, white, and yellow, filled half of Harry's truck bed. This Wednesday, June 13, pyracanthas filled the rest of the space. Once these were in the ground at St. Luke's, she'd return, filling hers and everyone else's truck bed with hydrangeas in full flower.

She parked near the graveyard at St. Luke's. Wearing her kid gardening gloves, she quickly unloaded the bushes.

Dee Phillips, Ph.D., had designed the plantings for the peaceful, beautiful grounds. Harry and friends provided the grunt work, which Harry liked okay.

Miranda Hogendobber, using a tape measure, had carefully marked out the proper distance between the plants. Usually Miranda would eyeball it, but since these roses and pyracanthas would go in at the church, she wanted the plantings to be just so.

Susan, BoomBoom, and Alicia were digging the holes. A bag of Miracle-Gro, three watering buckets, and three measuring cups lay on the clipped grass. The hose from Herb's garage had been stretched to the max.

Tucker dashed to the graveyard. The cats jumped on the stone walls to watch the dog sniff tombstones.

"*And?*" Pewter asked.

"*No one's been here.*" By this, Tucker meant no dogs had peed on the tombstones.

"*Good. Best to respect the dead.*" Mrs. Murphy looked as Elocution, Cazenovia, and Lucy Fur bounded across the emerald green, the colors of their shiny fur made even more vivid by the grass carpet.

"*Hooray.*" The cats cheered as they reached the stone wall, all three bounding up, ready for a cat gossip.

"This pink is so soft." Miranda admired the color as she planted one of the bushes.

"It gave me an idea for the house," Harry said. "What if I planted roses all along the first fence between the barn and the pastures? I'd start with the deepest pink closest to the barn, and each successive rose would be a lighter shade until the very end, when it would be so pale, almost white."

Miranda and the others stopped for a moment.

"I don't believe I've ever seen that," said Alicia, who'd been all over the world. Now she was on her knees, putting in a yellow bush.

"I figure if it doesn't turn out as I like, I can always rearrange the bushes to a more conventional color scheme. I don't know. Just sort of hit me."

"Great idea." Susan thought maybe she'd try it at home, too, but she wanted to use white roses with slightly different colors deep down on the petal.

"Where are we going to plant the pyracanthas?" BoomBoom asked.

"Dee's plan, which is in my truck if you want to see the drawings, is to have those on the building walls that Herb can see from his office window. There are a few already there. We have to train them with, uh, espalier. What do you call it?"

"Fish wire and a trellis." Alicia laughed, since this technique used heavy cord or wire to support the growing branches.

"Right. I didn't do so well in French," Harry ruefully remembered.

"Because you hated the teacher," Susan laughed.

"Every time Mademoiselle Suchet said"—BoomBoom imitated their high school teacher's high-pitched voice—"'*Ouvrez la porte,*' Harry would stand up and go open the door just to piss her off."

"Harry?" Miranda chided her. "How could you do that to poor old Mademoiselle Suchet? Poor woman could barely walk, bless her soul."

"Such a pill!" Harry wrinkled her nose. "I did learn enough to read a menu in a French restaurant."

As the humans and cats talked and laughed, Tucker, nose to the ground, followed the various human scents throughout the enclosed graveyard. She'd follow one or another, inevitably winding up at a grave with flowers against the headstone. The intrepid dog was surprised by how many people had been to the graveyard in just the last two days.

Lifting her perfect corgi head, she said, "*Lots of traffic in here.*"

Elocution responded, "*The whole Petrus family comes once a week since Georgette Petrus passed.*"

"Had to be one hundred years old," Cazenovia giggled.

"She looked one hundred," Lucy Fur chimed in.

"Humans obey strict rules about their dead. Even if the person dies at sea, there are these rules and prayers and ceremony." Elocution knew these things because Herb had to provide funeral services—although not at sea, of course.

Pewter saucily tossed her head. "Wasteful. Think of all the animals that could eat those bodies. What good does all that protein do moldering in a coffin?"

Mrs. Murphy thoughtfully said, "That's true if the bodies are relatively young, but old Georgette was so full of drugs. Any animal that ate her would probably die, too."

They giggled, then Lucy Fur added, "Poppy reads a lot about other religions. He read this article aloud to us about Parsis in India. I think that's what you call them. They put their dead up on stilts, kind of on a canvas or something, and vultures come and eat them. It's part of their religion. Well, the vultures are dying from a rare bird disease, but not from the human bodies which they've eaten for centuries. Anyway, the Parsis won't change their ritual, and without the vultures, all these rotten bodies are lying above people's heads in the hot Indian sun. It's crazy."

Pewter wrinkled her nose. "Revolting." Her eyes brightened. "Want to hear something really revolting?"

"Can hardly wait," Tucker drily replied.

"Years ago at Halloween, I found a severed head in a pumpkin. It hadn't gone off yet, but the hair was full of pumpkin mush and the mouth spilled out pumpkin seeds." Pewter used the old expression "gone off" for the beginnings of decay.

"I was there." Mrs. Murphy didn't remember it quite as Pewter did, since Pewter made herself the center of attention.

"I was there, too," Tucker piped up. "The head was gross."

"I miss everything," Elocution whined.

"You weren't born yet," Cazenovia sniffed.

Reverend Jones walked out from the administrative offices of the church and strolled across the verdant lawn.

"He's got to lose weight." Cazenovia shook her head.

"Good luck." Lucy Fur's whiskers drooped for a moment. "That man loves to eat. He can sit down and eat a quart of ice cream."

"He's a big man." Tucker gallantly defended the beloved pastor.

"He doesn't have to be that big," Elocution said.

"Look at these beautiful roses." Reverend Jones swept his hand toward the gardeners as opposed to the roses.

Miranda smiled. "That honeyed tongue, but I do like to hear it."

The others agreed.

Harry said, "We'll get this done today and then put the hydrangeas in tomorrow so there will be color for the Flag Day celebration. Actually, as you know, June 14 is tomorrow, but we have to honor the flag on the weekend. It's the only way St. Luke's can make it work for everybody."

"It will be beautiful."

"If Flag Day were later, all those fabulous crepe myrtles lining the drive into the church would be in full bloom," BoomBoom noted.

"We'll think of another party for July." Herb smiled.

"Did Craig Newby get the flags?" Susan asked about their fellow vestry-board member.

A broad smile filled Reverend Jones's handsome face. "He found every flag we've ever had, starting with Old Glory. Big ones that he's going to hang off the roofs all around the inner quad. He swears he can do this without harming the gutters. It should look sensational. And, of course, he bought flags on sticks for every attendee. The flags for the graveyard for those who have fought in our wars are provided by the DAR and the Veterans of Foreign Wars. As you know, our parishioners who belong to those organizations knock themselves out."

"It is impressive." Miranda nodded. "And let's not forget the Confederate veterans."

"They'll have their flags, too." Then Reverend Jones focused on Harry and Susan. "Latigo says he'll give me eight thousand dollars for my old truck. Victor told me that, yes, he could get it running again but given its age I should just go with a total loss. Latigo arranged it. I guess when you're the president of a big insurance company, you can do anything. Eight thousand dollars is a lot more than it's worth."

"Preacher's price." Alicia stood up, dusting off her gloves.

"Special interest for good works," Harry teased him.

"You all should get deals, then, with all you're doing. And, Harry, you said you'd come back Friday and mow, so everything will be perfect for Saturday."

"I'll be here with my magic zero-turn mower."

"So what are you going to buy?" BoomBoom wanted to talk trucks.

"Something big enough so you all can haul more plants." He laughed.

"Come on." BoomBoom smiled and winked at him. "What do you want?"

"Well, now, I have to take this slow. Check around, check what I can pay per month. I like the new Dodge. Really like the interior. I don't know. You girls can help me when things settle down."

Susan watched as the cats leapt off the wall to chase butterflies and one another. "When do things ever settle down in Crozet?"

26

Saturday, cool at 6:00 A.M., promised to turn up the heat and humidity as the hours wore on. Rising at her usual 5:00 A.M. in the summer, Harry patted herself on the back for mowing and weed-whacking at St. Luke's yesterday morning, as the day was cooler.

After drinking her first cup of coffee and feeding Mrs. Murphy, Pewter, and Tucker, she returned to the bedroom. Fair, on his side, head nestled in a goose-down pillow, remained sound asleep.

"Poor guy," she whispered to herself.

He'd gotten a midnight call from a frantic horse owner. The big expensive dressage mare she'd purchased a month ago was colicking. He finally got back home at 2:00 A.M. She heard him take a shower. When he crawled into bed, she'd rolled over and he told her all was well.

Tucker, always wanting to be beside Harry, said, "He'll be awake in a little while."

Harry looked down at the small dog she loved so much and smiled. Although she hadn't a clue as to Tucker's prediction, she knelt down, kissed her friend, then returned to the kitchen.

Tucker really did know when Fair would awaken. As Fair's skin cooled down or heated up, the dog detected changes in his scent. No matter the season, Fair usually woke up sweating slightly.

"How come you got the beef?" Pewter paid no attention to Harry returning to the kitchen.

"I don't know. How come you got chicken?" Mrs. Murphy responded to her peevish friend.

"I want some."

"Pewter, go ahead." The tiger cat backed away from her dish, and Pewter dove right in.

"Hey! Hey, what are you doing?" the gray cat yelled, mouth full so she dropped food on the counter.

"You're eating my food. I'm eating yours."

"I didn't say that you could eat my chicken!"

Early it may have been, but Mrs. Murphy's patience was already thin as a bee's wing. She hauled back, giving Pewter a real swat—claws out, too.

Pewter, no wimp, stood on her hind legs to box. Terrible words were spoken. Neither cat would back down. Tufts of fur flew all over the kitchen counter.

Harry fed them breakfast up there because, when she turned her back, Tucker would steal the cat food. Good as Tucker was, she loved cat food. It contained a higher fat content than did dog food. Supper, however, was different. They all ate a light supper on the floor because Harry, preparing food, remained in the kitchen. Mornings had the pretty woman rushing all over the place.

Now it looked like a fur blizzard.

"Stop it!"

The opponents ignored Harry.

Fair, with a towel wrapped around his waist, bed head, and slippers on his feet, more or less stumbled out. "Jesus, sounds like the cat house at the zoo."

"*I am a lion.*" Pewter whacked Mrs. Murphy on her side as the tiger whirled around.

"*A lion of lard!*" Mrs. Murphy shot back.

The combat escalated. Harry grabbed the kitchen broom. With a sweep over the floor, she caught the tiger cat under the butt, pushing her out the door to the screened-in porch.

Pewter flew after Mrs. Murphy, but Harry stood in the doorway, greeting her with the broom face. Pewter, moving fast, smashed right into it.

"*Ha!*" Mrs. Murphy gleefully observed.

Once back on her feet, Pewter leapt over the bottom of the broom. Mrs. Murphy blasted out the animal door in the outside porch. Pewter got caught with the flap swing back and fell backward. This so enraged the gray cat that she spit like a llama.

Tucker, dumbfounded at the vehemence of the fight, sat on her rear end.

Even Fair was impressed. He walked to the screened-in door.

Harry joined him. "They're totally nuts."

"*I'm not going out there to stop it,*" Tucker declared.

The two cats ran in big circles. Then they ran through the barn. The horses stopped eating in the pastures to observe the kitty NASCAR races.

Shortro, hay still in his mouth, said, "I didn't know cats could move that fast."

Tomahawk shook his gray head. "Especially the fat one."

The fat did tell on Pewter. Finally, she slowed down. Mrs. Murphy sat about thirty yards distant from her on a fence post. They glared at each other.

At the top of her lungs, Pewter bellowed, "I hate you. I hate everybody. I hate the whole world!"

She turned, thumping back to the house, each determined step heavy on the ground. She reached the walnut tree, paused for breath, and saw Matilda hanging by her tail, looking straight down at Pewter.

"You don't hate me, do you?" The blacksnake laughed mischievously.

Pewter's mouth opened, but nothing came out. She hit her turbo, zooming into the house, where she collided with Fair, his towel falling off.

"Speaking of being nuts." Harry put her hand over her mouth, laughing so hard her sides hurt.

"I am not nuts. I just happen to have them." He laughed, too.

"For which I am grateful." She handed him his towel and, as he wrapped it around his waist, she gave him a hug.

Still laughing, they sat down at the table. She poured him coffee.

"Eggs, cold cereal? This short-order cook is taking orders."

"Hmm, cold cereal." He smiled at her. "We've had our entertainment. Flag Day can't possibly top the cats."

Later, the cats managed a truce. If they hadn't, Harry

would not have taken them along for the day. They sat in the back of the Volvo station wagon. Silent.

Tucker curled up in her riding bed. She, too, shut her mouth, feeling that sooner or later the feline tinderbox would explode.

As they approached the church, Fair noticed the hydrangeas along the drive. "Honey, the place looks beautiful."

"We all did it. St. Luke's needed a pick-me-up. Dee Phillips created such a lovely plan."

"Isn't she Episcopalian?"

"Kissing cousins, Episcopalians and Lutherans."

Fair twisted around and checked on their passengers. "Not a peep."

"Good." Harry parked on the lower level.

As the humans walked up the terraced path to the interior quad, the two cats and Tucker followed. The Very Reverend Jones loved animals, so anyone's animals who behaved were welcome.

Once inside the inner quad, both Harry and her husband stopped.

"Fabulous!" Harry exclaimed.

As promised, Craig had hung the flags from the roofs. The various numbers of stars bore evidence to our growth as a nation. At one end of the quad—the administrative end—he'd also hung flags from the nations that first gave us colonists: England, Ireland, Scotland, Wales, France. Since Germany did not become one nation until under Bismarck in the nineteenth century, there wasn't room to hang the flags of all the various small German states. Craig did, however, hang the flag of the Austrian dual monarchy, as well as the flag that now represented all of Africa to African Americans.

"How smart he is." Fair rubbed his chin.

"I would have never thought of the parent nations, for lack of a better word." Harry enjoyed watching the slight flutter of the flags.

The pyracanthas stood out from the stone building that Herb could see from his office. Clear fishing line had been set up so the branches would grow on it, creating straight horizontal lines. The church side of the quad, covered in wisteria that had already bloomed, offered deep shade. In glorious symmetry, St. Luke's looked especially beautiful today.

Elocution, in her office window, looked out. None of the cats appeared eager to mix with screaming children all waving their little flags.

Pewter stopped under the window. *"I've had a horrible day."* Whether or not any of the other cats wished to hear Pewter's lavish lament wasn't going to stop the gray fatty from going on and on.

Mrs. Murphy, in contrast, stuck with Tucker, who loved children. This canine affection was returned. One little boy gave Tucker his flag. The dog patriotically ran all around the quad, flag in mouth.

On long wooden picnic tables in the middle of the quad was true summer picnic fare. Miranda, although not a Lutheran, had helped with all that. Everyone attended this gathering: Catholics, Baptists, Jewish families from the temple in Charlottesville. Flag Day at St. Luke's was not to be missed.

The veterans saluted the flags at a short ceremony

before food was served. Victor Gatzembizi was an Air Force veteran, though he had not seen combat. However, heroically enough, he now paid for transportation for those elderly vets who might otherwise have difficulty attending. Mostly their families brought them, but some lived in nursing homes.

Sipping a cold one after the ceremony, Fair slapped Victor on the back. "Thanks. Having those World War Two veterans here is an inspiration for the rest of us."

Latigo strolled over. "Vic, I'll be sending you more work after the holiday."

Fair wasn't sure if Latigo was joking or not. "What do you mean? You think there'll be more accidents from Flag Day? It's not a drinking holiday. Not like Memorial Day," Fair remarked.

"Any holiday is an excuse," Latigo replied in an even tone. "I was actually thinking about the Fourth of July. Always a lot of accidents then." He asked Fair, "You didn't serve, did you?"

"No, I headed straight to vet school after undergraduate. I often think I missed one of life's central experiences—for men, anyway."

"All I heard was 'central experiences.'" Yancy Hampton joined them.

"Didn't serve in the military." Fair drained his long-neck.

"Navy," Yancy stated. "I've even been thinking about going back in. They're offering tempting packages to those of us who made captain or above."

Victor's eyebrows raised. "I learned a hell of a lot in the Air Force. I was in transport and they taught me about engines. But you'd go back? Why leave a thriving business? And, hey, it's the assholes above you and the idiots below."

"That's anywhere." Yancy waved his hand dismissively. "I'd go back to get away from home. Next weekend is my daughter Stephanie's wedding. Around my house there's been just about as much estrogen drama as I can handle."

Latigo's daughters were the same age as Stephanie, all the girls having attended St. Anne's. "Stephanie's pretty reasonable."

"It's Barbara." Yancy mentioned his wife.

"Ah, yes, mother of the bride." Victor whistled, then added, "Good luck, Yancy. Fair, I'm going to tempt your wife."

Harry had walked by with a few other vestry-board members.

"She tempts me daily." Fair smiled.

"WRX STI. Great deal." Victor started to move in Harry's direction.

"You'll torture her," Fair rejoined.

"I know." Victor left as the three other men watched.

Yancy turned to Latigo and got down to brass tacks. "Do natural disasters greatly affect your business?"

"Yes," Latigo replied seriously. "Any disruption affects insurance, but I don't have the kind of massive claims that life insurers or property insurers do in situations like floods or tornadoes. In ways, auto insurance is pretty cut-and-dried because we have the blue book to value our cars and trucks."

Yancy, drink in left hand, slid his right hand into his

pants pocket, jingled keys. "Because I buy some crops ahead of harvest, like futures trading, I factor in weather. Not that you can predict anything with accuracy, but large changes like El Niño, stuff like that, I factor it in. Every little thing can affect harvest for good or for ill. 'Course, I don't think there ever was insurance for corn worms." He took a sip.

Fair listened with interest to Latigo's reply. "As you know, the government does offer some insurance for crops—"

Yancy interrupted. "Better than nothing, I suppose, but I'd hate to depend on it."

"Me, too. The payment is always inadequate to the damage, and there's plenty of people who will tell you the same thing about auto insurance. We undervalue their cars, undervalue repairs, use less-skilled labor. The funny thing is, NHTSA—the National Highway Traffic Safety Administration—hasn't had an update on wheels since 1974. Back then wheels were steel. So we've got some seriously outmoded standards."

"Well, that just might make it easier for you to be dishonest," Yancy impolitely answered.

Stiffening slightly, Latigo said, "I'll assume the 'you' applies to the industry and not me personally. Actually, what creates problems is people expecting the government to take care of them. Well, if wheel standards are damned near forty years old, isn't it clear either they don't care, or they don't know enough to care, or they're too venal to care? I know that safety standards are vastly different for a steel wheel than for one made primarily of aluminum. When my field agents assess damage and repair costs, I can tell you they're far more accurate than any federal goon ever is."

"Didn't know about that," Yancy simply replied.

"People have no idea, no idea at all." Latigo laughed derisively.

"The technology changes so rapidly. How can you keep up with it? I know the government can't." Fair was curious.

"Fair, let me tell you something." Latigo, one inch shorter than Fair's six foot five, looked level at him. "What's changed is computers running cars. Engines haven't changed. Alternators haven't changed. Fan belts haven't changed. The internal-combustion engine is about perfect. Materials change. Oh, maybe the angle of setting an engine under the hood will change, but a piston is a piston."

"Never thought of it that way," the vet replied.

"I have a garage full of great cars. My Porsche 911 is a little bit of heaven. I have a gorgeous old restored DeSoto. Walt Richardson restored it, actually. I have my own muscle cars, and for my wife I bought a 1957 Thunderbird in aqua and white. I love cars, I love engines, and I love insuring them. What I don't love is my industry being demonized, made into a target."

Yancy was thoughtful. "If I have one misshapen grape in a bunch, someone will call Albemarle's health inspector on me. I wasn't kidding when I said the Navy looks good again."

Fair, dangling his longneck bottle, asked, "Latigo, what would you say is the real purpose of insurance?"

Right back at him, Latigo said, "To spread risk.

We've had forms of insurance since the second millennium B.C., and the purpose is always to spread risk."

Just then Harry trotted up to her husband, pulling him away from Yancy and Latigo.

"Honey, you're a little flushed. Do I look that good to you?" Fair teased.

"Victor Gatzembizi is the devil himself. Twenty-seven thousand dollars for the WRX STI. The loan would be about twenty-three thousand if I went to the bank. Of course, I'm not even thinking about it. Given all that Nick put in it, that's an incredible price. Fantastic car. Great reviews in the car mags. He's ruined my day."

"No, he hasn't. He has given you something to think about. You love cars."

"Twenty-seven thousand dollars with a blown tractor to repair? Hell." Harry looked confused, sad, a little angry all at once.

"There is the tractor." Fair sighed. "That's farming. One thing after another."

"What would I ever do with a pocket rocket?" She looked up at him imploringly.

"For one, you'd enjoy yourself. You only go 'round once."

Aunt Tally reposed in a comfortable chair under a tree. At one hundred she deserved that. Her friend Inez Carpenter, DVM, two years younger, sat next to her. Big Mim rushed and fluttered about, being her usual imperious self. Her daughter accepted all the happy hugs from those who now knew she was pregnant. Blair—no cigars this time—handed out Zippo lighters with the Stars and Stripes on the chrome casing.

"I want you prepared when the baby comes. You'll need to light your cigar." Blair gave Fair and Victor each a lighter, then gave one to Reverend Jones, and he joined them.

"Thanks, Blair," Herb said. His flame flared up high. "But if I use this thing, I'll burn my eyebrows off."

Blair took the lighter back and showed the reverend how to adjust the flame.

After the food, everyone sat for a bit to let it settle.

Mark Catron had played the clarinet for the Charlotte Philharmonic Orchestra before moving to Albemarle County. Now he stood up and, using his bugle, he blew them to order. Mark could play anything

Reverend Jones stood next to the trumpeter with the bright blue eyes. "All right. We're ready to divide up for the capture-the-flag teams. If you all look at the ticket you were given when you got in the food line, it will have a number on it."

There was a rustle as people searched for their tickets. Purses opened and shut. Men fished in their back pockets.

"Odd numbers are the blue team. Even numbers are the red team. You'll have tails in your color, like in flag football. BoomBoom Craycroft will hand out the blues; Alicia Palmer, the reds. The timekeeper is Susan Tucker. She has the whistle. When the air horn blows once, play. Blows twice, stop. Our referees, Harry Haristeen and Craig Newby, will be wearing referee shirts and blowing the standard whistle."

Harry and Craig appeared in shirts with vertical black-and-white stripes.

Is there an American who doesn't love playing capture the flag on Flag Day? The whole crowd repaired to the area outside the inner quad, the cemetery anchoring its far side. This giant rectangle had been marked with lime to the dimensions of a football field.

At one end was a red flag the size of an American flag. At the other end, a blue flag, also large. Each team lined up opposite its colored flag.

Each team was given time to elect their captains. Aunt Tally kept the stopwatch after people moved her chair to the field's edge. Susan held the air horn to signal quarter- and halftimes.

Both elected team captains were popular high school seniors at Western Albemarle High School.

"Is everybody ready?" Reverend Jones called out in his deep voice.

"Ready," the captains responded.

Reverend Jones raised his hand, dropped it.

Harry blew the whistle at the exact moment. The chaos began. If a red ventured into blue territory and his or her flag was snatched, the person had to go behind the opposing team's end line, in purgatory.

Pewter haughtily strolled to the cemetery wall, jumping up to observe the silly game. The three St. Luke's cats joined her.

People yelled, screamed encouragement to teammates. Onlookers clapped and shouted.

Fifteen minutes into it, the air horn blew, signaling

the end of the first quarter. The teams had two minutes to catch their breath and rethink strategy.

Already, half of each team was behind the opposing end line. One of the peculiar rules of capture the flag was that you were set free if someone from your team slapped your hand. Given that the liberator was in enemy territory with a small team flag stuffed in a waistband, the liberator risked becoming a prisoner, too. If one had speed, it was pretty easy to run up and grab the team colors, which hung out two feet from a four-inch-wide waistband. It was like a donkey tail.

The captured reds now lay down on the field. One had to lie down with feet touching the end line and reach out to hold the ankle of the person in front. In this way the captives formed a human chain. It was all within the rules. The closer the chain stretched to the fifty yard line, the greater the chance that someone would be able to free the captives. They'd then rejoin the game, giving them an obvious advantage if the other team's players were still held prisoner.

The whistle blew; play resumed. The faster players remained free. The intensity grew. The sidelines erupted.

"*Humans invent some funny games, don't they?*" Cazenovia mused.

Mrs. Murphy sauntered down, jumped up on the stone wall at a distance from Pewter but within speaking range of the Lutheran cats.

"*I'm not speaking to you,*" Pewter huffed.

"*Good. You're a bloody bore.*"

"*I resent that,*" Pewter snapped.

"Come on, you two. We want to enjoy the day," Lucy Fur, with authority, spoke.

Pewter jumped down into the cemetery just as the reds were freed, their chain having grown longer so it was easier to have a free player touch a captured player without being captured herself. A huge roar went up. "I hate them all," she grumbled. The gray cat walked to the far side of the cemetery, toward the large old stately tombstones.

Mrs. Murphy moved closer to Elocution, Cazenovia, and Lucy Fur to chat.

Pewter sat for a moment on the back side of the large Trumbull tombstone, a huge recumbent lamb on top of it. She sniffed. Sniffed again.

"Hmm." She walked around the tombstone—and stopped cold.

Leaning against the carved family remembrance, bolt upright, was a young man, eyes staring into space. Dead as a doornail.

"Hey! Hey!" Pewter shouted.

Of course, the other cats paid no attention, so she tore through the graveyard and screeched to a halt at the bottom of the wall. "There's a dead man in here."

"They're all dead." Cazenovia laughed.

"But someone is leaned up against a tombstone!" Pewter panted.

Mrs. Murphy jumped down and ran to her friend, anger forgotten. The two cats hurried around the Trumbull monument.

Mrs. Murphy put a paw on the dead man's leg, looked intently at what she could see of the corpse. "No wound. No blood. How did he die?"

Pewter also stared at the body. "Could he have been strangled?"

"His eyes would be bloodshot," Mrs. Murphy replied.

Pewter wailed, "Why does everything happen to me?"

No point in arguing, so the tiger just nodded. The two cats raced across the well-tended graveyard.

As they sailed over the stone wall, Mrs. Murphy called over her shoulder to the three cats, "Dead body at the Trumbull monument."

This was too good to be true. Cazenovia, Elocution, and Lucy Fur hopped down to run in the opposite direction.

Calling out before she reached Harry, Mrs. Murphy hollered, "Tucker. Tucker, I need you."

All the commotion surrounding the game drowned out her voice.

The two cats reached the dog, and Mrs. Murphy rapidly filled her in on their discovery.

"I was the one who found the body," Pewter corrected the tiger, who had said "we."

Stifling the urge to smack the gray cat, Mrs. Murphy simply agreed, then ordered, "Tucker, take Mom's hand. Pewter, you and I need to get behind each leg, stand on our hind legs, and push. Sooner or later, she'll get it."

Tucker, on her hind legs, grabbed Harry's hand gently in her mouth. The two kitties started pushing. Standing just inside the limed sidelines, Harry resisted them.

"Guys." Harry shook off Tucker.

Fair, amused by their antics, returned his attention to the evenly matched game. The contestants were now showing the effects of hard running.

"*Mother, pay attention!*" Mrs. Murphy screeched as loud as she could.

Tucker barked, taking Harry's hand again, leading her a few steps.

"What is wrong with you all?"

Arms across his massive chest, Fair looked down at the animals. He could read their behavior better than most humans could. Not that Harry was oblivious to their methods of communicating, she just had never been accused of being overly sensitive.

"Honey, I'll follow them. You can't leave your ref duties."

"*Damn, these people are hard work.*" Tucker allowed herself a brief complaint.

Looking at the dog, Pewter unleashed her claws. "*It's refreshing to hear you not defend Mom for once. You're always sticking up for her.*"

"*I love her, although at this moment I'm loving her a little less,*" the dog replied.

"*They're all idiots, even her.*" Pewter retracted her claws, since Harry had taken advantage of a time-out and called to BoomBoom to fill in.

She handed off her ref's shirt to BoomBoom and followed the threesome. "I'll be right back."

The cats ran ahead, occasionally stopping and looking back. Tucker followed them. The animals hoped this would encourage the two people to move faster.

The cats jumped on the stone wall. Tucker raced to the iron gate, wiggling underneath.

Fair lifted his wife up on the stone wall.

"I can climb," she said.

"You can, but why deny your husband the pleasure of feeling your body?"

"Oh, you big, strong thing."

This playfulness abruptly ended when they rounded the Trumbull monument. Gathered there were all the cats. Tucker barked once for good measure.

Harry's hand flew to her mouth. It was Bobby Foltz.

Fair was smart enough not to touch the body, but he knelt down for a closer look. "Dead, obviously."

He reached into his back pocket, pulled out his cell-phone. Although not on call this weekend, he knew that certain of his clients preferred only him and would fuss if they couldn't reach him—hence, he carried the damned phone. He dialed the sheriff's department.

"Honey, what would you rather do?" Fair, once finished, asked his wife, whose curiosity was now overtaking shock. "Stay with the body or go tell the reverend to move people into the inner quad?"

"You're a medical person. You stay. I'll go." She hurried back through the graveyard, looking over her shoulder. "Tucker, come on."

Harry filled in the reverend with the news as the blue team came within a whisker of winning.

Reverend Jones said to Harry, "Let them finish the game. It will be much easier to move everyone in. I have to present the trophy anyway." He paused. "This is just terrible. What in the world is going on?"

Harry then ran along the sidelines to go and ask BoomBoom to help after the game.

As Reverend Jones had anticipated, herding people into the stunning inner quad after the game proved easy.

Tucker was a big help, snapping at people's heels. The corgi did this respectfully. Harry was too distracted to call her off.

Once in the inner quad, Herb presented the trophy to the triumphant blues, then said, voice commanding, "We've had a bit of an accident. I ask that you all go home, and, Craig, as people leave, please have them sign a—Susan, get a notebook from the supply room. Have them sign the notebook with their name and the names of their family members. I'm sorry to do this, folks, but all of this will be clear later. We need a record of who was here today, as best as we can get one."

The crowd grumbled in confusion, and then sirens split the air.

Cooper had intended to come to the celebration but was delayed, thanks to an accident on the old bypass. Fortunately it wasn't serious. She'd picked up Fair's call and informed Marcie, the dispatcher. Rick would arrive shortly after her, she hoped.

As people left, the murmur became a roar, especially when they saw Coop's vehicle fly down to the reverend's garage. She hit the brakes and jumped out.

Cool in a crisis, BoomBoom continued to move people along. She glanced back at Harry. "Whatever happened must be big."

Harry simply nodded.

Susan stood at one end of the quad with the notebook. She, too, quizzically looked at Harry, who made the wrap sign with her forefinger.

Thanks to the vestry-board members' expert people-management skills, the place was cleared out in twenty minutes. By that time, Harry had run back to the grave-yard.

Standing on the big quad looking down, BoomBoom asked Alicia, Susan, Craig, and Reverend Jones, "What's going on? Should we go down there?"

Herb grimaced slightly. "No. Let's wait up here for the sheriff. There's always the danger of evidence being trampled."

"What do you mean? Evidence of what?" Alicia inquired in an even voice.

"There's a dead man propped up at the Trumbull tombstone. Let's wait here. If Rick needs us or wants us, he'll let us know."

"Of all times and all places," BoomBoom blurted out. "No wonder Harry's face looked so white."

Staring into the dead man's eyes, Cooper wasn't saying anything. She was puzzled by the disposition of the body.

"I can't disturb him. We've got to wait for the team." She checked her watch. "Dammit to hell."

"Neat work. No marks," Fair observed.

"No marks that we can see. It is remotely possible that he sat there and had a heart attack."

"He looks awfully young for that," Fair rejoined.

"Well, we can't dismiss anything until the report comes back from the Office of the Chief Medical Examiner."

Rick arrived within ten minutes. Slamming the door of his squad car shut, he hurried over to the small group at the grave.

"Not happy," Elocution observed.

"Finding bodies affects their equilibrium," Lucy Fur sagely opined.

Pewter sat up straight. "A dead human always means trouble. It's not like a squashed squirrel on the road. The fellow seemed familiar, but I can't quite place him."

The forensics team arrived right after Rick. Weekends were slow, but the department maintained a skeleton crew. Rick had learned long ago that the damnedest things could and would happen on weekends.

The forensics team's Nina Jacobson carefully observed the body. She donned thin rubber gloves while asking her two assistants to move the body slightly away from the tombstone. She then carefully examined his back.

"No obvious wounds. No gunshot, knife, blunt trauma."

Tucker lifted her nose in the air. "Skull."

"Ah." Mrs. Murphy agreed, for she, too, could smell the very faint signature of fresh bone.

Nina, no slouch, peered at the back of the fellow's neck, ever so slightly brushed back his hair at the nape of his neck, then moved higher. "There it is."

Rick and Cooper moved closer to eyeball where she pointed.

"So it is." Fair whistled.

Rick, voice crisp, said, "Someone drove a thin needle or ice pick from the base of his skull into his brain. One hard, hard blow. Instant."

Fair knew how fast death could be when the brain

was invaded. "But surely not here. It wasn't done in this graveyard."

Rick grimaced. "No. I think not. Who would sit still while someone pierced his brain? Dammit, this last month has been just, just . . ." His voice trailed off.

"A bitch." Cooper finished his sentence for him.

"Whoever killed him wanted to show off," Rick said. "Someone is playing games with us. Sooner or later someone from the celebration would have wandered into the graveyard."

"Let's be thankful no children found him," Harry breathed out.

"I found him." Pewter walked over, brushing Cooper's leg.

"I guess this killer likes drama." Cooper looked at Rick, who shot a look at Nina.

The team placed the body on a stretcher.

Hoping for more attention, Pewter piped up, "Why do these things happen to me?"

"Karma," Mrs. Murphy fired back.

27

"You never know." His tools as neatly laid out as a surgeon organizes scalpels, tweezers, and probes on a tray, Dabney Farnese was talking about death.

"No, you don't." Harry sat on an upturned Winchester ammunition wooden crate in the equipment shed while Dabney stood on a small stepladder next to the John Deere.

In his mid-seventies, Dabney Farnese couldn't keep up with the volume of his work. Making it to Harry's within two and a half weeks was fast for him. So few people repaired older-model tractors that Dabney could have worked twenty-four hours a day if humanly possible.

Before her, Harry's parents had used Dabney's business and were good customers. He always enjoyed seeing Harry, remembering the little girl from long ago who wanted to repair tractors with him, grease smeared on her nose, hands, and clothing.

Farnese, an Italian name, was easy for people to recall, plus Farneses had lived in Virginia since the Revolutionary War. Dabney, no interest in history or genealogy, never brought up how long his people had lived in the Old Dominion, but others found it fascinating. His children dabbled in their family history, finding what everyone finds: brave people, some bright, some dumb as a sack of hammers, most honest, a few not.

"You just make sure, Missy," he told Harry, "that you aren't found. Let the Sheriff do his job and you steer clear of the business." He carefully lifted out the entire hydraulic pump. "Would you like to provide a funeral for this hard-used hydraulic pump?"

She laughed. "I could hang a wreath on it."

"Very respectful. Do you remember when your father fried eggs on Johnny Pop?" Dabney recalled the old tractor from the fifties, which had an exhaust pipe on the left side of the engine, with a lid on top of it. When you drove the tractor, the lid would *pop, pop* as the exhaust escaped. That particular tractor would have run into the twenty-first century, except that Harry's dad started it up one spring day without noticing a bird's nest filled with eggs scrunched in the exhaust pipe, the lid slightly ajar. By the time he figured it out, not only was there a mess, he'd driven into a ditch, making yet another mess. He finally traded the tractor in for a newer model less inviting to birds.

"Never heard my father cuss so much." Harry laughed. "Actually, Mom fired off a few choice words herself when he drove into that ditch. At first we didn't know what had happened. All we heard was our collie barking, barking, and more barking. By the time we got outside, Dad had crawled out from under the overturned tractor. Lucky he wasn't hurt. It was pretty funny—those things are, after enough time passes. I suppose, in a way, it will be funny someday that we found that young man Bobby Foltz in the cemetery. Convenient. All they'd have to do would be to dig a grave right there."

"Know him?"

Harry shook her head. "Not really. I saw him race at the drag strip. Passed him at ReNu."

Dabney removed the hoses. "Did you like him?"

"He seemed nice enough. Now that's three men dead who worked at ReNu."

"Read in the papers where the guy who owns the shop has offered a ten-thousand-dollar reward for information leading to a conviction." Dabney wiped his hands on a red cloth, unpacked new hoses, set them on his big tray.

"A lot of money." Harry whistled.

"Also said this fellow is establishing scholarships in honor of the dead men, for kids who want to be mechanics."

"What a good thing to do." Harry listened to the bluebirds who'd made a nest outside the shed in the back.

"Wish somebody would create scholarships for tractor repair," Dabney said.

"John Deere should be naming scholarships after you. You can repair anything." She thought a moment. "But I suppose you're taking business away from the dealers. They charge an arm and a leg for repairs."

"I don't have their overhead," the shrewd Dabney announced. "Don't want it, either."

"Thank you for driving out on a Sunday. You're saving my bacon, 'cause I've got to cut my hay."

"You're lucky it hasn't gone to seed—nor have you." He winked.

"Elevation. I'm sometimes two weeks behind farms at lower elevations, and I'm almost three weeks behind the farms near Richmond. Most times that's a help. In the dead of winter, maybe not."

"You mentioned over the phone that Fair was going to take out a loan."

"I talked him out of it. He was worried we'd lose our hay crop. It's such a good one this year, but I said, hang on, honey. He leaves the farming to me. We each have our spheres, as he calls them. But I raised the money by selling my sunflower crop—futures, sort of—to Yancy Hampton."

"I don't believe that organic-farming crap." Dabney carefully inspected the new hoses on his tray, then removed the new pump, meticulously checking it.

"I do and I don't. Farming without some form of pesticide is hideously expensive. Birds, bugs, little viruses, can ruin a high percentage of your crop. Plus, Dabney, the produce doesn't look as pretty as the agribusiness produce."

"That's true. Real apples are a lot smaller, might have a little blemish on them. Might have a worm, too." He lifted his shoulders slightly. "How does anyone expect the world's bursting population to be fed without genetic engineering?"

"Don't know." Harry kept to the old ways, so she truly didn't.

"I bet I've been to half the farms in Virginia in my long life, repairing John Deere tractors. The changes I've seen." He shook his head. "The worst was in the eighties, when the government pretty much turned on the small farmer. God bless anyone who managed to hang on. Your family did."

"Sometimes I think it killed Mom and Dad. They worked so hard to save this place. It took its toll. I have a husband whose income doesn't derive from farming, so I can keep the old home place going. Still, sometimes I get overwhelmed. Maybe that's why I get caught up with mysteries, wanting answers. Takes my mind off these huge economic forces. Nature, the government, a crop across the ocean, can affect my crop prices. I mean, there's just little me."

"Yep." He breathed in the fresh morning air, for a cold front had swept through during the night. "Mystery is one thing. Murder is another. You read too many books when you were a kid."

"Nancy Drew." She smiled. "Mother would get after me to read serious fiction. Bored me stiff, which set her right off. Can't help it." She held up her hands in supplication.

"Here. This isn't a mystery, but let me show you something." He held out the hydraulic pump. "This is a genuine John Deere pump for your 2750. It hasn't been cheaply produced in India or somewhere else in Asia." He lifted an eyebrow. "For one thing, your tractor is twenty-four years old, which means it's too old to get fake aftermarket parts for it. Don't part with this tractor.

Those countries have a real incentive to produce cheap aftermarket parts."

"Are the fake parts defective?"

"Not necessarily, but they aren't as good. The steel's never as good, and moving parts are often not packed in thick-enough grease, or there's a rub years later because the calibration isn't perfect. Often, when you pick up a motor part not made by the original manufacturer, it's a hair lighter. Another clue is the fitting holes. If you removed an engine element or, say, this hydraulic pump and saw that the bolt holes were maybe a little elliptical, that would mean aftermarket. They had to fuss with the original hole to make it fit."

"I did try to look at the hydraulic pump. Chipped my tooth," Harry joked.

Dabney laughed, then returned to the subject. "Buy the specs. If a model goes out of production, the manufacturer often doesn't want the bother of producing the old parts. So they sell the specs for old models. It's easier to use the tooling equipment to produce newer parts, I guess. Now, John Deere doesn't do that, but—and it's a big 'but'—some of these overseas people are smart enough to hack into computers and just plain steal the specs. Anything on a computer is not safe. Hell, even the FBI's been hacked into."

"I never thought about that—industrial theft, I mean."

"Billions. No stopping it, either. If I order a part from John Deere, I talk to the same guy I've been working with out there in Illinois for decades. I've got the real thing. Same with Ford. I call Ford, not a dealer here."

"You're not branching out and fixing old trucks, are you?"

"No, but I'm sure fixing my own. Well, I've just nattered on here, haven't I? But it frosts me, frosts me good, because American businesses are being screwed. If they don't want to make the old parts anymore, that's their damned dumb choice, but foreign companies stealing our new stuff?" He bit his lower lip for a minute, then stood back on the small ladder to recheck the site for the new pump. "If you take care—and I know you do—you'll get twenty, maybe thirty years out of this pump. Those hoses, you might have to change those earlier. Your old ones lasted eighteen years. A small piece of one hose is missing. Wonder what happened to that? No matter. I'm putting in all new hoses. No point in a new pump and worn-out hoses."

Harry watched as Mrs. Murphy and Pewter left the barn, heading in the direction of the shed.

Tucker slept on the concrete floor of the shed. That concrete floor had cost Harry's dad plenty, but it, too, held up. She questioned Dabney some more.

"Yep. Indians are building decent tractors, a lot more horsepower for the money. A heck of a lot better machine than those Russian tractors that hit the market ten years ago, but John Deere is the Rolls-Royce of tractors. Spend the money. Buy the best."

"I'm with you there. You were telling me about models where the manufacturer no longer makes the parts. I see these magazines for old Ford parts, old Chevys. Looks like a big business. How is that different?"

"In some cases those are parts that a businessman

bought from a local dealer. The car dealer no longer had the space to store mirrors, alternators, you name it, for cars from the forties, fifties, et cetera. In other cases, someone with skill can reproduce those parts."

"Why is that different?"

"Well, for one thing, the original manufacturer has a warranty on the parts. If you buy a 1950 Chevy block, a John Deere block, a Harvester, it still is under warranty. But let's say I have an aftermarket tractor part made in China. The manufacturer gives you a warranty, right?" He looked at her. "The part is defective. Are you going to go to China to sue? I don't have to tell you where I bought the part, nor does any repair shop. I'll save money using cheap aftermarket parts. Like I said, you have a model that's old enough, you're okay, plus I would never do that. I only use genuine parts."

"I had no idea."

"No one does, really." He paused. "Someone remodeling an old car loves it. It's irrational. Someone repairing a tractor needs it. Someone repairing a new car or a new tractor needs it, and usually pronto. A man spends more on his young mistress than on his middle-aged wife." He glanced down at her. "Maybe that wasn't the best comparison."

"I get it. No apology needed. Men are doing it all over the world."

"One woman is expensive enough. Why two?"

"Dabney, you're awful."

"That's what Doris tells me." He laughed.

"You couldn't live without her."

"That's the truth. Hand me that ice pick."

She held it up for him as he gingerly cleaned out a hole. "That's how they think Bobby Foltz was killed," she said. "Ice pick or something thin, they think."

"I wouldn't have looked."

"Nothing to see." Harry shrugged. "Not like Walt Richardson, whom Reverend Jones, Susan, and I found at ReNu."

"I don't even want to look at dead animals on the road."

Three hours later, everything replaced, Dabney ran the tractor, declared it fixed, and Harry handed him a check for $5,319. She said a little prayer of thanks for her sunflowers. This prayer didn't include Yancy Hampton.

The organic grocer could have used her good wishes, for his middle daughter was very expensively married that Sunday. The reception was at the Randolph Inn, and the caterer misplaced the chicken. After that debacle, Yancy wanted to replace his hysterical wife, who dissolved in a discombobulated fit of anger and raw nerves.

Yancy remembered what his mother used to say about his father: "Divorce, never. Murder, yes." Gave him a shiver. There'd been enough murders.

28

"*C*harleston, South Carolina." Latigo Bly walked across the inner quad with Reverend Jones.

The two men had come from Reverend Jones's garage. Neither one wanted to pass close to the cemetery. Instead, they walked at the edge of the large outer quad, reaching the low fieldstone retaining wall. Herb opened the white-painted half-moon gate, stepping into the rich green space. "Well, I'll be," Herb said, in response to Latigo's mention of Charleston.

Satisfied that Reverend Jones had evidenced interest, the tall man continued, "It was in 1732. However, this first American insurance company only offered insurance against fire."

"I always thought the first person to start an insurance company was Ben Franklin." Reverend Jones had to take bigger steps to keep up with the long-legged Latigo.

"That was later, in 1752. He founded the Philadelphia Contributionship for the Insuring of Houses from Loss by Fire." Latigo chuckled. "No fool, Mr. Franklin. He refused to insure bona fide fire hazards, which meant all wooden houses."

"Guess he still made money."

"A resourceful, creative man." Latigo reached the arcade, the stone arches adding to the sense of order and harmony.

"A highly sexed man, too," Herb said, then quickly added, "Recent history books make much of it."

"Sex sells," Latigo said without emotion.

"Maybe you should try it in the insurance business," Reverend Jones teased him.

"Sure works in yours. Aimee Semple McPherson, for starters."

"Well, if it worked for religious revivalists, it's got to work for you. Insurance isn't a—how shall I put this a lively business? No singing, dancing—"

Latigo cut in, "Or praising the Lord."

The two laughed as Reverend Jones opened the outside door to his office. Asleep on the sofa, curled up together, the three cats lifted their heads, dropped them again.

"Please sit down." Herb motioned to a comfortable club chair. "Can I get you any refreshment?"

"No, thank you. I dropped by to give you the check for your truck." He reached into his pocket, retrieving an ecru envelope, business logo on the upper left corner.

"I didn't expect this so fast." Reverend Jones opened the envelope with his fingernail, pulled out the check. "Latigo, this really is more than that truck is worth."

"It has scrap value."

"Thank you. Thank you very much." Herb replaced

the $8,000 check, slipping the envelope into his pants pocket.

"As for a new truck," said Latigo, "this is a good time to buy. Folks are staying away from the gas guzzlers, so truck sales are slow. You should be able to drive a good bargain."

"That they are, but the church needs a big truck. As you can imagine, the upkeep on a place this old consumes a considerable chunk of our budget. I'll buy the truck in my own name, but, of course, we'll use it for necessities here." He leaned back in his chair. "Nothing seems to get cheaper, does it?"

"No. Doesn't the church provide you with a car?"

"They do, and it's a big help." He swept his hand toward the triple-sash windows, wide open. "What a beautiful place to work, to live. Can't put a price on that, and what preacher is in it for the money?"

An eruption of laughter roared from Latigo. "All of them on TV."

Reverend Jones smiled at the corners of his mouth. "I don't consider them ministers. I think of them as hucksters. Revealing my prejudice here, but I am an ordained Lutheran minister, so I have high educational standards. Plus, I don't think one should use the Good Lord for profit."

"I do." Latigo smiled. "I pray daily."

This time it was Reverend Jones's turn to laugh uproariously. "I'll pray for you." He patted his pocket wherein he had slipped the check. "You've got one good deed fresh in St. Peter's book." Then he smiled again. "And I'm sure many, many more."

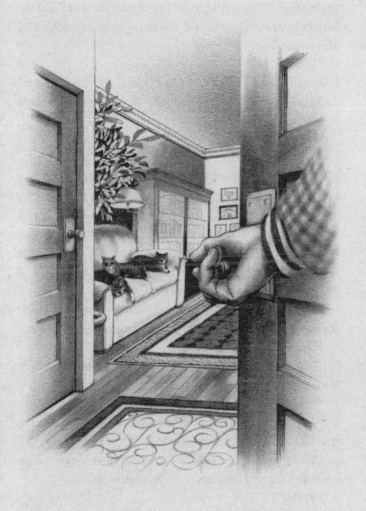

Latigo surreptitiously checked the Napoleon clock on the mantel. "I've got to run. Let me know what you do buy. I certainly hope you'll continue to insure with Safe and Sound."

"I will."

As Latigo left, Lucy Fur raised her head. *"Poppy's happy."*

"A new truck," Cazenovia purred. *"New leather seats to scratch. Heaven."*

Herb dialed ReNu.

"ReNu Auto Works," Kyle intoned.

"Kyle, this is Reverend Jones. You have my 1994 Chevy half-ton there. I'd like to come down tomorrow and clean it out thoroughly. I didn't do that when it was towed. Just too upset about it. Will that be okay?"

A short pause, then Kyle replied, "Sure. I'll tell the boys to leave it alone."

"What would they do with it?"

"Strip it. There will be good parts in it even though it's old. The boss sells the older stuff to specialty houses."

"Specialty?"

"Places that work on old vehicles, trucks. Plus there are warehouses for old parts."

"I see."

"And then the boss sells the truck for scrap. Scrap metal's up right now, so he's happy."

"Well, you don't stay in business if you don't find ways to make the money, beat the tax man."

"Right."

As Reverend Jones hung up, he thought to himself that the few times he'd seen or spoken to Kyle, no sliver of enthusiasm ever disturbed the young man. The other thing was, Kyle never said good things about ReNu. He didn't say bad things, either.

He dialed again. "Harry."

"Rev."

"Will you go down to ReNu with me tomorrow?"

"Sure. What's up?"

"I need to clean out the old truck before they trash it. I was so mad when the truck went out on me, I didn't think to take all my stuff. I don't even know what I left in there."

"Glad to help."

"I don't want to go there alone, truth be told."

"I understand. I really do."

"Okay, then. Mmm, ten too early?"

"No. I'll pick you up."

29

"*R*elieved?" Reverend Jones enjoyed the smooth ride of Harry's Volvo station wagon as they left the church to go into town.

A silence followed this. "Yes. I was sure I was fine, but yes." Harry waited another moment. "I have gained even more respect for doctors and nurses who deal with cancer."

"It's all around us. Our various church groups provide comfort. The men's group surprised me."

"You didn't think they'd talk about how cancer affected them?"

"I thought the men who had been afflicted with cancer would. But the new group, the one for men whose spouses, family members, have cancer or have had it, that's been the surprise. And your husband holds it all together."

"He never talks to me about it." Harry wasn't offended by this.

"Sometimes, Harry, there are things a man can only say to another man, especially in a situation like this. To tell your wife, daughter, sister, best friend, of your fears while she's in the middle of battling this disease, well, most men feel this would make it worse. They feel their job is to hold you up, not focus on fears."

"I believe that. But Fair's helping?"

"He has a knack for getting other men to open up."

"Maybe because his patients can't talk, he's learned to read the signs. I think he can read people as well as he can read horses."

"*Can't read me,*" Pewter called from her snuggle bed behind the driver's seat.

"*Sure he can.*" Mrs. Murphy, next to her, contradicted the gray cat. "*All you want is tuna and catnip.*"

"Mom," Tucker whined from the back, "*they're at it again.*"

Harry heard the slight snarl between the cats. "If I have to stop this car to break up a fight, there are going to be two unhappy cats. Do you hear me?"

There was not a peep, but Herb laughed loudly. "My three run the church and run me." He paused. "They're very faithful cats."

"*That's because you don't have a diva like Pewter.*" The tiger couldn't resist.

Harry looked at the rearview mirror just in time to see a gray paw swat the tiger on the side of the head. "Damn."

Herb turned around, booming in his deepest preacher register, "That's enough."

The two culprits froze, deciding to call a temporary truce. Pewter was already plotting her revenge for when they got home.

"Thanks," said Harry. "You even scared me."

"Takes a lot to scare you, but you sure scare the rest of us. We never know what you're going to get into."

"The truth," Pewter agreed.

Harry pulled onto the back ReNu lot, cruised the parked vehicles yet to be repaired. "Sure are a lot of accidents in Charlottesville. Look at all these cars and trucks."

"Inattention. People take their eye off the road constantly. There's cellphones and texting, but I actually think the worst is those maps."

"What maps?" Harry's eyebrows moved toward the middle for a moment.

"What do you call it? My truck's so old, doesn't have it. You know, a screen and a map pops up."

"Navigation system. GPS." Harry found Herb's old truck and parked at the end of the row wherein it sat. "Each carmaker gives it a special name. BMW calls it iDrive, which performs more functions than a visible map. Mercedes has their name. Some makers call it a driver interaction system, which takes too long to say."

The reverend unbuckled his seat belt. "Well, I say they're responsible for a lot of accidents. If you don't know where you're going, pull over and look. Don't do it while driving."

"You're right, but people aren't going to do that. They're going to look at that screen and bam! It only takes a split second." She lifted the back door to let air in.

The animals stayed, since the asphalt was hot. Heat caused more pain than bitter cold. They did move to the rear of the back to watch as Reverend Jones and Harry—

one carrying a large garbage bag, the other a carton—
approached the 1994 Chevy half-ton.

Herb had brought his extra key. He unlocked the
driver's door, then walked around to unlock the passenger door. "Shouldn't be too much work."

It wasn't. Harry removed his gloves, maps, a small
air-pressure gauge from the compartment on the driver's door.

Reverend Jones opened the glove compartment to
take out papers, leaving the manual behind. He put the
extra key in there. His good sunglasses greeted him.
"Ah, thought they might be here."

"You lose more gloves and glasses."

"Doesn't everyone? Why do you think children's mit-
tens are attached to their coat sleeves?"

"Got a point there, Reverend."

Within fifteen minutes, they'd cleaned out both the
debris and the more-useful items. Harry, alert per usual,
pulled down the visors, removing a few papers and one
bright goldfinch feather. She held it up, the light hitting
the brilliant yellow edged in deep black.

"Ah." Herb took it from her fingers.

"Think he killed it?" Pewter asked, eyeing the reverend.
Was he a bird killer?

Tucker replied, "He can't even kill a cockroach. He found it on
the ground."

"Maybe Cazenovia killed it." Pewter grinned, ever hopeful
for avian murder.

"Possible." Mrs. Murphy nodded. "What could he have left
in the engine?"

Harry, leaning into the engine, was carefully studying the old but good V8. For decades, General Motors had manufactured sturdy, long-lasting truck engines. In the old days, the rap on the GM truck motors was they were more complicated to fix. You had to pull out the Chevy engine, because things were hard to get to. The Fords proved less difficult; hence, the service bills were lower. That, however, had changed toward the end of the twentieth century. With today's computer readouts, all any mechanic had to do was hook up to the mobile unit. Ninety-nine percent of the time, a precise diagnosis made the task of repairing the fault much easier and the engine no longer needed to be removed to identify the malfunction. That one percent of the time when it did was when a garage needed someone's special talents, like the late Walt Richardson's feel for an engine.

Harry lacked that feel, but she possessed mechanical sense and some real ability.

"Dead?" Reverend Jones sighed.

"The engine? No. It's your radiator that's done for. Let's take your stuff back to the Volvo. I brought my toolbox. All I want to do is lift out this radiator."

"Why?"

"Won't take long. I'm curious as to what's behind the radiator. I can't see that anything has pierced it from the front. It's rare, but a part can dislodge or something could be stuck behind the radiator. A radiator is easy to pierce compared to an engine. The radiator is exposed. Your pistons are not."

Reverend Jones didn't give a fig about the radiator, but he assented.

Within minutes Harry was half in, half out of the engine. Standing on a broken concrete block she'd found, she had unbolted the radiator. Lifting it up, she put it on the ground. Then she checked the bolt holes. Next she examined the radiator. Didn't look smashed.

Jason Brundige had seen her from the garage, its bay open for the cooling breeze. He hadn't been informed by Kyle that Reverend Jones and Harry would be cleaning out the truck.

He placed his large screwdriver on his toolbox and strode out purposefully.

Sammy Collona observed this. Went back to work.

Jason walked up to Harry. "What in the hell are you doing?"

"We cleaned out Reverend Jones's truck."

"What's that got to do with the radiator?"

Herb, ever the gentleman, came to Harry's rescue. "I informed Kyle that I had left personal items in the truck and told him when we'd be here."

"Like I said to her, what's the radiator got to do with it? I put that radiator in your truck two years ago." A note of defensiveness crept into Jason's now-too-loud voice.

Sammy, hearing this, hurried inside to Victor's office. Fortunately, it was a day when Victor was in the Charlottesville shop.

"I'll take care of this." Victor dismissed a now-worried Sammy and quickly walked back to the parking lot. "Apart from his mouth"—he indicated Jason—"is everything all right?" Victor apologized to Reverend Jones and Harry.

"Fine. I didn't mean to cause upset." Reverend Jones's voice soothed.

"I know that. Jason's a watchdog type and everyone's a little edgy." Victor glanced at the radiator on the ground. "You're not taking that, are you?" He laughed.

"No." Harry took a step toward him. "My curiosity got the better of me. It's a two-year-old radiator, so I just wanted to look it over. Looks okay, but I'd need to study it better."

Victor knelt down. "It does look okay. Well, I'm sorry for your inconvenience, Reverend Jones. Latigo told me he wrote this off as totaled so you might be able to buy a newer truck. Good as these old babies are, this one's been hard used."

"I'm sorry," Harry said. "I really did seem to get under Jason's skin."

"No apologies necessary." Victor stood up. "Reverend, tell me what you buy. CarMax down in Richmond has very good deals on used cars and the histories of every vehicle. Now, if you want a new truck, there are a lot of choices right here in Charlottesville."

"Yes, there are. I'll be sure to let you know."

Victor walked back, stopped in the garage. "Jason, don't ever embarrass me like that in front of Reverend Jones."

"How was I to know?" he moaned. "She's a nosy bitch. She'll cause trouble."

"First of all, Harry Haristeen is not a bitch. Nosy, she is. Causing trouble?" He shrugged. "I hope not, but she's one of those people who can't leave well enough alone once her curiosity is triggered."

"Right," Jason mumbled as Sammy looked on.

Victor returned to the front of the building.

Sammy said, "Jason, all you did was call attention to the damned radiator. That was pretty stupid."

30

After the cold front passed through over the weekend, everyone enjoyed the perfect weather. But then on Monday, the heat shot back up. The stifling temperature and the close, humid air dispirited one and all.

Harry, bush hogging on her repaired tractor, stopped in the middle of the large pasture behind the crops, the smell of the new-cut hay field filling her nostrils. Cursing herself for saving the big pastures for later, she turned off the motor, stepped down—hand on what she always called the "Jesus bar"—and swung to the earth. Her soaked T-shirt clung to her. She might have won a wet-T-shirt contest, although Harry's mind never worked that way. If someone else brought it up she might make a crack about it, indulge in a little sexual innuendo, but she wasn't a person who thought a lot about erotic things. It's doubtful she would have been different if born male. "Tunnel vision" best described her way of seeing her day.

Focusing now, she lifted off a long polo whip that she affixed by the tractor seat with two welded small

"U"s. She'd slip the whip through them and secure it with rawhide.

The cats sat high in the hayloft. The upper hayloft doors were open, as were all the downstairs doors and every stall door, just in hopes of catching the hint of a breeze. They watched as Harry walked through the mid-thigh orchard grass, with white clover underneath.

The hay wasn't the finest horse quality, but it would do okay for cattle. She'd sell out of her seven-hundred-pound round bales by February. The quality was good, but Harry, fussy about nutrition, only square-baled her alfalfa–orchard-grass mix for the horses. She also had twenty acres in timothy and alfalfa. Perfect hay. Naturally she'd cut and baled that first, having gotten half of it up before the hydraulic pump expired.

Susan, happy to be outside, was running the spider-wheel tedder, turning cut hay to dry while Harry mowed down the cattle hay. Susan had always loved farm work. When they were kids, she'd often begged Harry's parents to let her help.

Harry and her friends were bound by hoops of iron. It wasn't just the years, it was the accumulated births, passings, victories, defeats—the sheer intensity of the experiences they'd shared. They knew one another's weaknesses and strengths. Observing the various generations, they noticed downright peculiarities popping up again and again, parent to child, and so on. Even if there was a Nobel Prize for intelligent farming and Harry had won it, it wouldn't mean as much as what she felt for her friends and what they felt for her. Naturally, she believed that her friends had more peculiarities than she did. They felt the same way about her. Never was there a shortage of laughter.

Even with her husband. Sometimes the two of them would laugh so much they'd fall out of bed. Fair's motto was "If you can't laugh while making love, you aren't making love." Well put, Harry agreed.

"She's methodical." Mrs. Murphy admired Harry's system.

Pewter observed Harry, who was now off the tractor and swinging the polo whip, the grasses bending over. Carefully, Harry covered much of the field she intended to cut. She did this in sections. Her whistle carried even to the hayloft.

"She is. Humans learned to be patient and precise from us. They watched us hunt, stay still, figure out where the quarry is. They're alive because of us, you know." Pewter puffed up.

"Hoo. Hoo. Hoo," Flatface, on her nest in the cupola, called down. "Cats aren't as important as owls. The Egyptians carved beautiful friezes of us. The Greeks put us in their myths, and I remind you, Fatty Screwloose, that we are sacred to Athena—an owl accompanied her. No cat traveled to Mount Olympus."

Pewter, voice low, grumbled, "I hate it when she calls me Fatty Screwloose."

Mrs. Murphy whispered, "Keep it to yourself. She's strong enough to pick you up in her talons. Flatface is powerful and smart—very, very smart." The tiger cat then called up to the huge owl, "You're right, but there was a tiger cat in baby Jesus's cradle. It was so cold we kept the baby warm."

"Might could be. Human stories interest me. Some of them are beautiful. With others, you can tell right away they're off their nut. Leda and the swan. Now, I tell you, why would Zeus seduce a woman as a swan?"

"Bet you're right." Pewter decided to humor the big girl.

"He would have come down as an owl." Flatface issued this judgment with absolute conviction.

The owl looked through the slats in the cupola.

The cats, too, saw the doe and fawn run away from Harry.

"Good she did that," Mrs. Murphy said.

"The fawn so often gets killed." Flatface turned her head at that odd angle that birds can. "They hear that fearsome racket, but the mama has told the baby to stay. She runs away, thinking she might well divert the danger, and, wham, the fawn is ripped up by the equipment. If Harry had killed that fawn, she'd be a wreck for all this week."

"She knows animals. Softhearted, so softhearted." The tiger cat smiled. "She gives to the animal shelter. Tight as she is, she'll give money to panhandlers even. I wish she wouldn't."

"Why?" Pewter asked.

"So many of those people lie. They can work. A lot of them are drunks. It's a scam. I don't like to see her fall for a sob story."

"Why don't they just die?" Pewter remarked. "Any animal that doesn't find its food, work for it, dies except them. They keep everyone going no matter how useless. It's sick." Pewter watched as Harry reached the edge of the pasture, which bordered the strong-running, deep-sided creek. "Well, isn't it?"

"I don't know if it's sick, but it's wasteful." Mrs. Murphy considered the subject.

Flatface called down, "Humans think human life is more important than any other kind of life. Ego. All ego."

"Harry's not like that. She treasures life. Susan, Fair, and BoomBoom

do, too." Mrs. Murphy felt a flash of pride as Harry crossed back to the tractor and waved to Susan, careful to walk in her same steps so as not to tramp down more hay.

"The exceptions prove the rule," Flatface countered, then called down, "Someone's coming. I don't know who it is."

A snoozing Tucker awakened when the car reached a quarter mile from the house. If awake, the dog would have heard the tread all the way down to the mailbox, almost a mile away.

"Intruder."

Harry heard the bark. She called to Susan, climbed up on the tractor, and—grateful the hydraulics were working—lifted the non-rotating bush hog up off the ground, as she'd shut off the PTO. Then she drove back to the house—where she beheld the alluring WRX STI.

"Harry." Victor Gatzembizi greeted her, stepping out of the Subaru. "You could appear in a John Deere ad. You look darned good on a tractor."

Swinging down, she replied, "Thank you. Victor, I am so sorry for all your troubles. Come on in and let's have a cold drink together."

"Thank you, but I've got to get back to the shop." He turned as another car approached. "Jason's driving me back."

"How about if I give you both cold drinks to go?" She ran into the house, returning with two cans of iced tea. "Nothing's as good as the tea you make yourself, but these aren't so bad."

"Thank you." Victor took the cans and walked back to Jason, who was driving a Nissan Altima, newly repaired and out for a test spin.

"Nice car. I see so many of those on the road," Harry remarked.

"Nissan, Subaru, Toyota. Good cars, but I'm telling you, the Koreans are catching up fast. Really fast." Victor reached into the shiny black WRX STI and pulled out the keys, handing them to her. "I can't stand to look at this car right now and neither can Mrs. Ashby. You keep it, drive it until after July fourth, and then tell me what you think."

Harry hesitated a moment, thought about the circumstances. "I really don't see how I can afford this, but I'll keep it until then. I can imagine that seeing Nick's car might be difficult."

He shook his head. "Three men, all from my shop. I can't find any connection other than that they worked for me. Not one of them played around with drugs, stuff like that. I even had a wild thought about one of them bringing in illegal immigrants. I've tried to think of anything that would be high profit, against the law. What is there but drugs and workers?"

"Prostitution."

"Harry, I know Bobby, Nick, and Walt didn't go that route. Watching porn, well"—he shrugged his shoulders—"probably, but paying a hooker? No."

"I meant running a high-class or even low-class hooking ring. I bet you there'd be takers in the audience at drag racing."

An astonished look crossed his regular, pleasant features. "Uh, I never thought of that. Anyone ever tell you you have an unusual mind?"

"Fair and my friends, all the time." She laughed. "But

you said illegal, and I assume high profit. That's all I can come up with."

He folded his hands together. "It's driving me crazy."

In the background, they heard the rumble of the truck as Susan drove the spider-wheel tedder, still at her chores.

"I can imagine."

"I knew those guys, I really knew them. By the way, the report from the chief medical examiner's office said Bobby was full of Quaaludes. He couldn't have defended himself. I never saw him take any drug. He had to have been purposefully drugged, then killed."

"I truly am sorry."

"I've hired special security for the shop. I can't really afford it, personally, for Jason"—he nodded in the direction of the Altima—"Sammy, or Lodi. I've advised them to always have someone with them when they travel. I've even suggested they not drive. Have a family member take them to work and pick them up—at least until this is solved."

"Good advice." Harry felt the keys in her hand. Someone—Nick, likely—had hung a lucky rabbit's foot on the key chain.

After more chat and another thank-you from Harry, Victor and Jason drove down the long driveway. Harry felt the temporary use of the car was also a peace offering for Jason's behavior the other day. She couldn't wait to tell Susan, to give her friend a drive, but first Harry marched right in to the kitchen and took the rabbit's foot key chain off the key. She put on a key chain of her own, with a little flashlight hanging from it.

That rabbit's foot was anything but lucky.

31

"This is fantastic." Susan, while hardly a car enthusiast, still appreciated the acceleration of the WRX STI when she mashed the pedal to the floor.

"That's why it's called a pocket rocket. Handles like butter." In the passenger seat, Harry grinned.

Harry wanted to treat Susan for turning hay in the unremitting sun. What Harry had just cut needed at least two days to cure, partly to let the blister bugs run out. Susan had turned yesterday's cutting. They showered after that sweaty job.

They'd known each other all their lives—sisters, really. Neither woman had siblings, a rare occurrence for their generation. Kindergarten, grade school, high school, Harry and Susan did everything together. They did attend different colleges but spent summers together and even went to Europe upon college graduation. Susan's people had more money than Harry's, but Harry's wonderful mom and dad saved for a year to send her overseas as a graduation present. Susan was a business major, while Harry studied art history. Like most traveling young people, they enjoyed and endured many adventures. They returned to their native Virginia with a deeper appreciation of their own state and country, as well as a wider view of the world. Both had learned that every country has gifts and every country can do many things better than we do.

"Do you know how many years it's been since I drove a stick shift?" Susan slowed for the intersection with Route 240.

As she lurched forward, one of the Zippo lighters with a flag on it given to the men by Blair Bainbridge slid out from under the seat.

"Given that you're knocking the fillings out of my teeth, I'd guess it's been a good twenty years."

Laughing, Susan replied, "That's about right. God, it is fun, though. I really feel like I'm driving the car."

"Remember that Dodge Dart you had junior year?"

"Tinker Bell." Susan smiled. "Hey, Tinker got me where I wanted to go." She paused. "With some help from you and BoomBoom. She suffered from chronic conditions."

"Brake fade, numb steering, faulty timing, bald tires. Tinker was a basket case."

"Half the time so was I. Why anyone looks back on their high school days with fondness is beyond me. Every day was an invitation to a new drama."

"Well, every day you fell in love. You were a hot mess."

"You always had Fair. But you were still a mess." A gleam shone from Susan's eyes, which never left the road.

"Oh, we all were. What scared me the most was taking the college boards."

"You aced them. Got you a scholarship to Smith."

"Scared me to death. Actually, I do sort of look back fondly sometimes. When we were tiny, we saw the world as so wondrous: butterflies, horses, shiny cars, listening to the car radio. But high school was more about emotions for the first time—adult emotions, I guess."

"Coming from you, that's a statement."

"Why?"

"Harry, I think of you as a part-time adult."

"You know, I could cancel our lunch, even if you did turn my hay. *Mean.* You are just hateful mean."

Susan laughed. "The truth hurts."

They cruised along, secure in the love of deep friendship, cruising down Memory Lane, as well.

Susan pulled in to the parking lot of The Blue Mountain Brewery, their favorite place. The restaurant, on Route 151 in Afton, had good food and was much less expensive than any equivalent place in Charlottesville.

Charlottesville was working hard on appealing to the foodies, the result being an array of restaurants with small portions artfully displayed, followed by big bills.

Once settled in their booth, orders given and tall, ice-cold glasses of Coca-Cola in their hands, they jabbered about this, that, and who shot the cat, to use the old Southern expression.

When Susan's rather big BLT arrived, a moment of guilt affected her. "I have no self-discipline. How can I lose weight eating bacon?"

"Oh, Susan, shut up about your weight. You look

great. If Ned still revs his motors when he sees you, there's nothing to worry about."

"That's the best way to look at it."

With a devilish smile, Harry added ever so sweetly, "And, Susan, a little fat fills the wrinkles."

Susan took her unused fork and jabbed Harry lightly on the hand. "You'll eat those words instead of your salad. You're too skinny anyway."

"A woman can never be too rich or too thin," Harry replied. "Who said that?"

"Someone who lived an unhappy life. Some days you have to eat fat or fried chicken or even a little sugar. I really do try to limit myself, but if I gave up everything, I'd be downright miserable."

"A lot of women sure are." Harry speared a wedge of egg. "Susan, I've been thinking."

"God, no."

"Really. This is serious, and I can tell you, knowing it will go no further. I can't get the murders out of my mind. With my dumb luck, I found two of the corpses. Well, the cats and dog found the second one. But no one can believe they're unrelated anymore."

"No." Susan's eyes widened. She knew that Harry, in part because she didn't have to observe law-enforcement protocol, often stumbled upon connections before others did. Then again, Harry often got it nearly right but not right enough, to the sheriff's discomfort.

"I've investigated the gambling angle—gambling rings—as best I could. I called Tessa Randolph, who works at the Bellagio in Las Vegas. You remember her. Anyway, she told me that, no matter what type of illegal gambling, there has to be a drop or a mule, a place where the money is bet or a person who takes the bets. The drag track could be a good spot for an operation like that. But I can't find a thing there. I've hinted to Sammy at ReNu that I want to bet. He races at the track, so I called him up. He said he didn't know anything. He could be playing dumb."

"You're not the brightest, honeybun."

"Well, do you have another suggestion?"

"Yes. Don't call anyone at ReNu, for starters. We pay taxes, so Sheriff Shaw and Coop will deal with it. If there's an illegal ring, you just tipped them off."

"Yeah," Harry paused, "but it bothers me that I've seen these dead men. I didn't know them, but seeing them so close to life, so recently dead, it's eerie, know what I mean?"

"I think so. All right, Harry, what have you got?"

"Questions. I've been in an early-morning fog. I could see shapes. Little by little, that morning fog is lifting. What I saw was that this could be tied to gambling or drugs, but now I don't think so. But I definitely think it has to do with whatever the mechanics know at ReNu. Of course, that could still be gambling and drugs, but—I don't know why I think it has to do with some kind of specialized knowledge. I've asked Coop to slip me the report on Tara Meola's death."

"That was an accident."

"Was, but I want to read the disposition of her car."

"What do you mean?"

"A deer caused her death. Official version, and indeed it likely was the catalyst, but I think there's more to it."

"Oh, come on, Harry, she wasn't murdered."

Taking a deep breath, then a deep swallow of Coca-Cola, Harry lifted her eyebrows just slightly. "Her air bags deployed."

"Hell, yes, they did. That's what they're for. A deer crashed through her windshield."

"But when did they deploy? Look, when Miranda and I careened off the road, the air bags blew up. She couldn't see. How she got us to the side of the road and stopped, I have no idea. Air bags are supposed to deploy in a collision. We had no collision or hard bumps really. They shouldn't have deployed. Miranda's a lot better driver than I thought—not that I'd say that to her, because then I'd let her know I had qualms about both her abilities and her age."

"Sometimes you actually can do the right thing." Susan smiled at Harry.

"I'm trying. I've got to find out about Tara's car."

"You're not going to trouble her parents?. Harry, you can't do that."

"I won't. I really would like to talk to them, but I promise I won't. I asked Herb a little about it, since he's been calling on them. She was insured by Safe and Sound."

"So are a lot of other people. It's a huge mid-Atlantic company."

"A very successful one, and we all more or less like Latigo Bly. Somehow, though, it's hard for me to completely trust a man who changed his name legally from Alphonse to Latigo."

Susan put down her BLT lest she drop it, she was laughing so hard. "Harry."

"Really? Latigo? He could have changed his name to Tom, John, Robert. If he wanted to sound younger, how about Jordan? But Latigo?"

Susan laughed all the harder. "Dakota, Travis, Brett, Randy, Caleb. Are those in the same category?"

"No. They're generational, but Latigo? Have you ever heard of anyone named after a rope?"

"You're right. He could have picked a horse—Secretariat. Secretariat Bly."

The silliness escalated, which meant it was turning out to be a perfect lunch.

On the way back, Harry drove, loving the short throw between shifts. "Victor is Lucifer. He knew I'd fall in love with this car."

"Anyone who knows you would know you'd go gaga over high performance. Didn't take a rocket scientist. BoomBoom driven it yet?"

"I'll pick her up at the concrete plant tomorrow."

"Think this car's haunted?"

"No." She climbed Afton Mountain. "I think about Nick, though, sitting in this seat."

"It will do me no good to tell you to be careful."

In her own way, Harry was being careful. She didn't tell Susan what her hunch was, because she was afraid it would set her friend off and, also, she was far from sure. Why cast a shadow on a seemingly good person until one was sure?

So Harry changed the subject, a favorite tactic. "Yancy Hampton is coming back to check out my ginseng in

July, when the little berries show up. Do you know in some places ginseng is bringing five hundred dollars a pound! Growers in New York get that—not all of them, but they're averaging between three hundred and four hundred dollars a pound."

Drily, Susan said, "Yancy isn't going to offer you that."

"I know." Harry shifted into fourth gear. "I have both cultivated and wild ginseng down by the creek. Ginseng loves it there, with all the shade and moisture."

"Takes ginseng a long time to produce seeds, doesn't it?" Susan remembered sitting down at the creek with Harry as children, dipping their toes in the cold water.

"Three to four years. But, remember, my wild ginseng is well established. The cultivated stuff I planted last year—well, I have a wait on that."

Susan changed the subject. "Ever miss the P.O.?"

"All the time. Really was Crozet's hub."

"Yeah. The new building is big, clean, and light, but you can't hang out there like we could at the old P.O. George Hogendobber used to give us licorice sticks. Who would have ever thought you'd graduate from Smith College and become our postmistress?"

"Not me. I thought I was filling in until I found my real job and the postmaster general found a real post-mistress."

"You never talk about it." Susan looked at her friend's profile.

"What's to say? The new building outgrew me, I guess. Couldn't take Mrs. Murphy, Pewter, or Tucker to work. Those two cats could roll the mail carts as well as I could." Harry smiled. "Everything's changed, Susan.

Sometimes I feel old. I know I'm not, but . . . oh, I don't know."

"We have memory now. We can compare things. Couldn't do that at age six."

Harry thought about that. "Change is life, I guess."

"It is." Susan took a breath as Harry shifted around a curve, sliding nicely. "Show-off."

"Couldn't help it." Harry laughed. "Ever go into the café at Fresh?"

"Couple of times. He's done a nice job. Sometimes I see friends. Sometimes I don't. I think Yancy hoped it would be a central place, but who goes into an organic market? People with some money. Nobody poor can pay those prices."

"Got that right. I really don't like Yancy. Can't put my finger on exactly why he rubs me the wrong way."

"Me, too."

"You play golf with Barbara. You like her."

"I do. But she's a nervous type. And she never talks about him. Not one word, which I think is a bit strange. It's not as if you and I and the rest of us don't occasionally discuss our significant others."

"Or insignificant others."

"That, too."

They were still laughing when Harry pulled in front of the barn.

"Why didn't you take me?" Tucker asked as the two women disembarked. Harry leaned down to pick up the cigarette lighter, reminding herself to call Victor, since it must be his.

" 'Cause you rolled in horse poop," Pewter helpfully suggested.

"Do you know, Pewter, when you talk, your belly sways from side to side?"

"Do you know, Tucker, when I'm behind you, tailless thing, I see things I'd rather not?"

32

*H*arry and Susan had just set foot in the kitchen when the wall phone rang.

Harry picked it up. "Hello."

"You'll never guess," Franny breathlessly spoke. "They found my tires."

"Where?"

Susan helped herself to iced tea, then moved next to Harry to hear better.

"A warehouse at Zion Crossroads."

At the junction of I-64 and Route 250 in Louisa County was Zion Crossroads. For so many years it had been sleepy and nondescript, but in the last ten, it had morphed into a hotbed of business, food, and gas. I-64 could carry one all the way to St. Louis if traveling west. Then it turned into I-70, rolling through until the Rockies. Even those drivers on a short hop to Richmond pulled in, grabbed a Coca-Cola or coffee, and stretched their legs.

The old lumberyard was still there, but to the locals it seemed yet another storage business appeared every day. Good for the coffers of Louisa County.

Susan offered Harry a sip as she got her ear close to the receiver.

"Susan's with me. A real eavesdropper." Harry smiled. "How did they find the goods?"

"Well, Rick put out a report, went all over. Computers really are amazing, and one of the girls at the cash register at McDonald's remembered a semi stopping. Nothing unusual there, but she looked out as the driver pushed up the big door in the back and two men jumped out. She saw the tires. Didn't think anything of it. An officer from the Louisa County Sheriff's Department mentioned to her that the storage units popping up were great places for contraband. She'd read about the robbery in the paper, remembered it, and told the officer. Anyway, they managed to convince the U-Store-It owner to open the bigger units."

"Thought they had a double lock. The storage key plus the unit owner's key."

"Harry, they do, but we all know those units aren't that hard to break in to. The storage owner checked his books first, discounting anyone he personally knew, then cut the locks off the others. Presto! Bingo!"

"Isn't that something? So whose name was on the unit?"

"That's just it. False name. Paid cash. We can hope they come back at some point to remove the tires, when the contraband is not so hot, but that presupposes no one will talk. A big hope."

"True."

Susan said into the receiver, "When do you get your tires back?"

"Don't know, but they're in Albemarle County now, wherever Rick puts stolen goods. Bet he had to rent a big unit. I can't imagine the sheriff's department routinely has enough space for stolen goods as large as mine. But isn't that something? One alert citizen. I'm going out there and giving that girl a new set of tires."

"What a nice thing to do." Harry was always impressed by Franny, who unfailingly did the right thing.

"Anyway, couldn't help myself. Had to call my group support buddy."

"We'll celebrate after this week's meeting." Harry took another sip of Susan's cold tea. "Franny, do you know where totaled cars go?"

"To auto heaven, where else?"

"Smarty. I assume that when a vehicle is written off as totaled by the insurance company, it's towed to a salvage yard and the insurance company owns it."

"Makes sense, but insurance isn't my field. I just know I pay too damned much for all my policies."

"It's cheaper to die. Then again, maybe it isn't. Isn't the average cost of a funeral seven thousand dollars?"

"Now, why do you know that? Harry, you're ghoulish. I don't want to know the cost of the average wedding."

"Twenty thousand," Susan called into the phone.

"That can't be right." Franny was horrified.

"I think it is," Susan replied. " 'Course, in Albemarle, it's probably more."

"Is your daughter in love?" Franny asked.

Susan's daughter, Brooks, was still in college.

"No, but Ned and I are planning ahead. We don't

want to be bankrupted when the time comes. Thank God our other child is a son."

"More power to you." Franny meant it. "I missed the reproduction boat."

"There's still time," Susan teased her.

"I sincerely hope not." Franny giggled, still buoyant over her good news.

"She's right, Franny. A woman in England gave birth in her sixties," Harry told her.

"You know," Franny became thoughtful, "it's wonderful. If a woman wants to do it, good for her. Used to be we only had but so much time, whereas men could go on and on. I wasn't ready at twenty. I'd be a disaster now. Oops, someone at my door. Harry, I'll see you at group."

"Great news, girl." Harry hung up.

"She'll need to be peeled off the ceiling." Susan reached into the fridge to refill her glass.

Three ice cubes clinked into a glass, tea over that, and Susan handed Harry her own glass.

"Susan, do me a favor. Call Vivien Bly and ask her where Safe and Sound takes totaled cars."

Sitting down at the kitchen table, Pewter now in front of her at eye level, Susan bargained. "Tell me why I'm doing this."

"*Are you going to eat anything?*" Pewter put on her sweetest puss face.

"Pewter, get off the table," Harry ordered.

"She's not going to listen to you." Susan stared straight into Pewter's gorgeous eyes.

"You really like me, don't you? I like you, too. How about some tuna? I like turkey, too."

"Fatty, fatty, two by four," Tucker sang under the table. The gray cat pointedly ignored the corgi.

"Harry," Susan demanded.

"All right." Harry sat opposite Susan, whose pageboy haircut looked so good on her. "I expect everything is taken out or off squashed vehicles and sold. The hulk is then sold for scrap. Logical?"

"Well, if they do it to human bodies, I'm sure they do it to cars," Susan agreed.

"I have a hunch. That's why I want to find Tara Meola's car. I looked at Herb's radiator and I, um, have a hunch."

"Tell me."

"Not until I'm more sure. I don't want to look stupid and I don't want to point the finger."

"I understand not pointing the finger, but looking stupid? You might want to revise that."

"I love you, too."

Smirking, Susan whipped out her cellphone, dialed. "Vivien, Susan here."

"Still on for Friday?"

"I am. I sure hope the heat has cooled down by the time we go out."

"Should. Well, that's what coolers on your golf cart are for. I can taste one of my frozen daiquiris now."

"I'll sure want one when we're done. Vivien, I was wondering if you could help me," Susan asked.

"I can try," she replied, a hint of eagerness in her voice.

"You and Latigo are still building Safe and Sound. You know auto insurance."

"It interests me. It's what brought Latigo and me together. His first wife, although she really did help start the business, wanted to spend his money. I want to make it," she forthrightly said.

"As you know, Harry and I serve on the vestry board at St. Luke's. Your husband kindly wrote the reverend's 1994 Chevy off. What happens to that truck? I assume it's stripped for anything of value."

"Yes, it is. Sometimes we tow the vehicle to a salvage yard. If the motor and other parts are quite serviceable, we tow it to ReNu, where those parts are removed, sometimes refabricated, if you will, or simply put on the shelf until they can be used again."

"So they're rebuilt?"

"Sometimes they don't even need that. They're serviceable with a little fixing up. But what's left if they're not serviceable is always sold for salvage. As you know, those prices go up and down like waves in the ocean. Anything having to do with cars, steel, rubber, oil—the prices are volatile. Last year, metal salvage went through the roof. Our profit from that salvage shot up seventeen percent."

"I'd throw a party."

Vivien replied, "I bought a new set of clubs."

"What salvage yard do you use?"

"Haldane's Salvage in Stuarts Draft. There used to be yards on Avon and Avon Extended." She cited a street in Charlottesville. "The congestion, traffic especially, made us switch to Stuarts Draft. Easier to get the vehicles in."

Stuarts Draft is a small town between Charlottesville and Staunton.

"You've satisfied our curiosity. See you Friday."

Harry walked over to the wall phone, pulled a phone book for Augusta County out of the drawer, located the salvage yard in the yellow pages, and dialed.

After ascertaining that Safe & Sound had dropped off fifteen vehicles at Haldane's Salvage in the last two months, Harry asked, "Do you know who used to own those wrecks?"

"Most times we do," said Mildred Haldane. "We have paperwork on everything—what's been removed, what's left," the older woman replied with pride. "We're environmentally concerned. No battery-acid leaks around here."

"That's a big job."

"It is, but we're the best."

"Would you mind checking your records to see if you have a busted-up Explorer once owned by Tara Meola?"

"Pulling it up right now." Silence followed. "Still here. Hasn't been crushed yet. Now, that's a process if you've never seen it. A big car reduced to a metal cube—a big cube, but it's amazing."

"Ma'am, that car was stripped down, right?"

"Oh, yes. Had two wheels left. Even the steering wheel was removed."

"Why were two wheels left?"

"The other two cracked. These days, wheels are one unit. In the old days, they were steel. Now it's all aluminum, one unit. They're lighter, so it saves gas. That's why it costs about four hundred dollars to replace them. Tires, easy. Wheels aren't anymore."

"Cracked?"

Happy to be knowledgeable, Mildred chirped, "See it all the time. Cheap stuff. You'd be surprised at what I see down here. Sometimes they've been welded, which changes the molecular structure. Makes it brittle. See copycats of the original wheels—you know, cheap replacements. People can't tell the difference."

"The two cracked wheels—could they have been replaced?"

"Cheap, cheap, cheap. Looks just like they came from Ford, though. The destroyed wheels were replacements from an earlier accident. I'd bet on it. Whoever originally owned this Explorer probably did that," Mildred clucked.

"Ma'am, thank you. You've been very helpful." Harry hung up the phone, stood leaning against the counter. "Susan, I'm getting the picture."

Vivien was also getting the picture. Susan's highly unusual questions alerted Vivien to something brewing. Miserable as Latigo's philandering made Vivien, she loved him. She'd protect and stand by him.

He didn't deserve it.

33

*M*rs. Murphy slept behind Harry's computer. Pewter sacked out on the tack trunk, while Tucker lay flat in the center aisle of the barn for the cooling breeze. Crickets chirped, and the peepers in the pond sang loudly, melodious songs punctuated by deep bullfrog calls. Flatface lifted off her nest, venturing out for one of her evening food runs.

Thin tendrils of charcoal clouds floated above the Blue Ridge, now looming and dark. All those thousands and thousands of miles away, white-hot stars sent down their light to shine over those once-mighty mountains. Flatface, flying low, never gave the history of the Blue Ridge Mountains a thought. This geographic phenomenon was all the huge owl knew. Most humans didn't give the mountains a thought, either, but those who did knew that, before our species walked on earth, the Blue Ridge soared higher than the Alps and the Rockies. The Atlantic Ocean rolled much closer to them than today.

Harry sat glued to her computer. No T1 lines served her rural community, or most rural communities, for that matter. She had to use an ntelos Air Card, which, though better than nothing, could be slower than she wanted.

"Dammit, hurry up."

Mrs. Murphy opened one golden eye. "*Mama, you need to go to bed.*"

Checking the bed-table clock, Fair thought the same thing. He'd fallen asleep reading *The Utility of Force*, which he'd been intending to read for years. A good read, but he was so tired he conked out, the book falling on his muscled chest.

Setting it aside, he rose and slipped his robe on. Harry wasn't in the kitchen or the living room, where she'd sometimes fall asleep reading, especially in winter in front of a roaring fire. Walking to the screened-in porch, he spied a light spilling out onto the pasture. She was in the tack room.

Stepping out, he observed the ever-changing sky, the silver stars punctuating the late-June night. Somehow, those June and July nights never seemed as pitch black as a January night.

"Honey."

Startled, she looked up. "You scared me."

"It's one in the morning. Come to bed," Fair said.

"I lost track of time."

He grinned devilishly. "Are you out here watching porn?"

"No. I leave that to our congressmen." She laughed. "Come inside and pull up a chair for a minute."

"I'm trying to sleep." Pewter lifted her head.

"I got to thinking about Tara Meola's Explorer and Herb's truck being classified as totaled. Made no sense to me, since I knew the Chevy was still pretty good and, after talking to Coop, the Explorer had sustained damage but she thought a repair might be possible."

"Uh-huh." He had no idea where she was heading.

"I also knew that both vehicles had been repaired at ReNu for very minor infractions a few years before those later accidents."

"Define 'minor infraction.'" He pulled his robe tighter, for the night air had a little chill.

"Six months before she was killed, Tara Meola rolled over a concrete divider in a parking lot, screwing up a wheel. When Coop investigated the fatal crash, she also investigated Tara's driving history, asking Safe and Sound to pull up her VIN number. Insurance companies can run a VIN number through for prior claim information. A dealer can't. A dealer can run the title, get some idea of vehicle history. That's it."

Fair said, "So no one knows the true history of the car."

"Kinda. I can't figure it all out. What I do know is there are no rules or legislation concerning aftermarket prices and therefore no reliability statistics or safety information. Also, no one admits using aftermarket parts for repairs."

"Yes." He was still wondering when she was coming to bed.

"The other thing is if a car is totaled and the insur-

ance company writes it off as totaled, there is no investigation. You don't know what went wrong with the car."

"Presumably there was a collision of some sort."

She turned to him. "What if the collision was caused
by a cheap remanufactured part? What if, say, you are hit
like Tara by a deer and the part cracks, gives way, you
name it? Also, that Explorer had a repair from a prior
owner's small accident—at least according to Mildred at
the salvage yard. I'm onto something, but I don't know
exactly what yet. I think Safe and Sound is part of it.
Why three men are dead from ReNu has got to be connected to the insurance company."

"There's no reason that Latigo Bly would murder or
have murdered three mechanics."

"We don't know that. Seems to me that old profit
motive has reared its head up again."

"How'd you find this aftermarket stuff?"

"Searched all over the Internet, using 'cars,' 'collisions,' 'auto.' Finally found the website for the Automotive Education & Policy Institute." She had found
incredibly useful information at www.autoepi.org.

"That's what you've been reading all this time?"

"There's a lot of fascinating stuff here, and I'm working hard to absorb it all. Kinda overwhelming, really, but
what I get loud and clear is this: If someone smashes
into our Ford dually, we'll be directed by our insurance
company to go where repairs are cheapest. The company
may not pay the full repair at a shop not on their preferred list. And those 'preferred' shops are where they
use copycat parts. But we'll never know it. Wouldn't you

rather have the truck repaired with a genuine Ford part, even if it costs more?"

"Yes, but we aren't paying. Well, I suppose we do pay with our premiums."

"Right, and so does every other American paying those premiums. The insurance company wants to retain as much of that premium as possible, so they go with cheap repairs."

"This makes my head swim. Come on, go to bed. You won't be worth squat tomorrow if you don't."

"You're right. I got carried away. Even if I had a year, I don't think I could master all this."

"It is disturbing." He stood up, leaned over, and turned off her computer. "Now, look, you go to Cooper with this. Don't go off half-cocked."

"I won't," Harry promised.

Mrs. Murphy, Pewter, and Tucker padded behind the humans. They felt quite sure that Harry would soon forget her promise and do something stupid.

34

*H*arry finished her farm chores. Hot and muggy, the late-June day would only grow more stifling in the later afternoon. She had spoken to Coop that morning, telling her what she'd found at the Automotive Education & Policy Institute website.

Coop vowed to pursue this further by checking other collision repair services, talking to other insurance agents.

Harry was restless, though, and thought she might just cruise around and poke into things herself. The WRX STI tempted her. She hopped into the powerful vehicle, putting Tucker in the back. The two cats sat in the seat next to her.

"*This car's too low to the ground.*" Pewter preferred the truck.

"*So are you,*" Tucker told her from the safety of the backseat.

"*Ha-ha,*" the gray cat sarcastically replied.

"*We can stand on the seat, put our paws on the dash. It's not so bad.*" Mrs. Murphy enjoyed any ride, regardless of cab height.

"Hard for Pewter to do. Sixty percent of Pewter's weight is in the rear, like a Porsche," Tucker said.

Pewter leapt through the space between the front bucket seats. Tucker bared her teeth, but the gray cat jumped on her back, rendering those fangs useless.

Harry cut the motor and whapped both dog and cat.

"I've had enough of this. Three weeks of nonstop fussing and fighting. One peep, one tiny little peep, and I am throwing you two out of this car."

Both looked up at the angry human. Harry leaned back into the driver's seat, which felt like a cockpit to her. Pewter returned to the front seat. Harry was falling in love with the car but was in anguish, too, because she wasn't going to buy it. They weren't starving—Fair had work, thank heaven, for many didn't—but money was tight.

The souped-up 2.5-liter four-cylinder turbo awoke with a pleasant rumble. Its six-speed manual transmission thrilled her. She wished her truck, as well as the Volvo station wagon, had a manual transmission. These days, finding manual transmission wasn't easy: There were a few models of BMW, but not one Mercedes that she knew of. Most all family cars forced the buyer into automatic transmission, which burned more gas, although manufacturers declared the computer chips saved gas. Harry wondered, did the car manufacturers think that because someone had a family they didn't like to drive, really drive? One could row through gears without being a maniac.

She, however, possessed a few maniacal qualities be-

hind the wheel of a heart-throbbing, terrific acceleration machine.

She and her little family climbed to the top of Afton
Mountain on Route 250, turned left onto I-64, and
drove to Stuarts Draft. Going left off the Fishersville
exit, she turned onto a commercial road filled with big
metal-box buildings. Haldane's Salvage was a small brick
building. Outside on the chain-link fence was a big sign:
RECYCLED CARS, WE GO GREEN. A big stoplight was painted
on the sign, with its green light glowing. She pulled in.

Mildred expected Harry, as she'd called ahead. Mildred Haldane also expected the pets, which the kind
woman allowed in the office air-conditioning.

Mildred was as round as she was tall, but nevertheless it was with considerable energy that she marched
Harry to the huge yard out back. It was bounded by
chain link with thin wooden slats inside, the fencing to
hide the view of crunched cars, as well as the view of
the real cruncher. At the back of the lot, Leyland cypress
trees hid some of what many considered an eyesore.
Row after row of eyeless trucks, cars, even a few golf
carts, greeted Harry. Harry didn't find the auto graveyard offensive. Some vehicles bore testimony to terrible
crashes; others looked tired, with rusting bottoms and
paint faded by the sun.

"Don't get too many people who are interested in salvage," Mildred rattled on, coral lipstick shining. "My late
husband and I started this business in 1972. Not much
out here then, so we could buy a lot of land. We figured
there'd always be cars and there'd always be collisions.
Little did we know that one-car families would become

two- and three-car families. We boomed with that." Mildred swept her arm over the lot. "Fifteen acres."

"Impressive. You and—"

Before she could finish, Mildred filled in "Drew."

"You and Drew had vision."

She shrugged but liked the compliment. "Tell you what, young lady, they don't build cars like they used to. Come on, let me show you." Mildred led Harry down to a trim yellow shed, hopped into a new golf cart, and drove Harry to the very back. "Now, this is my antiques graveyard. Drew and I never had the heart to crush them when they'd come in."

"Look at that!" Harry saw a Plymouth from 1948, then an old Model T Ford—no windshield, no fenders, but unmistakably a Tin Lizzie. A Model A squatted next to the Lizzie. Rolling fenders on Buicks from the fifties were parked next to the old Nashes and old Rancheros, a Ford truck–car combo. They may have been useless, but the design, the bones, gave evidence to the aesthetic of the times.

"Here." Mildred tapped an old Dodge bumper. "Real steel. Go on, tap it."

Harry did as she was told. "That could take a bump or two."

"Tell you what"—Mildred's eyes squinched up—"I learned more about motors, car design, and safety while taking cars apart—kind of like construction in reverse. It's true: No fuel injection, simple engines, and the shocks often left a lot to be desired, but these babies were cars. *Real* cars."

Harry sighed. "You're right, Mrs. Haldane. Everything's been cheapened, and the excuse is making cars lighter so as not to consume so much gas."

"Call me Millie. Well, if you want to talk about pollution," Mildred put her hand on a jutting hip, "what about industrial pollution? Plastic, plastic made to look like aluminum, plastic, plastic, plastic. Ugh." She threw up her hands. "So many alloys in the metals, you can't call it steel. The public has no idea, no idea at all. Well, I may be a dinosaur, but I lived when the big boys ruled the road, and, honey, it was fab-u-lous."

Smiling broadly now that she'd expressed herself in no uncertain terms, Mildred motioned Harry back into the golf cart. "You asked about the Explorer. Let me show it to you."

Within two minutes, they'd pulled up to the SUV.

Mildred climbed out surprisingly agile given her weight. She bent over, pointing to the wheels.

"Yes, I see it." Harry viewed the damaged wheels.

"No cracks like that if these wheels were made by Ford. These were made in China. Some are made in other Eastern countries, but China has the ability to crank out lots of cheap stuff. They can fool a lot of people. Here, I can prove this to you without a doubt."

Back in the cart, Mildred, driving at as fast a clip as the cart could go, pulled up to piles of wheels, a big pile on the left, one on the right.

"Hope no one ever drops a cigarette here." Harry's eyes widened.

Mildred laughed. "They'd better be more afraid of me than the fire. Okay, the wheels on the left are genuine parts: on the vehicles when sold from the dealership, or, if replaced, then the driver made sure to duplicate the tires recommended by the carmaker. GM, Ford, BMW, Subaru, Chrysler, Jeep . . . you get the idea. The ones on the right are knockoffs. Now, let me show you." The short lady picked up a wheel—not light—without a grunt. "You take it."

Gingerly, Harry took the proffered wheel, getting as dirty as Mildred in the process.

Neither woman much cared about the rubber smudges or grease. Two motorheads from different generations had found each other.

"Should I put it back on the pile?"

"Yes, indeed." Mildred picked up a wheel, same size, from the right pile. "Try this."

The difference in weight, immediately apparent, surprised Harry. "I can't believe it."

"Believe it." Mildred's coral lips snapped shut. "Now, looking at these two piles, can you tell the difference?"

"No, ma'am, I can't."

"Come on." Mildred pointed to the cart again, and soon they were back in the office. "These are well-behaved animals," she said, once they'd all settled in.

"Thank you."

"*I'm well behaved. The others are dreadful,*" Pewter purred, rubbing against Mildred's leg.

"Honey, like I said, not too many people are interested in my work here, in how cars are made today. They should be. Their lives depend on it. Now they focus on new models, focus on the makers, but they don't focus on parts. There are only crash standards for the original manufacturers' parts. I'm not one for regulation—I think we're overregulated—but here's a case where there's nothing. I can fix your car with a plastic part made to look like metal. Will it hold up in a crash? No."

"I had no idea, and I love cars. Until you handed me those wheels, I couldn't have known what you were talking about."

Mildred grimaced. "It's like the mortuary industry. People don't want to think about dying, and they don't want to think about car wrecks, either. It's not a part of their daily life until it happens to them."

Harry nodded.

Mildred scrutinized Harry, then continued, "Here's the thing, and I go 'round about this. All carmakers want you and me to replace damaged engine parts with their parts, electrical stuff, and so on. They guarantee those parts. Aftermarket parts are a lot cheaper, so people can get their cars repaired cheaper. Some folks would say that's good because if you use only, say, GM parts, then GM has squeezed out the copycat, so that's no competition. The consumer loses. I understand that." Mildred paused for full effect. "But what's more important: anti-monopoly or your safety? 'Cause I sure can tell you, the Chinese don't give a fig about your safety, and I'm thinking the insurance companies don't, either."

"Why?"

She exploded, "They don't care about safety and they don't want to cover big repair bills."

"Yes," Harry agreed. "Wow, what a mess."

"The insurance companies are bleating about consumer choice, the carmakers want to protect their reputations, and maybe they do want to shove out the copycats, but I tell you what, I see poorly made cars; trucks come in here even after stripped and still have blood on them. Gets to me every time."

"It would me." Harry changed the subject. "Are you the only person working here? This is a big place."

Mildred leaned against the counter. "No. Have two fellows working here; sent them off to bring me a late lunch and get some for themselves. I have two kids; 'course, they're in their forties now. Drew and I sent them both to college. They don't want no part of this business. Don't want to get their hands dirty."

"This is a good business." Harry emphasized "good."

"Young people are different now. Forty is young to me. No one wants to work with their hands." She peered at Harry again, noting the dust on her jeans, a few pieces of hay in her hair. "Not many want to farm, either."

"Millie, I wouldn't be farming if I hadn't inherited it. No way could I afford land, the equipment, seeds, and fertilizer and make a go of it."

"Sucks," Millie succinctly responded. "Tell you what, though, your mama and papa sure were lucky to have a girl who wanted to keep the family business going. I don't know what I'm going to do. I know I should retire, but this is my life. What would I do? Watch I Love Lucy reruns?"

"She was the best." Harry grinned.

"That she was." Mildred shifted her weight. "When the economy comes back up, I reckon I will sell the business. Don't rightly know."

They chatted a bit more, then Harry thanked her profusely, making a mental note to send over some special canned foods she'd put up last year. Harry knew she'd be back. Something about Mildred touched her. She didn't dwell on it, she just knew she'd be back.

Mildred gave her a big hug as Harry put her hand on the doorknob, the three furry friends at her feet.

"Millie, what do you drive?"

"Ha." Mildred clapped her hands. "A big-ass 1962 Impala convertible. They can all get out of my way."

Driving out of the salvage yard, Harry pictured the round little lady in the big Chevy.

Bored with I-64, she drove to Waynesboro the back way.

"Hey, let's go to the drag strip. No one's there."

Tucker's brown eyes registered worry. *"You'd better not do anything with this car."*

Fifteen minutes later, the black WRX STI glided onto the grounds of Central Virginia Hot Rod Track. Harry drove right up to the Christmas tree.

"That's a lot of lights," Mrs. Murphy remarked.

"I so want to do the quarter mile." Harry's hands gripped the steering wheel. "Well, I can't. It's not right to do that in a car I haven't paid for, but how can I do it otherwise? I mean, they'll never let me race here, and I shouldn't. I really shouldn't."

"Don't," Pewter howled. *"You do enough crazy stuff."*

"What the hell?" Harry exclaimed. Coming around the bleachers in front of her at a fast clip was a charcoal Porsche 911. She checked her rearview: Behind her was a yellow Camaro. Harry couldn't see the drivers, but she knew if she didn't do something she'd be trapped. She put her foot on the brake, gunned the motor, took the brake off, and shot down the track so fast that the Porsche braked hard.

"*Something's wrong,*" Mrs. Murphy cried.

Tucker, trying to balance herself, looked through the two front seats. "*They're trying to trap her!*"

Pewter, crouching on the footwell behind the seat, shouted, "*Make her stop.*"

Mrs. Murphy summed up the situation. "*If she stops, we're toast.*"

The jet acceleration gave Harry confidence. At the end of the quarter mile, she turned sharply, skidding out, for the Porsche hung hot on her tail. The Camaro driver seemed to hesitate. Perhaps he had the brains to know if he tried to block her she'd plow right through him, maybe killing them both.

Harry had guts: She called his bluff. The Camaro accelerated out of her way, and she felt the shock waves as she blew by that beautiful yellow tail. As she rocked by the Camaro, she saw Latigo Bly behind the wheel.

Harry now headed for the state road, praying that someone would see them and call the police. No way could she reach her cellphone.

She was running for her life, very glad the seat belts were good.

She hooked left, skidding out again. This time the Camaro disappeared, only to reappear emerging from the back way into Central Virginia Hot Rod Track.

Fearlessly, Harry aimed straight for him again. Latigo

backed up in a hurry, stones flying from under the wheels.

As they were not yet near housing or commercial buildings, her two pursuers had two miles to bring her down. Given the quality of their cars and the skill with which they handled them, they just might succeed.

Sweat poured down her forehead, between her breasts. Senses razor-sharp, she'd never felt more alive than at this moment.

She heard the beautiful yowl of the 911 coming up on her right, on the lip side of the road, which was wide enough to take the car. She recognized Victor Gatzembizi in the gorgeous 911. On her left, the Camaro hurtled down a paved two-lane road. Both cars closed in. She was between them now. She couldn't take her eyes off the road for an instant.

The Porsche bumped her as the Camaro swerved close to her. The smaller car shuddered but took it. The pursuers drove about a foot away, then came toward her again to slam the hell out of the WRX STI. Harry hit those brakes, which bit into the pavement. The screech of the wheels had to have been heard in Richmond. So quickly did the pocket rocket stop that the Porsche and Camaro crashed into each other. The big Chevy shouldered the Porsche right off the road at such a high speed that the Porsche plowed into a field, but it didn't turn over. The Camaro, right fender now bent into the right wheel, made a screaming sound as the tire blew. The car spun around, stopping like a wounded animal. Latigo leaned out the open driver's window with a gun and fired a shot Harry's way. He missed, the bullet skidding over the Subaru hood.

Harry took off, speeding toward Waynesboro. Eventually she slowed, grabbed her phone, dialed 911. After giving the location of the two wrecks, she pulled into the Rite Aid parking lot to calm down.

"*That was close.*" She reached over, putting Mrs. Murphy in her lap and turning to pet Tucker.

"*I could have been killed,*" Pewter cried.

"Pewter, come on up here. Come on."

Wobbly-legged, the gray cat, belly low, slunk into Harry's lap. She'd peed on herself, but neither Harry nor anyone else said a word. They'd near done it themselves. Then Harry called Cooper.

"Coop, I'm in Augusta County—Waynesboro, at the Rite Aid. Victor Gatzembizi and Latigo Bly tried to kill me. I'm safe, I think. Will you come get me?"

"Hang on." Harry heard Coop hit the siren and start roaring through Albemarle toward Augusta County.

By the time Cooper reached Harry, the animals were cleaned up. Harry had gone into Rite Aid to get bottled water for everyone and had bought a little plastic bowl and some paper towels for cleanup. Behind the counter Belinda—a pug owner and animal lover herself—pretended not to notice the cat-pee smell on Harry.

It wasn't until Harry saw Coop that she about cried, her relief was so great. Coop shot out of the squad car, saw the scar marks on the right side of the Subaru, the thin bullet line on the hood.

"Jesus Christ, Harry, what happened?"

Harry explained as best she could, from the beginning. "How did they know I was there?"

"Easy, neighbor. Someone slapped a tracking device on your car. Same thing as on hunting-dog collars. They've known where you are ever since Victor Gatzembizi dropped off this car." Cooper leaned into her squad car, called the Augusta sheriff's department.

She identified herself and gave the location of the accident, asking if anyone was there. If so, were the drivers safe? Could they give her a positive ID?

She clicked off the phone. "Victor Gatzembizi and Latigo Bly."

"I was so stupid. So incredibly stupid!" Harry leaned against the car, put her head in her hands. "How could I not have known?"

"Hindsight is always clear." Coop put her arm around her friend. "The good news is you're alive. Mrs. Murphy, Pewter, and Tucker are alive." She looked over the car. "I think you can drive this thing home."

"This car saved my life."

"That and the fact that you can drive." Cooper hugged her with the arm draped over her shoulder. "Wish I'd seen it. We'll get this figured out. Those two will have their asses in the slammer. Rick and I will pay them a visit later. Come on, girl; I'll follow you home."

"Can I ride with you?" Pewter meowed loudly.

"Pewts, Mom needs you. The worst is over," Tucker counseled.

"Why does everything happen to me?" the gray cat wailed.

35

Rays slanting through mountainsides and steep ravines, the golden late sun pierced the eastern meadows and pastures along the Blue Ridge.

"Why is it that the light before the sun sets is so much richer than at any other time of the day?" Harry wondered aloud to herself.

Her friends had gathered at the farm this Saturday before the Fourth of July to rejoice in her escape, talk about the capture of the two culprits, and, of course, talk about one another.

Fair, like 90 percent of American men, showed off his considerable grilling skills, ably assisted by Reverend Jones. Since the reverend loved to eat, you wanted him helping you. Anyone who likes to eat is usually a good cook.

Cooper brought fresh greens to make a salad. Alicia and BoomBoom brought all the biscuits and also a big cake. Other friends dropped by, had a drink, and left. The place had buzzed, but now it was those closest and dearest, eating, drinking, laughing, and perhaps enjoying the recent scandal of Yancy Hampton being caught falsifying his organic foods.

"It isn't all that terrible," Alicia defended him. "So he sells some genetically modified foods. Big deal."

Franny Howard jumped into the conversation. "False advertising. String him up by his shoelaces." Franny plopped down with a thud.

"He wears sandals," BoomBoom quietly replied.

"Jesus boots," Franny giggled.

"Franny, you're in a mood." Cooper pointed to the huge salad bowl.

Franny did get up to investigate.

Trolling along the two picnic tables placed together, she filled her plate and a salad bowl. "I'm happy Harry has solved the crimes and I'm happy my tires are home."

"Laying rubber, are you?" Fair pointed a long grilling fork at her.

Franny shook her finger. "Don't go there."

Reverend Jones, happiest when among his friends, sat down with a long, cool summer drink, into which he had added two raspberries and fresh mint. "Coop, when are you and Rick going to reward our girl here? She apprehended two dangerous men."

"I'm not sure I'd use the word 'apprehend,' but she did bring them to justice, so to speak."

Harry pointed to the WRX STI. "That car did the trick."

They knew the details, but all asked to hear it again, so Harry, who couldn't help herself, spilled all the details once more.

"Nothing about us," Pewter lazily said, having eaten offerings from the people plus what she could steal.

"Wasn't much we could do in the car except hang on," Mrs. Murphy added. "This was one time we couldn't help her."

"Wild ride." Tucker grinned.

On a different branch than Matilda, who reposed higher up now, perched the blue jay, Pewter's nemesis. Brazenly, the bird swooped down, flew over the table, stopped for a split second, then flew back up into the tree with a morsel of fresh-baked bread.

"Blue jays don't like bread. They like seeds," Susan, a birder, said.

Fair laughed. "He hasn't read Audubon."

The blue jay then opened his beak, letting the bread drop. "I can do anything. You can't catch me."

"Did you see that?" Harry's mouth fell open.

"Cheeky fellow," Reverend Jones roared, then held up his hands. "Lord, is this your way of telling us we aren't the crown of creation?"

"Listen to him." Pewter sat upright. "He gets it."

The blue jay jumped off and flew sideways, one wing toward the ground, right in front of the gray cat. Pewter's whiskers moved with the air current. Then he returned to the table, this time plucking a seed off one of the special biscuits.

Harry, hands on hips, stood up. "What good are you cats? This is your job."

"You get upset if we kill birds," Mrs. Murphy fired right back.

The blue jay, sitting a bit too near Matilda, swallowed the seed. Matilda opened her jaws and flicked out her tongue. The saucy bird dropped a few branches below. He wasn't done yet, but he wanted that juicy seed to settle for a moment.

"You two look lame," Tucker ever so helpfully said.

"Well, you try to get him." Pewter was incensed.

"I'm not a cat. Not my job." The corgi dropped under Fair's chair.

"We wouldn't have you," the gray cat snidely spoke.

As the three animals complained to one another and about one another, the blue jay began to imitate other birds for the joy of irritating everyone.

He was successful.

Ignoring the racket, Reverend Jones asked, "Coop, what have they confessed to?"

"That's why I drove out here, to find out," said Franny. "Did Victor and Latigo steal my tires along with their other crimes?" She gleefully shoved divine barbecue into her mouth.

"No," Cooper replied. "It's going to take time to crack your case. Is it a large interstate ring or is it local? We'll get it, Franny, just give us time."

"Bet you will." Alicia licked her fingers, while Boom-Boom rose to get her a small little wet towel at the end of the table.

"The three remaining mechanics, Jason Brundige, Sammy Collona, and Lodi Pingrey, want to save themselves, and they want to prove they didn't kill anyone, so they've been singing like canaries."

"Do you think they did kill their co-workers?" Reverend Jones asked the tall deputy.

"No. I'm pretty certain Victor and Latigo did the killing. And that's what Jason Brundige is saying. The murders weren't professional grade, if you will, but they were clever, bold, and left no fingerprints. These two thought they were clever by using a different M.O. for each murder. Jason said they killed Bobby together, just like they tried to kill Harry together."

"The killings were messages to the others," Harry simply said.

"Yes," Coop replied.

"Messages about what?" BoomBoom had returned to her place at the table.

"'Shut your mouth. Don't get greedy.' The mechanics knew what Victor and Latigo were doing. And they were well paid to shut up." Cooper swung one leg over the long wooden seat so she now sat at the end of the table facing all of them. "The mechanics received big payoffs to keep quiet about the substandard parts. In return, they received a cut of the action. Now that we have forensics accountants in law enforcement, we can find the holes in anyone's books eventually. Walt started the ball rolling. He wanted more money to keep silent. Not only did he try to shake down Victor and Latigo, he tried to shake down his co-workers. No love lost there."

"How much do you think the whole scheme made?" Franny inquired, ever interested in profit.

"Millions. We can only work off percentages—in other words, the cost of genuine manufacturing parts versus the cost of knockoffs—but the profit is huge."

"So Latigo sent clients to Victor?" Fair finished his steak, thinking he'd done a great job, which he had.

"He did. Both men profited handsomely, obviously.

Jason indicated that first Walt got greedy, then Nick and Bobby wanted more. Nick stupidly threatened to tell the media about the Chinese parts, the whole scam. A collision-repair shop is under no obligation to identify whether parts are from the original manufacturer or aftermarket. All Victor had to do was undercut his competition by fifteen percent. Latigo referred everyone to Victor. Both made a lot of money." Cooper then pointed to Harry. "What really tipped you off? You were ahead of us."

"When Herb's truck was declared a total wreck, I knew it had many years left. That's why I went to the lot and pulled out the radiator. I knew it wasn't right, because the drill holes to fit it had been altered. They were elliptical, and for that I thank Dabney Farnese. When he came to repair the John Deere, he told me about substandard parts for tractors, especially the holes. He said they were dead giveaway signs, because a substandard replacement part never fit exactly right. The holes had to be altered, and he said those alterations tend to be elliptical instead of perfectly round."

"So that was it? My radiator." Reverend Jones reached for a cupcake with thick vanilla icing.

"But I became surer about my theory when I drove over to Haldane's Salvage and Millie Haldane showed me cracked wheels, two of which were on Tara Meola's Explorer on the lot for scrap. Safe and Sound uses Millie's salvage yard. That lady knows a whole lot. By the time I left there, I knew, I just knew, but I couldn't prove that Safe and Sound was behind it. If Tara's Explorer had had true Ford wheels, there was a chance she might have lived when she veered off the road. The copycat wheels cracked.

"And when Miranda went off the road, it was a wheel problem. She'd had that wheel replaced the year before."

"Where is Miranda?" Franny loved the older lady.

"Choir practice. Her choir has been asked to sing at the swearing-in ceremony on the Fourth of July at Monticello." Harry mentioned a moving event at Mr. Jefferson's home, where people became American citizens.

"What an honor." Alicia smiled.

"She has a solo, too. That beautiful, beautiful voice," Reverend Jones added.

"Why did declaring Herb's truck a total loss alert you?" Franny was curious.

"No investigation when a vehicle is declared totaled. My curiosity must have set off those two. They didn't want me to go over the truck. I mean, Victor towed the Chevy out of St. Luke's right away. I should have smelled a rat when he dropped off the WRX STI. He had a tracking device in the car. He knew my every move in that Subaru. I never imagined that. I was really dumb."

"Well, stubborn is closer to the mark," BoomBoom said.

"I was too dazzled by the WRX STI. It was easy to track me—you can watch a person's movements on your phone GPS; hunting guys even get map printouts with their dogs' trails overlaid on them. That's what they did to me. When they knew I was in an isolated place where they could get me, they did. They'd obviously shadowed me to Millie's and knew I was getting close to the truth."

Reverend Jones thought out loud. "Greed, one of the

seven deadly sins. You might have been the fourth victim."

"Thank God my baby can drive," Fair said. "She's the NASCAR type." He wiped his hand on the wet towel. "They never imagined she could control a car as well as they could."

"I could have told them that." BoomBoom smiled. "Reflexes like a cat."

"Not even close," Pewter responded.

The blue jay swept down on all those people at the table, making off with more delicious seeds from the tops of some muffins.

"That damned bird!" Franny allowed herself a curse.

Franny, who knew Millie Haldane, asked Harry, "What'd you think of Millie?"

"She's lonely, you know. She knows a lot. Cooper, I'd pay a call on her or use her for an expert witness once you have a talk with the prosecutor. Actually, I want to see her again, too."

"A real character." Franny nodded.

"Look who's talking." Susan giggled, then became serious. "Harry, I think our phone call to Vivien Bly tipped them off, too. I mean, tipped them off that you were getting closer. I bet she ran straight to Latigo and told him everything. We should have thought of that. Just because we know he's a two-timing you-know-what doesn't mean she doesn't love him. Maybe she doesn't know."

"She does," Alicia said with conviction. "She's going to stick by him; she'll try to come up with alibis. Just wait until this goes to court."

"How can she do that?" Harry threw up her hands.

Quietly, Reverend Jones replied, "How can she not? We have thousands of years of written history extolling women who put their love for a man before the common welfare. She was being a 'good wife.'" He looked at the celebrants intently.

Harry plowed right in. "It's one thing if infidelity occurs, but it's quite another if you know your husband or son or daughter is killing people. How can what she's doing be construed as good?"

"It's a confusing issue. Standards are shifting," Alicia wisely stated. "Personally, I don't know what I'd do. I mean, do any of us know until it happens to us?"

"She'll run the empire when he goes to jail." Franny shrugged.

"Well, it's entirely possible she'll be on the carpet, too. How much did she know? Is she an accessory?" Cooper knew all too well how these things worked.

"This will drag on and drag on," said Franny. "In the meantime, Harry's got a Subaru WRX STI, because I doubt anyone is going to think to take it back at the moment. Safe and Sound owns it, right?" She laughed.

"Guess they do," Harry replied.

"Well, make hay while the sun shines," Franny enjoined her.

"That's just what I've been doing." Harry swept her arm to indicate the cut hay fields, to much laughter.

Just then, the blue jay returned. The light on the iced-tea pitcher, mirrored almost, fooled him, and he flew smack into it, falling between the glasses and the sugar and lemon.

For a fat girl, Pewter burned the wind jumping on that table.

She'd just put her paw on the bird's plump chest when Harry scooped her up.

"*That's my bird. I've waited years for that monster!*"

Fair picked up the bird, stroking its head, feeling its neck. "Not broken."

A bright black eye opened. The blue jay moved his head.

Pewter wriggled in Harry's arms, her rage escalating.

"Get your tail out of the cake icing." BoomBoom gingerly picked up the tail.

"*Mine. That bird is mine!*" Pewter reached out.

"No," Fair said, as he plucked a baked oat off a muffin and put it into the bird's beak. Then he threw the blue jay up. A flutter of wings and the thief landed on his branch.

Swallowing the oat, he stared straight down at the distraught gray cat. "*Ha.*"

"*I will kill you,*" Pewter vowed. "*I don't care how long it takes. I will kill you.*"

Mrs. Murphy walked over to her emotional friend, leaned on her shoulder, and said, "*Pewts, don't you worry. Someday that blue jay will get his. You know that crime doesn't pay.*"

Dear Reader

I sometimes worry that readers mistake my characters for me. For what it's worth, I'm pretty middle-of-the-road and am appalled at the entrenched dishonesty, self-centeredness, and lack of concern for our citizens that I perceive in Washington. That loss of confidence and belief knows no party, really. I think most of us are stunned.

In the interests of clarity, I am not Harry, although we share a love of farming and nature. In most other respects, we are markedly different. Still, Harry and I both live in central Virginia, where people are not liberal. They aren't to the right of Genghis Khan, either. Sure, a few are, but most are not. By and large, the residents of Virginia adhere to Jefferson's ideal: "That government is best which governs least."

Thank you for keeping up with Sneaky Pie and the Crozet family. My hope is that Sneaky Pie will run for president. I trust her; she's sensible and reliable.

As for me, I'm doing my best to keep body and soul together, as are you. No matter what folly humans are committing, the great blue heron flying in front of a sun setting behind the Blue Ridge Mountains restores me. I hope you have something equal to such beauty in your life.

Always and ever,

Rita Mae Brown

Dear Reader

Cats do like riding in cars and trucks, but we need to learn to do it as kittens. If I'm not looking out the dash, I like to get up in the rear window.

This story interests me because of zooming around with my human. I've even ridden in her lap when she drives the tractor. Not often, as it's a rough ride, but I do like the view from high up.

Pewter, on the other hand, only goes along for the ride because she's afraid she'll miss something. If she gets scared, she makes a mess. She should just stay home.

Hope all is well where you are.

Yours,
Sneaky Pie

Dear Reader

She's full of poop, not me! I can ride with the best of them.

Sincerely, honestly, truthfully,
Pewter

Acknowledgments

Erica Eversman tops the list, but she tops my list always. The Automotive Education & Policy Institute is hers (www.autoepi.org). This good woman drove all the way from Akron, Ohio, to stay in my barn, calling it headquarters despite no air-conditioning or Internet service. She soldiered on in punishing heat, brought me all manner of hard copy, and had the incredible patience to explain just what's at stake with this issue.

We are so accustomed to seeing any of the Big Three auto manufacturers as the bad guys. In this case, they are not. For one thing, they don't want you to die in their vehicles. Let's leave it at that.

Thanks seem inadequate for all that this tall, blonde smarty has done for me and by extension for all Americans, although you may not know about it. Erica and others are fighting the good fight for auto safety.

Mrs. Donna Packard, Academic & Professional Services, always prepares my manuscripts. For this mystery, she actually researched some agriculture questions. Nothing like a last-minute call. She came through, but then Donna always does, whether it's for her profession, her children, her husband, or her friends.

Thanking a jewelry store—well, is there a woman who doesn't love a good jewelry store? Keller & George has served Charlottesville for well over one hundred years. Bill Liebenrood of Keller & George, whom I think of as the Big Cheese, asked me to kill him off in this book so he wouldn't have to go to work anymore. Only Bill. I like him so much I just couldn't do it, but perhaps in subsequent books I can make him suffer.

I am especially grateful to Bill and Gayle Lowe for their kindness to me during a spectacular reversal in my life. It didn't help them, or Keller & George, either, but they handled it with their good humor and grace, and I am forever in their debt.

Wherever you live, I hope you are surrounded by good people, as I am here in central Virginia. You see people in business circumstances, social, and it's pleasant. But when the you-know-what hits the fan, I am overcome with just how helpful and genuinely caring people are. Even better, how they are all busting with ideas, many of which find their way into Sneaky's books.

Lucky cat. Lucky me.

Ever and always,
Rita Mae

Turn the page for an exclusive sneak peek
at Rita Mae Brown and Sneaky Pie Brown's
next Mrs. Murphy Mystery

The Litter of the Law

Coming in hardcover and eBook
from Bantam Books

*W*hen they were courting, Fair Haristeen, doctor of veterinary medicine, would pick up his wife, Harriett— "Harry"—and they'd go on a Saturday drive. He'd be bruised from Friday night's football game. She'd be dirty from the stable. Now in their early forties, they'd steal a Saturday and cruise the back roads in central Virginia.

Mrs. Murphy, the tiger cat, Pewter, her gray, overweight sidekick, and Tucker, the corgi, looked out the window from the backseat. The three animal friends usually accompanied their people everywhere except in high heat. On a day like today, windows down a crack, the three could sleep or chat while the humans talked.

"Perfect," Fair replied.

October 12 proved a ravishing fall day, early fall, for the summer warmth lingered late this year. The forest looked spray painted with yellow, orange, flaming red, deep red, old gold.

"Hey, Miranda got the respiratory flu." Harry mentioned a former co-worker and dear friend. "She's swearing that drinking electrolytes will cure her. She saw it on TV."

"We've got plenty of quacks now." He grimaced. Fair shook his head. "Electrolytes will help, but our beloved Miranda seems susceptible to quacks."

Watching the passing scenery, the cat Pewter noticed a lovely yellow clapboard farmhouse. *"Quack. Duck. Why call a crook a quack?"*

"I don't know," Tucker replied. The corgi was well-used to Pewter's inquiring mind. *"They also use the term 'snake oil.' A quack sells snake oil. It's confusing."*

"Ha." Pewter let out a whoop. *"If they'll buy snake oil, maybe we can get our human hooked on catnip."*

"She won't sniff catnip," Tucker replied with dignity. Someone had to stand up for Harry.

"They can learn," the gray cat spoke with conviction.

"Pewter, sometimes I think you're cracked as well as fat," the dog unwisely said.

"Fat?" Pewter raged.

"You need a seat all your own. Every time we take a turn the flab on your belly sways." Tucker growled.

Pewter lashed out, a quick right to the shoulder.

Tucker growled, showing her fangs.

"That is enough!" Harry turned around.

"I haven't done a thing," Mrs. Murphy said, distancing herself from the combatants who then rounded on her.

"Brown noser!" Pewter whacked the tiger cat, who gave as good as she got.

The hissing and barking irritated Fair to the point

where he drove to the side of the road near Hester Martin's vegetable and fruit stand.

Harry got out of the car, opened the back door. "I am going to give you such a smack."

All three animals jumped to the far back of the Volvo station wagon. She opened that back lift so they jumped into their original seats.

Slamming the back door, Harry cursed as Fair couldn't help but laugh. She walked over to the driver's side; he had the window down. "They know how to pluck your last nerve," Fair said, laughing.

"Yours, too. I didn't pull the car over." Harry looked down the road at the produce stand, a small white clapboard building with a large overhang, goods displayed in orderly, colorful rows. "Hey, let's get some pattypan squash. Bet Hazel still has some." She walked around, getting in the car's passenger side before turning to face her animal tormentors. "If I hear one peep, one sniff, one hiss while I am shopping, no food tonight. Get it?"

"*Hateful.*" Pewter turned her back on Harry.

As Tucker hung her head, Mrs. Murphy, the tiger cat, loudly defended herself. "*I didn't do one thing.*"

"*Of course not, the perfect puss.*" Pewter curled her upper lip.

Fair coasted the car to the stand where Hester— wearing an orange apron, black jeans, and an orange shirt—talked to customers, most of whom lived in Crozet or nearby.

"I'll stay here." Fair knew how Hester could go on, plus Buddy Janss was there, all three hundred pounds of him, and he could outtalk Hester.

Orange and black bunting festooned the roof over-hang. Scarecrows flanked the outdoor wooden cartons overflowing with squashes, pumpkins, every kind of apple imaginable. Inside one could buy a good ham and cheese sandwich. Little ghosts floated from the rafters, big green eyes glowed in the room's upper corners. Brilliantly gold late corn, huge mums, and zinnias added to the color.

A sign, almost as big as Buddy, sat catty-cornered to the entrance, announcing the community Halloween Hayride to raise money for the Crozet Library. No doubt Tazio Chappars, an architect, designed the impressive sign. She worked hard for the library and the sign really grabbed you: from a large drawn skeleton, one bony arm actually reached out to get your attention.

Hazel looked up. "Harry Haristeen, I haven't seen you in weeks."

Buddy turned. "How'd you do with your sun-flowers?"

Buddy, a farmer who rented thousands of acres along with his own holdings, enjoyed getting reports about Harry's foray into niche farming. Who knew better than Buddy the cost of equipment and implements for wheat, corn, soybeans? Harry knew she'd made a wise choice in focusing on sunflowers, as well as a quarter acre of petite manseng grapes and ginseng down by the creek which divided her property from the old Jones farm.

"Pretty good," she said, not wanting to brag that this year's yield of sunflowers was her biggest yet. "How's your year so far?"

He hooked his thumbs in his overalls. "Tell you what, girl, that mini drought thinned out my corn crop. I did better than most because my lower acres got enough rain, others didn't. Never saw anything like it. On one side of the road the corn would be twisted right up, and on the other just as plump as you'd please. Lost most of the corn behind the old school houses."

Hester jumped in. "Government's fault. All that stuff they have circling around up there in space. Gotta affect us."

Both Harry and Buddy nodded politely for Hester was a little in space herself. Sometimes she was way out there. Middle-aged, with glossy light brown hair hanging to her shoulders, she applied just enough makeup to draw attention to her healthy good looks. Every small town as well as big cities have Hesters; it's just they can't hide in the small towns. Good-looking people, often bright, but they don't quite fit in and often they never marry. Hester had gone to Mary Baldwin College, excelled in her studies, but came back over the Blue Ridge Mountains to run this roadside stand. Her parents had built it more as a hobby than a business but it flourished. Her father had been a banker. Her mother ran the stand. She seemed happy enough, engaged with a steady stream of regulars, classmates, and tourists.

Buddy kindly semi-agreed. "What scares me is what we don't know. I mean just in general, look at this drought and hey, we came out a lot better off than they did in the Midwest where everything burned up. Right now our water table is good. I planted more corn because I think it will stay warm longer. I'll get it harvested and, if not, I'll make a lot of critters happy." He let out a booming laugh.

Hester asked, "You've got crop coverage, Buddy? After the drought of 1988, surely you started paying for an insurance policy, revenue protection."

"I do. I elected an eighty-percent revenue protection policy. Yes, I did learn from 1988 but, girl, every time I turn around I'm writing another check and I see my return diminish. Farming gets harder and harder," said the well-organized man, a true steward of the land. "Just to keep up I have to plant more acreage. Plant an early crop, then come back and throw soybeans down. I feel like I'm running to stay in place."

"Think we all do," Hester agreed.

"Only way I can buy or rent, and renting makes sense in the short term, is to sell some of my land closer in to Crozet or Charlottesville."

Hester's shoulders snapped back. "Don't do that, Buddy. Don't ever do that."

Harry didn't want to keep Fair or the arguing animals waiting. "Before I forget, Hester, do you have any pattypan squash?"

"I do. Wait until you see it." Hester nodded to Buddy who winked at Harry.

The two women walked inside where there was a gorgeous array of crooknecked squash, acorn squash, and Harry's favorite: cream white pattypan squash that looked like scalloped discuses.

"Beautiful! And the right size."

"Right about now the pattypan is usually over, but with this year's long, long summer, still getting some. The melons are over though." Hester thoughtfully replied, "I do so love melons. Before I forget now, you and Fair are buying tickets for the hayride. You must. The library is built but there's a lot to be done. We need $59,696 just for adult computers and, oh my, the adult area needs tables and we need furniture for a quiet reading room. The list is endless."

"Of course, we'll buy tickets. I'll even buy tickets for Mrs. Murphy, Pewter, and Tucker."

"If that gray cat of yours gets any fatter, I'll have to find a special wagon and pony just for her." Hester laughed.

"You're looking pretty Halloweeny yourself, all orange and black."

"Oh, this is just my warm-up. Next week I'll be out here in my witch's costume."

"So long as you don't scare customers away."

"I could be a Halloween fairy except I've never seen a Halloween fairy."

They laughed as Harry picked out two succulent squashes, paid at the cash register run by Lolly Currie. Harry knew the ambitious young woman was looking for a better-paying job, but making ends meet at the fruit stand until then.

Back on the road, Fair grinned. "That was the shortest time you have ever spent at Martin's stand."

"Buddy Janss helped me out because as soon as I paid for my squash, he came back to chat up Hester, about late produce deliveries. I swear, Buddy has put on more weight. His chins now have chins."

"Buddy may be fat but he's light on his feet. He was a hell of a football player in high school and college. It's a pity but retired linemen run to fat so often."

"Boxers, too." She watched rolling hills pass by.

"*Maybe you should go live with Buddy Janss,*" said Tucker, knowing this would cause a fight. "*The two of you could be Team Tubby.*"

"*Don't.*" Mrs. Murphy counseled in vain.

"*Bubble Butt. Poop breath!*" Pewter hissed loudly.

Harry twisted around in the front seat just in time to see Pewter hook the dog's shoulder with one claw.

"*Ouch,*" she yelped.

"*Next. Your eyes.*"

"Pull over, honey," said Harry. "There will be fur all over the car if I don't stop this right now."

He pulled over on the two-lane road which runs into Garth Road. The north field was jammed with corn. Morrowdale Farm usually put these fields in good hay but this year row after row of healthy corn filled them and they had somehow escaped the small drought.

Opening the door to again castigate the backseat passengers, Harry remarked. "This has to be one of the best run and prettiest farms in Albemarle County."

"Sure is."

They looked out to the scarecrow in the middle of the field, currently being mobbed by crows.

"I thought scarecrows frightened crows?" Fair shrugged.

"Those crows are having a party. Look at that. Pulling

on the wig under the hat." Harry laughed. "What are all those birds doing?"

Fair stepped out of the car to stare intently as a crow plucked out an eyeball.

"Honey, that's not a scarecrow," he said.